Mrs. Hudson
and the Wild West

By

Barry S Brown

Paperback ISBN 978-1-78705-976-4
ePub ISBN 978-1-78705-977-1
PDF ISBN 978-1-78705-978-8

Published by MX Publishing
335 Princess Park Manor, Royal Drive,
London, N11 3GX
www.mxpublishing.com

Cover design by Brian Belanger

Dedication

To Steve Emecz for his unflagging support and encouragement

Acknowledgment

I am greatly indebted to Arlyne and Marvin Snyder for their careful editorial review, resulting in many helpful suggestions and an embarrassingly large number of corrections.

Praise for earlier accounts of Mrs. Hudson's achievements:

"Each new book surpasses the others ... Some enterprising TV producer is missing out on a potentially great TV mystery series!"
Over My Dead Body Mystery Magazine

"... an inherently entertaining and fascinating read from beginning to end ... an enduringly popular addition to community library Mystery/ Suspense collections ..."
MidWest Book Review

"It is always a pleasure to recommend a Sherlock Holmes novel that retains the reader's interest to the very end. This one did."
Sherlockian.net

"... delightful entertainment with more than a dash of comedy. ... deftly juggles historical fact with fictional whodunnit."
Wilmington Star-News

"enormously entertaining ... Mrs. Hudson's a likeable character and disconcertingly credible."
The District Messenger – Newsletter of the Sherlock Holmes Society of London

"... an intriguing narrative ..."
Strand Magazine

And from the author's three children:

"Wasn't bad."

"I've read worse."

"Wait. He writes? Books?"

Mrs. Hudson Adventures

The Unpleasantness at Parkerton Manor

Mrs. Hudson and the Irish Invincibles

Mrs. Hudson in the Ring

Mrs. Hudson in New York

Mrs. Hudson's Olympic Triumph

Mrs. Hudson Takes the Stage

Mrs. Hudson and the Wild West

Chapter 1. The Littlest Horse Thieves

It was a sight unlike any ever seen on Baker Street. The man facing Mrs. Hudson on the doorstep of 221B was tall, muscular, ruggedly good-looking in spite of his more than 60 years, and wholly out of place on this or any street in London. Curls of white hair flowed beneath a wide-brimmed, high-crowned hat to the shoulders of a fringed buckskin jacket. On closer examination—and every passer-by turned to make closer examination—he could be seen to have full and flaring moustaches as well as a goatee that appeared destined to reach his breastbone given sufficient time. Boots that extended well above his knees completed the picture, although few in his early morning audience ever got beyond the buckskin jacket before recognizing the impropriety of their continued staring.

The man himself seemed wholly unconcerned about the spectacle he was creating. Indeed, if the truth be known he was well accustomed to it. It was, after all, precisely the effect he sought. For several days his arrival in London had been described in the dailies, always with accompanying artists' renderings, while his face in profile with goatee, and what everyone would learn was a Stetson hat, was on display on posters in the windows of nearly every shopkeeper who had a window, alerting all of the city and much of the countryside to the return, "for a limited engagement only," of Buffalo Bill's Wild West Show.

"I'm here to see Mr. Holmes, may I come in?"

Mrs. Hudson threw the door wide. "Please do, Colonel Cody."

She turned and led him into the parlor after first receiving the self-satisfied look she fully expected her words of recognition would produce. "Please seat yourself while I make certain Mr. 'Olmes is free."

In spite of her invitation, the man remained stiffly erect while she mounted the seventeen steps to the sitting room where Dr. Watson was hunched over his roll-top desk intent on capturing with utmost accuracy every detail of the recently concluded adventure of the left-handed calligrapher, every detail, save one—the identity of

1

the mastermind responsible for uncovering the calligrapher's killer. The person to whom that credit was misapplied was at the back of the room, in the space allotted to his laboratory, staring sullenly at a beaker half-filled with a greenish liquid.

"There's a visitor wantin' to see Mr. 'Olmes. 'E's someone who'll interest you both. It's Colonel William Cody, Buffalo Bill as 'e's called. From the looks of things, 'e's got a personal problem that's more than a little embarrassin'."

Watson put down his pencil and asked the question Holmes would die before posing. "Why do you say that, Mrs. Hudson?"

"E's comin' to see us, not the police, which indicates the problem is somethin' 'e wants to keep secret as best 'e can—meanin' it's somethin' that could be embarrassin' if folk learned about it. At the same time, it's bound to be somethin' 'e sees as quite serious or 'e wouldn't be comin' all the way across town at this 'our and on a day 'e'll be wantin' to be with 'is Wild West people preparin' things for tomorrow's openin' for the public. I'm thinkin' it's likely got to do with some piece of property that's gone missin', most probably stolen, and 'e wants us to look into it. If there was some kind of personal disagreement, 'e'd either take care of it 'imself, or e'd be duty bound to share it with the police. I'll send 'im up to see you and I'll be up later with a pot of tea and some fresh made scones."

Once more downstairs, Mrs. Hudson directed the still firmly erect Colonel Bill Cody to join Holmes and Watson while she put up the tea she had promised and gathered together the morning's baked goods. As she did, she fell into a reverie, reprising the events that had led to internationally known figures bringing their problems to Baker Street. Her colleagues would count the beginnings to more than twenty years earlier when they first took rooms at 221B, but she knew the beginnings came well before that.

In truth, she couldn't remember the first time she and Tobias first spread the *Evening Standard* wide across their kitchen table to select a crime for analysis. She had been the one to suggest it, she remembered that. At first, it was only to show an interest in his work, but it soon became the best time of her day. Tobias would choose the crime and then for an hour, often more, they'd have at it, sometimes challenging each other, sometimes joining forces, always honing his and developing her investigative skills. They determined what to look for at the scene of the crime, what questions to ask of witnesses and people who knew the victim, and the course the investigation would take depending on what was learned. He claimed to be just reporting what any constable would do. She knew better. Ever after, she would call him her "uncommon common constable." But not to his face. That would have been boastful, and Tobias did not do boastful—at least not about himself. He did, on the other hand, remark now and again about what a fast learner she was. And she believed him, because just as Tobias was slow to accept praise, he also wasn't one to waste it on others. She complemented their nightly sessions with regular trips to the British Library. There, her taste in literature at first raised eyebrows among the librarians. Later, finding no reports of horrific crimes involving knives, firearms, poisons, blunt instruments, or lethal falls, and no statement of the arrest of a middle-aged, short, stocky grey-haired woman bent on systematically reducing London's population, they filled her requests with only a nod to a nearby librarian confirming she was at it again.

Nor were studies of criminal behavior and its investigation Mrs. Hudson's only interest. Trips to the greengrocer, the butcher, the apothecary and post office were spent analyzing the people she saw and what their faces, their hands, their gait, their dress, and the way they dealt with others told of who they were and who they had been. When she shared her analyses with Tobias, he professed to being as impressed with her ability to read character as he was with her ability to plan an investigation. His hard-won praise emboldened her to intensify her efforts until one day, quite without warning, she felt herself to have crossed from conscientious student to confident practitioner.

And still it was little more than a parlor trick, and good fun on that account, until Tobias fell ill. The doctor said it was a blood disorder and there was no cure, and too soon Tobias was gone, and parlor tricks were put aside as was a great deal of her life.

It was a trip to the bakeshop months later, as she described it to Tobias during one of her biweekly visits to his gravesite, that she "returned to the land of the living." Before making her way back to that land, she had given up baking since she had no one with whom to share her baked goods and had taken to purchasing the decidedly inferior scones and breads available from Tyler's Bake Shoppe,

Tyler's having the sole advantage of being within easy walking distance of 221B. On one occasion, as she left the shop with her purchase, a man, just entering, tipped his homburg to her, and somewhat hesitantly asked, "Mrs. Hudson, isn't it?"

She recognized him instantly as the shy, fortyish librarian whom she knew from her observation to have an invalid wife at home and to be childless. She knew of his wife's disability first from the routine disarray of his clothing. Shirts seemed always in need of ironing, and the remains of breakfast were sometimes visible on both his shirt and jacket. That might have suggested a bachelor's existence were it not for the quantity of groceries and packets of powders from the apothecary she often spied under his desk afternoons, when he'd used his lunch break to go shopping. Her conclusion about a childless marriage was confirmed by the single small picture on his desk showing a younger, less harried man standing beside a smiling, pleasant looking woman. Family man that he was, had there been children, their pictures would undoubtedly have also found their way to a corner of his desk.

"It is, Mr. Pederson. I do 'ope you're well." Mrs. Hudson was inclined to continue on her way, but Mr. Pederson had other ideas.

"I must tell you we've missed you at the library. I hope there's nothing wrong."

Perhaps it was her knowledge of Mr. Pederson's situation and its similarity to her own, perhaps it was because his concern seemed terribly genuine and she hadn't shared her loneliness with anyone, perhaps it was some of both. Whatever the cause, she elected to speak of her loss with a near stranger on a London street outside Tyler's Bake Shoppe, albeit without fully revealing the strong feelings she still harbored.

"I'm afraid there's been an un'appy event, Mr. Pederson. I stopped comin' to the library when I lost my 'usband some months ago."

"Oh, how awful." Pederson's long face removed any doubt she might have had about the genuineness of his concern. "I am so sorry, Mrs. Hudson." And in a softer, no less urgent voice, "How are you coping, if I may ask, Mrs. Hudson?"

She forced a sad smile. "Oh well, each day perhaps a little better."

"Well, I'd like to think whatever it was you were working on at the library could be a help. You know you had all of us speculating about what it was you were doing. You seemed so earnest about it. I do hope you'll be coming to see us again to continue your studies—when you feel up to it, of course. It seems a shame to let all your hard work go by the wayside, and it might be that getting back to it can give you some relief. In this world you have to take what relief you can wherever you may find it." Pederson swallowed hard before continuing. "I hope I'm not being too forward, Mrs. Hudson. I do know something about losing the companionship you once had."

"Not at all, Mr. Pederson. Not at all. You've been most kind and understandin'. Just now, I should let you get on about your business, and I'll be gettin' on 'ome to see about mine. And I do 'ope to see you at the library sometime soon—maybe very soon."

It was not an idle statement. Pederson's comments had gotten her to thinking. She had, after all, put in a great deal of work and acquired a considerable level of expertise in criminal investigation. More than that, she owed it to Tobias to make certain his teachings, and all those nights puzzling out the mysteries in the *Evening Standard* would not be for nothing. By the time she got home she had the germ of an outlandish idea as to how she might proceed. By the time she took dinner the idea was still outlandish but had become fully formed. Two days later she placed an advertisement in the *Standard,* the *Times,* the *Express,* and the *Mail.* It read, "Rooms to let, good location, applicants should possess an inquiring mind and curiosity about human behavior." The plan was simple enough. The lodging house at 221B had long ago been leased by Mrs. Hudson and Tobias to be their home for now, and to provide an income from the lodgers they would accommodate after his retirement. Now, it would have a new role. It would become the site of the consulting detective agency she was determined to found. The newspaper advertisement would attract someone to act as the male figurehead a woman attempting to start her own business would require.

When the several respondents to her advertisement had been seen and judged, a tall, slender chemist appeared by far the best man to act as her face to the world. His high forehead and precise Cambridge diction suggested the necessary intelligence. His haughty self-assurance would, she felt certain, instill confidence in the work

5

of the agency. The physician who accompanied him provided a clear, if unexpected, bonus to his selection. Indeed, his quiet, levelheaded demeanor, and the steady hand she felt certain he would bring to their partnership put Mrs. Hudson in mind of her own dear Tobias.

A look to the teapot reminded her it was time for refreshments to be brought to the sitting room. Setting tea and scones on a tray together with a pot of strawberry jam, she climbed the steps to the sitting room to provide food and drink to the men and to divine what she could of the reason for Buffalo Bill Cody's visit.

"Ah, the tea, and some of your delightful scones, Mrs. Hudson," Holmes smiled his gratitude while Watson cleared a place to accommodate Mrs. Hudson's tray.

"You English and your tea," said the man in buckskin. "Is there anything more you need to know? Will you take my case?" He glanced for a moment to Mrs. Hudson. "We do understand that everything I've told you is in confidence." As if to make clear he need have no worry on that score, Mrs. Hudson continued methodically distributing plates, cups and saucers, seemingly oblivious to anything beyond her mundane household duties.

Holmes screwed his face to a look of utter confusion, then pretended a sudden inspiration. "You mean old Hudson," Holmes chuckled at the thought. "She's been with us for years. I assure you she's totally trustworthy. Try one of these delicious scones. It's something she does quite well."

In spite of Holmes's reassurance, Cody watched Mrs. Hudson complete her task and leave before speaking again. It frustrated the Baker Street trio's usual procedure. Normally, Mrs. Hudson's entrance would trigger Watson's request to read and make certain the notes he had been taking accurately reflected the client's report. His always accurate review would give her a clear understanding of the client's problem. This time, Mrs. Hudson would only learn the problem after the client's leaving. As it turned out, she didn't have long to wait. Within ten minutes, a grim-faced Colonel Cody made a rapid exit from 221B, only stopping briefly to make known to Mrs. Hudson his appreciation for the tea and extend his compliments on her baking. Moments later, the Baker Street trio was seated at Mrs. Hudson's kitchen table ready to consider the problem Cody had shared with them.

Watson set his notes on the table, but before beginning his recitation, thought it wise, if not essential, to lay the groundwork for the unusual action he and Holmes had taken in their meeting with Cody.

"Mrs. Hudson, Holmes and I need to acknowledge at the outset the colonel's difficulty is somewhat foreign to our experience. Nonetheless, we did feel that, if for no other reason than the simple courtesy of helping our much-celebrated American friend, we should take on the case he presented. In a word, we agreed to help him resolve his problem without having a discussion involving the three of us as we normally do." Watson cleared his throat noisily and continued without looking up from his notes. "His problem involves the recovery of his horse which appears to have been kidnapped." Still focused on his notes, he added, "the animal answers to the name of Duke."

Seeing that the grimace, which had been gradually forming across Mrs. Hudson' features, had now completed its journey, Holmes attempted a spirited defense of his and his colleague's action. "It's well to remember this type of crime is not completely out of our experience," Holmes reminded her. "It's not as if we haven't dealt with kidnappings before. There was Ludwig Viktor, the brother of the Austrian emperor, who, you'll remember, was held for ransom by a group of Bosnian separatists. And, closer to home, the grocer's daughter who was taken from her school."

Watson pursed his lips before speaking. "I'm not sure we can count that one, Holmes. You'll remember it turned out she had conspired with her boyfriend to kidnap herself."

The grimace gone, but with eyebrows now threatening an assault on her forehead, Mrs. Hudson stared a long moment at each of her colleagues. Both men recognized it was not a good sign. "You will recall that in each of those instances the victim was two-legged and capable of describin' 'is captors when it became useful to do so."

Holmes shrugged his unconcern with what he viewed as a minor point. Watson decided on another line of attack. "We felt it to be a rather special situation, Mrs. Hudson, or we would never have agreed to take the case without consultation. The horse in question is

7

the colonel's own animal that he rides in his Wild West Show. A very distinctive palomino that has been trained to perform and is 'integral'—to use the colonel's own word—to the success of the show. In a word, it is of considerable value to the colonel and he has promised a packet to get it back." Sympathy for an animal being held against its will having failed to move Mrs. Hudson, he hoped an appeal of a more practical nature might succeed.

Whether swayed by the promise of substantial reward or simply resigned to what appeared inevitable, Mrs. Hudson groaned her acquiescence. "Well, you've given your word, and to renege on it wouldn't be right, to say nothin' of its bein' bad for business if talk got around. So, what do we know about this 'orse stealin'?"

Watson seized on Mrs. Hudson's grudging acceptance and tried to instill an enthusiasm for the task she clearly lacked. "What we know is the story told to Cody by a very upset, very embarrassed stable boy, a youngster of about sixteen who is the son of one of the performers in the Wild West Show.

"The boy reported that late last night, after everyone had settled down and he was alone in the stable, there was a pounding on the door and a girl's voice calling for help and crying—at least it sounded to him like crying. He thought he had to let her in, if only to find out what was wrong. He didn't ask her name and all he can say about her is that she was probably about thirteen or fourteen, had sort of a long face, brown hair that went down below her shoulders in two twists where they were tied together, and that she was slender—'skinny' was the word the boy used. The girl told him her brother had fallen down a nearby embankment and couldn't get back up. She said she thought he had broken a leg. The stable boy felt he had to go with her. Besides which, he didn't see how there could be any danger with seemingly no one around, and her crying and carrying on was beginning to—again, the boy's words—'spook the horses.'

"By the time they had walked to the part of the embankment where she said her brother had fallen, they had gotten so far from the lighted area that the boy reported he could barely see his hand in front of his face. That was when the girl slipped away. A short time later he heard a noise coming from the stable and when he looked back, he saw Cody's horse with two riders. With the light from the stable, he's certain that one of them was the girl and he believes the other was somewhat smaller and a boy. It would seem that while the girl led the stable boy away from the barn, the boy—who was, of course, perfectly safe—went in through the open door, got a bridle on Cody's horse, picked up the girl who'd started back in the dark and the two of them took off riding bareback."

Watson closed his accounts book and finished his report. "Cody would like us to find his horse before noon tomorrow. He's scheduled to put on the show's first public performance at two that afternoon. As we know, there was a show yesterday for King Edward, Queen Alexandra and others in the royal family, and today was set aside to allow his people to recover from the celebration that followed yesterday's performance and prepare for the later shows. Holmes and I pointed out that a day and not quite a half was a good deal less than generous given what little we had to go on, but he was quite insistent on that point."

"We should probably start with questioning the stable boy," Holmes suggested. "There's a good chance that whatever's been done, he's part of it. He's young, very likely new to this kind of thing and should be easy to break down."

"I rather doubt the stable boy's involvement, Mr. 'Olmes. As you say, 'e's young and new to this kind of thing. If 'e was part of this kidnappin'—or 'orse-nappin'—one wouldn't expect 'im to return to the stables to face Colonel Cody and likely 'is own father, who you say is part of the show. Besides which, 'e's also new to this country and with the show just gettin' started, 'e wouldn't 'ardly 'ave 'ad time to recruit a pair of accomplices from a place 'e's never been or to 'ave scouted out somewhere safe to take the animal. No, I think our young stable boy is tellin' the truth and there's nothin' more we could 'ope to get out of 'im."

"Well then, Mrs. Hudson, what is your thinking about the horse-napping?" Watson asked.

"I believe it's exactly what it appears to be, Doctor. A prank organized by two children, almost certainly brother and sister since youngsters that age rarely form cross-sex friendships. They would obviously be subject to loose supervision, or more likely absent parents. Since the 'orse 'as not shown up, it is clear the children 'ave access to a barn where the 'orse can be kept. Moreover, they could not 'ave gone far without rousin' suspicion or tirin' the 'orse, meanin' the children and the 'orse are likely on a farm not very far from the exhibition grounds. It's only to the west of the exhibition grounds there's still farmland, so we'll need to ask people who live out that way if they know a farm where there's a brother and sister likely between eleven and fourteen years with the girl the older of the two. Somebody's bound to know them. When we find them, we need to remember they're just children playin' at a game and not scare them out of their wits. I'm thinkin' it might be well for a woman to be along to make it seem less threatenin'.

"We'll want to start within the hour. We'll need a carriage to go over the country roads. Can you arrange to rent one, Doctor?"

Watson nodded although neither Mrs. Hudson nor Holmes looked to him, all three knowing her words only sounded like a request.

By late morning they had arrived at the exhibition grounds west of the city. Ten years earlier it had provided a venue for Indians from the Empire of India to entertain and to acquaint the English with their culture; now, it provided a venue for Indians from the American West, together with cowboy trick riders and sharpshooters, to entertain and to acquaint the English with selected aspects of American Indian culture. They chose the road that took them due west from the exhibition grounds, passing patches of grassland and small clusters of trees, before coming finally to long furrows of unrecognizable plantings extending from the road to distant houses and barns. The farmhouse on the left side of the road being the first encountered, it became their initial stop.

It had been agreed that three strangers descending on the woman or man of the house might seem overwhelming and create unwanted defensiveness. It was seen as best for Watson to wait in the carriage while Holmes and Mrs. Hudson conducted the inquiry. It was reasoned that the name, Sherlock Holmes, might make clear the seriousness of their investigation while Mrs. Hudson's matronly presence—although no one used that term—might not only prove comforting with children, but might also loosen the tongues of adults who would otherwise be loath to speak to strangers about their neighbors.

10

Accordingly, Watson remained in the carriage, reining the horse to a stop just beyond the three steps leading to the farmhouse porch. Holmes and Mrs. Hudson climbed to the top step and were in the process of setting their faces to meet the situation they anticipated—Holmes's serious, befitting the search for horse thieves regardless of their age, and Mrs. Hudson's gently sympathetic, befitting the search for children regardless of their crime—when the woman of the house opened the front door. She was wiping her hands on a part of the apron she had scooped up for the purpose. She was tall, and thin, almost gaunt, and she too had set her face. Hers suggested a less than welcoming spirit toward her would-be visitors. When she spoke, the suggestion became fact. Words that might have sounded a greeting were undone by the tone in which they were spoken.

"Hello. Is there something I can do for you?"

"Good morning. My name is Sherlock Holmes, and this is Mrs. Hudson." Holmes paused to allow for an expression of recognition that never came. "We're here in search of a horse that seems to have wandered off in the company of two young children, a boy and a girl. We're searching for the horse on behalf of its owner."

The woman looked to them and then to the man in the carriage as if she was searching for the real motive for their coming. "And you think your horse might be here?"

Mrs. Hudson had doubts about any approach succeeding with the woman. but thought it worth trying a genial woman to woman exchange. "Nothin' like that, Mrs. ..."

There was a long pause, then a reluctant, "Walls. Mrs. Jeremiah Walls."

"Nothin' like that, Mrs. Walls, we don't know where the 'orse is, and we believe it's all nothin' more than a prank, but it's important we find the animal before the youngsters get themselves into real trouble. We're lookin' for a farm where the children—a boy and girl likely between eleven and fourteen are livin'." The sympathetic smile she had tried earlier resurfaced as she finished her appeal. The effort was marginally successful as Mrs. Walls became marginally amiable.

"Children can bring worry into a house. No question about that. Mr. Walls and I don't have any ourselves, mind you, but there's

11

nieces and nephews, a bunch of them." She shook her head disapprovingly, whether of their behavior or their existence was unclear. She then reverted to her earlier self. "I'm afraid I can't help you, Mr. Hines, Mrs. Hudson. I don't know anything about runaway horses or children. If that's all you wanted, I'll wish you good day and get back to my baking." With that, she turned so sharply, she missed seeing the man she knew as Hines tip his hat or the woman called Hudson smile her good-bye.

They climbed back in the carriage and, without words between them, headed for the farmhouse right of the road. Its owner, or more likely its owner's father wore an empty smile as he followed their progress to the edge of the farmhouse porch. Only then did the smile become a look of worried concentration as he struggled to determine who these strangers were and what they might want of him. His greeting quickly made clear the fruitlessness of their visit.

"If you're looking for my son, he ain't here. Don't know when he'll be back. Elizabeth's gone with him if you wanted to speak to her. There's just me and there's not much I can do for you."

This time there was no getting out of the carriage. All recognized the unpromising nature of the situation, but they had come this far and nothing would be lost by calling a question to the man. Holmes shouted to him, "How well do you know the families here about?"

"Families? What families?"

"I wanted to ask you about the other farmers who live nearby, whether any of them have young children—we're looking for a family with a boy and a girl somewhere between eleven and fourteen?"

"There's just the one boy, William. That's what he calls himself. William. Doesn't like Bill, just William. He went with them, my son and Elizabeth. My son is also William, but he's alright with Bill."

Holmes yielded to the futility of further questioning. "Thank you. We won't take up any more of your time."

The vacant smile returned as William's father and grandfather watched the carriage retrace the route to the main road. There was silence inside the carriage as each of its occupants dealt with the possibility that finding the two children, and the horse that answered to the name, Duke, might be a more formidable task than any had anticipated. As they pondered the situation, the carriage came to a point where paths branched off right and left of the main road. Watson held the horse in check while they stopped to consider whether to follow one or the other path or continue along the main road. After brief discussion, they decided to stay with the main road. The path to the right showed a patch of woods with no end in sight, the path to the left passed a vast lake with what appeared to be a farmhouse on its other side. The distance to that house, and the unpredictability of the road to reach it, made the decision an easy, if not entirely satisfactory one. Inquiries at the next three farmhouses on the main road did nothing to bolster confidence in the choice made. They hoped without conviction for better luck with the fourth.

Holmes and Mrs. Hudson ascended three steps to the wide front porch that seemed a staple of every farmhouse. Holmes's knock was answered by a girl of about fifteen with red hair, a wealth of freckles and a friendly open face. She pushed back rimless glasses that ever after appeared intent on getting as far down her nose as possible before getting caught and pushed back. She looked to the strangers with a half-smile. The single word she spoke was less a welcome than an expression of curiosity about their visit.

"Yes?"

Holmes smiled his most ingratiating before answering. "My name is Sherlock Holmes, and this is Mrs. Hudson. Are your parents at home?"

"They're in the barn." She nodded to a building some distance from the house while herself remaining framed in the doorway. "One of the horses is down."

Mrs. Hudson decided not to wait for the girl's parents. "We believe there's a farm somewhere near to 'ere where there's a boy and girl close to your age, probably a little younger."

Curiosity remained the dominant force but now was expressed with a note of caution. "Why are you looking for them?"

Mrs. Hudson continued. "We think they could be in some trouble. Nothin' really bad. They took someone's 'orse for play, but they 'aven't returned it yet. We mean to find the 'orse and get it back to its owner before they get into any real trouble."

13

The girl looked to Mrs. Hudson then to Holmes, a broad grin suddenly creasing her face.

"That sounds like Joy and Jonathan. They're always pulling stunts like that." Her lip now curled in teen-age disgust. "They're just children."

"Do they live near here?" Holmes asked.

"Not far, but you'll have to go back toward town. You'll come to a road where you can go right past a lake or left past some woods. Sort of a lot of woods. You want to go past the woods. After that you'll come to a farm, a pretty big farm—the Stockton farm. You'll want to be careful about Mr. Stockton. He's their father and he won't be happy when he hears what Joy and Jonathan have done."

Mrs. Hudson and Holmes nodded an understanding they did not fully possess, heartily thanked the girl whose name they still did not know and returned to the carriage, now confident their search was coming to an end.

As it turned out, the farm was only a short distance beyond the woods they had seen from the road, but the density of those woods made it impossible to get a glimpse of the farm until a last turn took them beyond the small forest. When they did come within sight of it, they were quickly struck by the difference between the Stockton farm and all the others. The difference began with the turnoff from the main road onto the dirt path leading to the farmhouse. Entering that path, one passed beneath a wrought iron arch holding within it the name STOCKTON in thick lettering. Beyond the arch they were guided to the front porch of the farmhouse by the neatly pruned wintergreen boxed hedges that lined both sides of the path they were to follow. Ending temporarily at the porch, the boxwood hedges could be seen to reappear beneath each of the farmhouse's ground floor windows.

The farmhouse itself was an enlarged version of those they'd already seen. While there were the usual two windows on each landing to the left of the entrance, there were three windows on each landing to the right an increase of at least two rooms over its neighbors.

Like all the others, the farmhouse was painted milk white; white seeming to be the only color available for painting farmhouses in the area. The windows were framed by dark shutters, and multiple chimneys protruded from a peaked roof.

With the success of their mission now in sight, Holmes and Mrs. Hudson came as close to bounding up the steps to the porch as the director of London's premier consulting detective agency could manage. Holmes made spirited use of the knocker on the front door but got no response. He shrugged his frustration and changed strategies, now calling in a loud, but he hoped not unfriendly voice, "Is anybody home?"

After a short pause, a somewhat tremulous female voice answered his question with a question of her own. "Who's there?"

Holmes looked to Mrs. Hudson with eyebrows raised and found her looking to him in kind. He continued his speech to the closed door in a voice he was certain carried to the fields beyond the house. "I am Sherlock Holmes and I wish to talk to you about Jonathan and Joy."

"What about them?"

It occurred to Holmes that, if this arrangement continued, he would be discussing improper and possibly criminal behaviors with an unknown number of unknown persons. With a nod from Mrs. Hudson, he sought to address that difficulty.

"Would it be possible for us to talk without having to shout past the door? I promise I won't detain you long."

Silence met Holmes's request and continued for a frustratingly lengthy interval. Holmes and Mrs. Hudson detected muffled voices beyond the door but couldn't make out the number of persons involved or what they were discussing. When the door was opened finally, it was not a girl with a tremulous voice who stood in the doorway. Instead, they were confronted by an intense young man they judged still in his teens, who viewed both Holmes and Mrs. Hudson with a suspicion he matched with the words he spoke. "What is it you want with them?"

"May I first know with whom I'm speaking. I've told you my name is Sherlock Holmes and let me introduce Mrs. Hudson." Holmes tilted his head in the direction of Mrs. Hudson lest there be any confusion about the person he was referencing. "My friend, Dr. Watson, is in the carriage below."

"Sherlock Holmes, the detective?

"I know of no other."

The young man's eyes widened, and he visibly gulped, but he was no more forthcoming for having realized the celebrity of his visitor. "And you want to see Jonathan and Joy. Why? They're just children."

Mrs. Hudson thought it time she entered the conversation. She looked beyond the doorkeeper, hoping to get a more cooperative response from the girl of about seventeen intently watching the exchange from a distance behind him. "There's a good chance the young people could be in trouble if we don't 'ave a chat." The warning given, she added a note of urgency to her voice while suggesting the relationship she suspected. "You're the children's sister, aren't you?"

There came a drawn out, "Yes," as if she was uncertain what she might be revealing with the admission.

Indeed, Mrs. Hudson already knew a good deal about her beyond her being the sister of the children they sought. Her hesitancy to open the door and the tremulous voice in which she answered Mr. Holmes, combined with the boy's presence at a time her parents appeared to be away, pointed to her involvement with a young man who had earned her favor but not yet that of her parents. In fact, the opportunity for his visit in the absence of disapproving parents likely led to the less than diligent supervision of the two young children, a responsibility that almost certainly fell to her in the absence of their parents.

The young man reasserted himself in the role of protector. "What is it that they've done—or that you believe they've done?"

The initial ready acceptance of the youngsters' misbehavior suggested to Mrs. Hudson a history of minor transgressions. It emboldened her to forego further explanation and move directly to the reason for their visit.

"Are you aware of a 'orse on your farm that doesn't belong to you?"

The question led the young man to take a long step back, pulling the door wide as he did, thereby, however unintentionally, giving opportunity for Holmes and Mrs. Hudson to enter the house. They seized the opportunity without concern about its origin.

Directed to what she took to be the parlor, Mrs. Hudson was surprised at the contrast between the prosperity suggested by the farmhouse's exterior and the modesty of the furnishings making up its interior. Chairs and the room's sofa were somewhat the worse for wear, showing occasional nicks and scratches inexpertly repaired. A low table bore the scars of a careless smoker without any pretense of repair. It was evident to Mrs. Hudson that the farmhouse owner cared deeply about outward appearance and spent money accordingly.

Having been identified as the sister of the two delinquents, and fully expecting there to be a strange horse in her family's barn, the young woman became both more cooperative and more decisive. She spoke first to her boyfriend. "Benjamin, I believe we need to talk to Joy and Jonathan now before my parents get home."

Benjamin nodded his grim agreement and left to gather up the two youngsters.

After seeing her visitors to seats on the room's sofa, she settled herself on an easy chair opposite and belatedly introduced herself. "My name is Olivia, Olivia Stockton. My parents are away for the weekend and I was left to watch Joy and Jonathan. I'm afraid I haven't been doing a very good job of it. They brought home this palomino they told me they had borrowed from their friend, Ethan, who lives a few farms over. I should have checked on it, but I was sort of busy." She blushed on hearing her own words, confirming Mrs. Hudson's judgment that her parents did not know of and would not approve of Benjamin's visit. "Anyway, if they did something wrong, I'm sure they were just being playful and didn't mean anything by it," she grimaced a moment before continuing, "although I'm not sure father will see it that way."

At that point they were joined by a somewhat breathless Benjamin, and two children who stared curiously at the two people on the sofa before turning their attention to their sister for explanation. Mrs. Hudson was now certain she was staring at what were very likely the two youngest horse thieves in all England— probably in all the Empire. Their sister chose, for the moment, to concentrate on a related but different concern.

"Aren't those the same clothes you people wore yesterday?"

Both children ignored the question whose answer was surely known to the person who posed it. Instead, the girl shrugged and asked a question of her own. "What is it you want?"

17

"These people want to talk to you and Jonathan. When that's done, we need to have our own talk."

The children, still standing, transferred their bemused expressions from their sister to the two strangers. Holmes decided it was time to take control of the situation. First, he again introduced Mrs. Hudson and himself, this time with a small smile meant to put the children at their ease. Since they were already at their ease the smile was wasted.

"It's my understanding that you have borrowed a horse." Holmes kept his small smile in service, hoping for its greater impact as he looked to each child for response. The boy met his gaze briefly before finding something of interest in the carpet at his feet. The girl did not look away and even mimicked Holmes's small smile. Like her brother, however, she said nothing.

Mrs. Hudson felt a sterner approach was in order. "What Mr. 'Olmes is sayin' is that we know you took a 'orse that belongs to somebody else, and that person has asked us to bring 'is 'orse back. I'm thinkin' we'll find the animal in the barn. I'm also thinkin' if the owner 'as to come out 'ere to get 'is animal, 'e could bring a constable with 'im and there'd be a lot more trouble than if the animal was brought back by the people who borrowed it."

The boy looked to the girl; the girl looked to Mrs. Hudson. When she spoke, it was to clarify a point. "It's not an animal; it's a horse."

Mrs. Hudson granted the point, trading the child's small victory for the implicit acknowledgment of hers and her brother's misdeed.

However, it was not Joy, but her brother, Jonathan, who made their guilt explicit. "We were going to return him later anyway. We just wanted to ride him a while. We fed him and gave him water and we scrubbed him down."

His sister nodded and supported her brother's words by staring defiantly at Holmes.

Olivia, sternly, if somewhat belatedly, assumed her supervisory responsibility. "How could you people do anything so crazy? What do you think will happen when father finds out about it?"

Joy again shrugged a response. "We can easy have the horse back to the exhibition grounds before he gets back." Then she looked meaningfully to her sister. "Just like you'll make sure Benjamin is out of here before father gets back."

Mrs. Hudson had the sense of watching an oft repeated conflict, both sides having things to hide from a common adversary. She wondered about a family in which the father was viewed by his children with such trepidation and the mother seemed somewhere out of view. Mrs. Hudson shook her head in silent disapproval and was thankful she could soon wash her hands of this family.

"As I'm sure Mr. 'Olmes will agree, the task now is to get the animal—the 'orse—back to its rightful owner and avoid anyone gettin' themselves into needless difficulty."

Holmes eased back into a smile as he and Mrs. Hudson continued in their unanticipated exchange of roles with Mrs. Hudson the unrelenting authority and Holmes the understanding ally. "I tell you what," he spoke in a low, conspiratorial tone, "if you take the horse to the exhibition grounds now, we'll give you a ride back home in our carriage."

Joy and Jonathan made a small nod to each other before addressing the others. Joy again spoke for them both. "The horse is in the stable. Only one thing. Me and Jonathan get to ride him one last time. We can do that taking him back to the exhibition grounds." The request won reluctant nods from Holmes and Mrs. Hudson.

A half hour later Colonel Cody had his horse back. After a thorough examination, he declared him "not the worse for wear." In fact, he thought the horse had been well cared for, and was amused by a prank that was not entirely foreign to his own youth. He forgave the children "provided they would never do anything like that again," and gave each of them an autographed placard of the Wild West Show. After smiling his appreciation to Watson and Mrs. Hudson, he vigorously shook the hand Holmes offered before placing in it the packet Watson had said they would be receiving. When that was done, the colonel gave all three open tickets to attend the show as his guest whenever was convenient and exacted a promise they bring Joy and Jonathan when they came—an addendum that brought broad smiles to the youngsters' faces and a clapping of hands by Jonathan.

19

The Baker Street trio then took Joy and Jonathan back to their home, where neither Olivia or Benjamin, or the children's parents were anywhere to be seen. They wished the children well and restated Colonel Cody's admonition to them to do nothing like that again, "that" being left purposely vague to encompass as broad a range of misbehaviors as seemed within the children's repertoire. They received neither goodbyes nor assurances that whatever "that" was, it would not be repeated. Neither omission surprised them.

Three weeks went by before any thought was given to the Wild West Show or the possibility of the Baker Street trio attending a performance. Their time and energies were entirely taken up with resolving the mystery of the eight dollhouses. Having uncovered the clue hidden in each of the dollhouses owned by the recently deceased Sir Henry Aspinwall, Eighth Earl of Pickery, and fitted those clues together, they had been able to discover the location of the last will and testament of the eccentric earl. That greatly relieved the earl's several heirs, some of whom would now extricate themselves from debt, while others would adopt a lifestyle long denied them that would ultimately thrust them into debt. That, however, was for the future. In the present, overcome with relief and gratitude, the earl's heirs bestowed on the members of the consulting detective agency their second packet in a month. Resolution of the mystery also left the Baker Street trio free to take advantage of Cody's invitation to attend his Wild West Show, which, courtesy, as well as curiosity, demanded. As it happened, however, before they could honor that invitation, a second, more pressing request arrived from the colonel.

The request was again delivered by Buffalo Bill Cody, once more in buckskin dress and Stetson hat, once more the sensation of Baker Street. On this occasion he was accompanied by two very recognizable children, each grasping a hand of the colonel. They smiled shyly to Mrs. Hudson who greeted them as Miss Joy and Master Jonathan as she admitted the unlikely trio. Cody looked to the stairs and Mrs. Hudson nodded, only regretting she would not see the looks on the faces of her colleagues when their unbidden guests entered the sitting room. Instead, she asked Cody whether he would like tea, the children whether they would like cocoa and all three whether they would like raisin scones. She got an affirmative response to each query.

When she later came upstairs with a well-stocked tray, she stimulated a brief competition between Watson and the colonel, ultimately won by the colonel, to relieve her of her burden and locate an empty place to set down the drinks and refreshments. Holmes affected a tolerant smile as he watched the small drama play itself out, then addressed himself to Mrs. Hudson who had turned to leave.

"Don't go just yet, Mrs. Hudson. Something's come up in which you may be able to play a small role. Perhaps you should have a seat while we explain the situation to you." Holmes offered no suggestion as to where she might sit, and it was left to Watson to remove the books occupying the seat of an otherwise inviting easy chair. When she was settled and had given Holmes her full attention, he resumed speaking, now affecting the air of an overlord giving direction to a somewhat slow-witted subordinate. Only Watson recognized the absurdity of the situation.

"It's a rather unpleasant turn of events and I hope you won't be unduly alarmed." Holmes paused to fortify himself with a sip of tea before sharing his potentially alarming news. "You'll recall we were at the Stockton farm a short time ago to recover Colonel Cody's horse." Mrs. Hudson lowered her eyelids by way of acknowledgment. "It seems there has been a far greater tragedy visited on the Stockton family." Out of the corner of his eye, Holmes looked to the two children sitting close together on the settee, both of them bolt upright, eyes wide with anticipation, their one-time brash behavior nowhere in evidence. Holmes looked again to Mrs. Hudson, and now continued in a softer tone.

"As I say, a great tragedy. Mr. Stockton is no longer with us. I'm afraid he was shot and killed just a little while ago. That led our two young friends," Holmes gently nodded toward the settee, "to leave home and find their way to the exhibition grounds where they sought out the colonel and asked to join the Wild West Show. It seems there had been some angry words with Mr. Stockton yesterday and they were afraid—totally without reason, of course—that they might be seen as somehow responsible for the tragedy." Holmes smiled indulgently to the children whose troubled expressions did not change. He turned his attention back to Mrs. Hudson but kept in place the indulgent smile.

"Under the circumstances, we thought it might be well for you to take the young people downstairs and perhaps give them some treats while Watson and I discuss the case with Colonel Cody. The colonel has been in touch with their mother, so she knows they're safe and we don't have to hurry them back. Colonel Cody has graciously offered to help in resolving the mystery since the young people saw fit to contact him. It was the colonel's idea for you to take charge of the young people. He believes that being a woman, you might have a natural rapport with youthful minds."

With difficulty, Mrs. Hudson resisted the temptation to respond to the opening Holmes provided. Instead, she gathered up Joy and Jonathan, and asked Watson to help her with the tray now restocked with cocoa and scones and suddenly grown unwieldy for one person to manage. She settled the children in her kitchen where they began a vigorous assault on her scones. She then walked with Watson to the foot of the stairs where he quickly outlined what little was known about the murder of Roger Stockton. The victim had gone for his customary early morning walk in the woods that separated his farm from that of his neighbor to the north. His body was discovered by his wife who had gone looking for him when he seemed gone overlong. She had told the children of their father's death, then called the police. Mrs. Hudson gave him a tight-lipped nod and said she would learn what she could from the children and that he and Mr. Holmes should learn what more they could from Colonel Cody. Once the children and Colonel Cody were gone, she continued, the three of them would meet to share what they had learned and to devise the next steps in their investigation. It was their usual procedure although Watson's somber expression made it appear he was hearing it for the first time.

Mrs. Hudson waited until Jonathan and Joy were sufficiently along on their cocoa and scones to have developed small brown moustaches, and for the worry lines they displayed early on to have all but disappeared. It was then time to discover what she could of their father's death. She took a sheet of paper from her purse and with a pencil in readiness, began her questioning.

"I wonder if you can tell me who lives at 'ome with you and who comes to visit?"

The children looked to each other before they responded. When they spoke, it was in the context of a small contest in sharing what each knew. Joy spoke first. "There's mam and Olivia. Of course, they live at home. And there's mam's brother, our Uncle Percy. He comes to visit pretty regular but only when our father's away. They had a big fight one time where Uncle Percy knocked father down. Anyway, that's what Olivia says." Joy's face puckered with a sudden thought. "I guess he'll come more often now. He's nice. His last name is Dickson."

"Which was our mam's name before she got married," Jonathan quickly added.

"And was your Uncle Percy 'ere last night or early this mornin'?"

Both children shook their heads in unison. After which Jonathan volunteered more names. "There's also Mr. and Mrs. Fiddleman. They sort of live here. Their home is over the stables. Mrs. Fiddleman is our housekeeper and Mr. Fiddleman works in the house and on the grounds. He's good at fixing things. Anyway, that's what mam says."

Joy felt further clarification was needed and elaborated on her brother's contribution. "She's our cook as well as our housekeeper, and he's her husband." She then turned back to her brother to add yet another name to their list. "And don't forget grandpa."

"I didn't forget, I was gonna say him next," Jonathan insisted in a voice a half octave higher and several decibels louder than was necessary to make himself heard.

Mrs. Hudson raised a question in a purposefully calm, soft voice in hopes of containing the small conflict. "What about your grandfather?"

Her effort was largely successful as Jonathan responded in a tone of near normal volume. "Grandpa is our father's father. He's very old and he stays in bed most all the time. Grandma died a long time ago. We didn't know her, but Olivia did—sort of. She doesn't remember much about her though."

23

Joy waited until her brother had finished, then again added a clarifying coda to his report. "Our mam is Olivia's mam's sister." She pressed her lips tight together, content that she had gotten in the last word on the subject.

It was for Mrs. Hudson, however, the first word on a new and surprising subject.

"Are you sayin' that your father was first married to another lady who was Olivia's mam, and that later he married that lady's sister and she is now your mam?"

Joy was only too happy to say again what she had just told Mrs. Hudson. "That's right. Olivia's mam died, so he married her sister to give Olivia a mam, and then we came along and she was our mam too."

"And 'ow old is your sister Olivia?"

"She's just eighteen. Her birthday was last month."

"And 'ow old are the two of you?

"I'm thirteen and Jonathan's twelve."

"'Ave you always lived on the farm?"

Joy nodded, "Always." Jonathan added, "We were born there. The farm has been in the family from way back, way before grandpa. Father says that now that I came along it always will be." He smiled brightly at his involuntary achievement.

"Except there's Benjamin and what father calls the 'awful Olyphants,'" Joy said. "You saw Benjamin when you came to the farm the first time," she reminded Mrs. Hudson. "He wants our farm, or really his father does. Which is why he wants to marry Olivia. Anyway, that's what father says, or anyway said, so he didn't let Benjamin come around. Except Benjamin lives one farm over just past the woods, so he and Olivia can easy work it out to see each other any time they want."

"Any time they want," Jonathan echoed and they grinned broadly to each other.

"Is there more cocoa?" Jonathan asked. "And scones?" Joy added.

Mrs. Hudson pushed away from the table to see about their requests. She filled their cups but had to substitute biscuits for scones much to the youngsters' highly visible disappointment. With that crisis passed, she followed up the last part of their discussion.

"Why did your father think these Olyphants want your farm?"

Joy shrugged while Jonathan bit off a piece of the biscuit he had selected. "He just does. It makes Olivia mad. She says Benjamin loves her and it's got nothing to do with the farm."

"'Ave Olivia and Benjamin been seein' each other for long?"

"For as long as I can remember," Joy said.

"Me too," Jonathan added after swallowing the last of his biscuit and palming another to have in readiness.

Mrs. Hudson was about to ask additional questions about the Olyphants when a familiar voice called from the top of the stairs. "We're done here, Mrs. Hudson. We'll be putting the youngsters in a carriage to get them home."

Mrs. Hudson filed her questions for use at a later time. She smiled the children out the door and into the four-wheeler Watson had hailed.

Tea replaced cocoa as Mrs. Hudson held a second meeting at her kitchen table. Holmes and Watson expressed the same disappointment over the absence of scones as did the children they replaced at the table.

After promising to correct that deficiency in the very near future, Mrs. Hudson asked, "'Ow was your meetin' with Colonel Cody? What did 'e 'ave to tell you?"

"Not a great deal, Mrs. Hudson." As if to confirm his words, Watson did not consult the accounts book he used for note taking as was his usual habit. "The colonel could only say what the children told him, and all the children knew is what their mother had told them—that their father had died in the woods where he went for his morning walks. That, and the fact that the children thought they might be responsible for his death because they had wished for it, and even prayed for it after their argument the night before. Cody finally convinced them that they had no responsibility for their father's death, and that their mother would be worried sick about them and needed to know they were alright. They agreed, but only after Colonel Cody told them that he would ask Holmes to help find the person who killed their father. According to the colonel, the children view Holmes as a great detective, what with his finding the two of them and the colonel's horse."

25

Watson paused for a moment, caught between a giggle and an effort to look properly sober. As amusing as the children's assessment was, he had to acknowledge that, largely on the basis of that assessment, and for the second time in less than a month, he and Holmes had broken the agency's rules and accepted a case without consultation with its director. With a damn the consequences flair, Watson blurted out their transgression.

"With all that, Mrs. Hudson, we didn't feel we could refuse the case. Besides, the truth is we have nothing on right now. I'm afraid, however, Cody couldn't really tell us much and we have very little to go on."

"We might 'ave somethin'," Mrs. Hudson smiled and sipped her tea, having decided to overlook her colleagues' action—at least for the moment. "Jonathan and Joy were most forthcomin'. There's things they talked about that will bear our lookin' into."

"They are, after all, children, Mrs. Hudson, "can we really take anything they say with confidence?" Holmes sniffed his disbelief.

"We'll try to stick with those things they saw themselves, Mr. 'Olmes, but you're right, we'll take whatever they say with a grain of salt except, of course, when it comes to their thinkin' about great detectives."

"I thought surely, in that regard at least, you found them insightful beyond their years, Holmes." Watson was finally free to give vent to the giggles he had been at pains to contain. Holmes regarded him with the disdain he felt the comment deserved.

"The situation with Mr. Stockton and the family is more than a little complicated. There's first that Mr. Stockton 'as been married twice, and the second time to the sister from the first marriage," Mrs. Hudson began. "Which is to say, when 'is first wife died, 'e married 'er sister. Olivia, the daughter we met when we were at the farm, is from the first marriage and Jonathan and Joy are from the second." Mrs. Hudson stopped to sip some tea, giving her colleagues time to sort through the relationships she had enumerated.

"As the children describe the family, they 'ave an uncle, Percy Dickson, who would be the brother of both the current wife and the last one. They only see Mr. Dickson when their father is away because there's been bad blood between Mr. Stockton and the uncle, which led to a fight between them some time ago—at least that's their understanding. There's also the children's grandfather, their father's father, who lives with them, but sounds to be pretty much confined to 'is bed and 'is room.

"There's others who, accordin' to the children, 'ad their problems with Mr. Stockton. You'll remember the boy, Benjamin—Benjamin Olyphant as it turns out. E's sweet on Olivia, and from the looks of things when we were there, she's sweet on 'im. Joy and Jonathan say they want to marry, but Mr. Stockton was against their even seein' each other, thinkin' the romance was part of Mr. Olyphant's plan to get 'is farm. It's my understandin' the Olyphants live just the other side of the woods that separates the two properties so it wouldn't be 'ard to join them up after a marriage—or a murder.

"In a word, gentlemen, we've got a number of people to sort through who 'ave or may 'ave a grievance of some sort with Mr. Stockton. And that's not to leave out the current Mrs. Stockton who would appear to 'ave 'ad a difficult life with Mr. Stockton and may stand to get a sizable inheritance to make up for it."

"What is it you suggest, Mrs. Hudson?" Watson asked.

"We've got the better part of the day ahead of us, Doctor, I suggest we decide who it is we want to talk to and what we want to know from them."

"It seems clear as well that we need to get to the scene of the murder before whatever clues may be there are trampled by the authorities," volunteered Holmes. "Hopefully, it's not already too late."

"I'm inclined to agree with you, Mr. 'Olmes. I think you and Dr. Watson should first travel to where the crime took place for what clues may be there. When that's done, you can go to the 'ouse and speak to Mrs. Stockton. Then, you should go see the Olyphants, which is to say Benjamin and his father, to learn what you can about their relationship with Stockton and whether there looks to be any truth to the stories about them 'avin' designs on the Stockton farm. We especially need to know where the two of them were earlier this mornin'."

She looked to each of her colleagues and gave them both a single message. "We'd best be gettin' started."

Chapter 2. The Investigation Begins

Stopping at the Stockton farm before going on to the scene of Roger Stockton's murder, Holmes and Watson were greeted by a Joy and Jonathan now relieved of the guilt they had felt for their father's death and more like the juvenile horse thieves the detectives remembered. Indeed, a short time earlier the two children had been warmly embraced by their greatly relieved mother after being brought home by Colonel Cody. There followed a prolonged period of caressing, petting and kissing, only interrupted by a breakfast made up of some of their favorite foods. Finally, when their mother had sufficiently satisfied herself about their well-being, they were directed to play outside while she and Olivia dealt with "all there was to do."

The children informed Holmes and Watson that policemen had arrived a little while ago and were now in the woods beyond their farm, a conclusion Holmes and Watson had already drawn from the two police carriages stopped a distance farther down the road. One would carry members of the Metropolitan Police to and from the crime scene, the other would carry Roger Stockton's body away from the crime scene. Accompanied by Jonathan's head-shaking agreement, Joy advised Holmes and Watson to stay this side of the woods to avoid finding themselves on Olyphants's land "which could lead to trouble." They thanked the children, told them they'd be careful, and continued on to the police carriages and the woods that separated the farms of the less than neighborly neighbors.

As Holmes had feared, the two police carriages had run over and through the tracks of other vehicles that had traveled the same grassless path. The midnight rain would have washed out others. Nonetheless, he asked Watson to stop their carriage so he could climb down and examine more closely what tracks there were untrammeled and available from morning. As he later described in his monograph, "Interpreting Carriage Tracks" (translated into four languages), he was able to calculate the number of vehicles that had passed from the tracks left behind, could judge the fullness of each from the extent of indentation left by them and could judge the size of the vehicle, and something of its type, by using the distance between wheels to determine width and length. Beside the Metropolitan Police carriages, Holmes calculated three vehicles had traveled over the path recently, one a carriage and two smaller vehicles, almost certainly buggies. The indentations from one of the buggies indicated it had traveled to where Holmes and Watson had come before turning around, the other buggy had traveled straight through, only stopping briefly nearby.

They parked their carriage near to where the police had parked theirs and followed indistinct voices for thirty or more yards into the woods to the crime scene. Three Metropolitan Police officers stood a respectful distance from the body of Roger Stockton. Two were constables, one holding a board, the other a blanket, both in readiness to remove the body after the physician's arrival and preliminary examination. The third was the ranking officer on the scene whose cheerless expression and slightly hunched posture were agreeably familiar to Holmes and Watson.

"Inspector Lestrade, this is truly a pleasant surprise." Then, paying due deference to the figure lying motionless between them, Holmes quickly added, "under otherwise most unpleasant circumstances."

For his part, Lestrade very nearly brightened at the appearance of his sometimes colleagues. "Mr. Holmes, Dr. Watson, I suppose I should not be surprised to find you both anywhere a murder victim turns up. But this is rather a long way from your patch. Tell me, if you would, how you happen to be here."

"You might say we're here on behalf of a friend of the family. I'd rather not say more than that out of respect for my client. All the same, Lestrade, had I known you were on the case, I wouldn't have come at all, knowing my presence to now be unnecessary."

"Well now, Mr. Holmes, I'm not saying you don't make a contribution every now and again. Besides which, you know I always welcome yours and the doctor's company."

Holmes made a small bow of appreciation before posing a question. "But it isn't like you, Lestrade, to be here this long after a murder or to be standing idly by. Are you waiting for a sudden inspiration?"

Lestrade's grimace made clear his dissatisfaction with the situation. "We are waiting the arrival of Roger Stockton's physician to allow for confirmation of the dead man's identity and for the doctor's judgment as to the time and cause of death—although frankly there's no great mystery about either of those. Nonetheless, we need his certification, and we need someone familiar with Mr. Stockton to officially verify that this is his body. Mrs. Stockton was clearly too distraught to be asked to come back to the murder scene and make an identification in front of witnesses. Indeed, Mrs. Stockton only contacted us some considerable time after discovering her husband's body because she was so upset. That gave us a late start to begin with. On top of that, it turns out the doctor was out on a case last night, and I understand he's not a young man, so it is taking considerably longer than I had hoped for him to get here."

At the last, Lestrade looked to Watson as if stirred by a sudden inspiration. "If you'd like to take a look at the body, Doctor, I'd take it as a great favor." Watson's quick response made clear he was glad to oblige.

Holmes thought it time to turn to a different line of inquiry. "While we're all here, I wonder what you can tell me about the dead man?"

"Not a great deal, Mr. Holmes. Just that he was forty-six, leaves a wife from a second marriage and three children as well as a sizable farm. I thought I'd leave it to later to question the family members more closely. No one is going anywhere, and I thought it proper to give them time to grieve. I did talk briefly to the Fiddlemans—they're the Stocktons' servants. They mouthed concern about Stockton's passing, but I'd have to say they were more concerned about their own futures. They made clear that, with Roger Stockton gone, they were ready to leave service and relocate. I told them they shouldn't plan on going anywhere until our investigation is complete. That's about all I know at this time. What have you discovered, Mr. Holmes?"

Holmes was disappointed in the meager information Lestrade had to report but was nonetheless resigned to share with him all he had learned at Mrs. Hudson's table. "A few things. As you say, Stockton had been married before—the first time to the sister of his current wife. The older child is from his first wife, the younger two from his second. At the time of his death he was having problems with the older daughter. She is in a romantic relationship with the son of Stockton's neighbor, a youngster named Benjamin Olyphant. Stockton thinks—or thought—a marriage would lead to the Olyphants gaining control of the farm and so was against their seeing each other. In fact, Stockton seems to have been in conflict with several people. He was estranged from his brother-in-law and he seems to have been at least as much feared as loved by his children. Nonetheless," Holmes let a sly smile show itself, "I think we can safely rule out the two younger children as likely assassins, although you may want to count the Yard's horses after they visit."

Lestrade's forehead crinkled in confusion but he decided against pursuing what was undoubtedly Holmes's small joke, instead he showered praise on the detective he viewed as without peer among men in the field of investigation. "You've done a good bit of my job for me, Mr. Holmes, and I do appreciate it." He turned to the man who now rejoined them. "Dr. Watson, is there anything you learned from your examination that you can share?"

"Some things, perhaps. Time of death is, of course, early this morning. Rigor is not very far along, nor has the body temperature dropped very far. The victim was shot twice with a small-bore shotgun. Once, almost certainly the first time, in the back just above the buttocks. It would have caused great pain and almost certainly led to Stockton's eventual death, but the killer would not, or could not wait. He rolled his victim over and very methodically shot him in what appears to be the very center of his heart. That, of course, killed him instantly. Mr. Stockton's valuables were left intact so robbery does not appear a motive."

As Holmes and Lestrade considered Watson's report, the rumble of a carriage sounded in the near distance, grew louder, then stopped. Lestrade identified its likely occupant. "That must be the doctor. As I was telling you, he was out late last night on a call to a farm some distance away which delayed his responding to our call. In any event, I doubt he'll be able to tell us anything you haven't already seen, Dr. Watson."

Watson smiled modestly and nodded his appreciation to the inspector. Holmes grunted agreement with Lestrade's comment, before voicing the concern he was feeling. "Watson, I suggest we wait long enough to introduce ourselves to Stockton's physician and for you to share your observations with him. As soon as we can, however, we should journey to the Stockton farmhouse to see if Mrs. Stockton is now of a mind to talk."

The doctor, for whom they had been impatiently waiting, was finally making his way along the same path through the woods that Holmes and Watson had trod a short time before. Moments later, Dr. Aloysius Montgomery was introducing himself to the three investigators, each man wearing a businesslike smile and giving the other the expected firm handshake.

Watson would later record in his journal that Montgomery was a man of at least sixty-five, who should be seriously contemplating retirement. His fatigue was evident in spite of a bravado meant to substitute for a display of energy. It crossed Watson's mind that this was the likely fate of a physician who stayed too long at his post where his post demanded availability to a widely dispersed patient population. A sallow complexion, combined with thinning hair, and clothes that seemed to hang from his slender frame completed the picture of a harried, overage physician.

Montgomery apologized several times for his lateness. He explained he had been to see a patient several farms distant the past night. He focused his attention on Watson as he provided greater detail. "A case of scarlet fever in an infant—the parents' first child— you know how that goes. I injected the child with Moser's serum, then had to stay the night to reassure the parents."

Watson did, in fact, know how that went although he would have phrased his awareness differently. Indeed, the doctor's lack of compassion for understandably worried parents served as further indication that Dr. Montgomery had likely remained in practice past time. He gave a quick nod, then changed the subject somewhat clumsily to share his observations with Montgomery. When he was done, the men from Baker Street explained their need to leave in order to continue their investigation. They wished Lestrade and Dr. Montgomery well; Holmes telling Lestrade he thought it likely they'd be seeing each other again in the near future. Lestrade grunted his certainty of it.

As Holmes and Watson expected, Penelope Stockton responded to their request to talk far more positively than she had to Lestrade's plea. They enjoyed a decided advantage over the inspector. Apart from having some additional time to recover from her early morning shock, Colonel Cody had made known to Mrs. Stockton the "playful transgression" of her children and the significant role played by Holmes, Watson, and a woman he understood to be their housekeeper, in that problem's quiet resolution. On their arrival a dry-eyed Olivia led them back into the parlor. There, they found Mrs. Stockton seated beside a square-jawed, stylishly dressed man in his mid to late-forties who a decade earlier would have been described as muscular, today would be described as stocky, and in another decade as stout. He sat a respectful distance from the widow on the sofa they shared, offering what support sad eyes that rarely left her and a tightly pursed mouth could provide.

With word of their earlier actions preceding them, they were greeted warmly by both Penelope Stockton and her companion. The companion spoke first, obviously feeling the need to explain his presence to the two visitors.

"My name is Alfred Thompkins. I'm a long-time friend of the family. I came to do what I could for Mrs. Stockton. We are, of course, familiar with your many achievements as an investigator ... as well as your work, Dr. Watson. And Penelope ... Mrs. Stockton ... told me of your assistance in what could have been an embarrassing situation involving Joy and Jonathan. Let me offer a belated thank you for that." He tried to accompany his words with a small smile but found the effort overwhelming and returned to the comfort of an unremitting solemnity. "Please, gentlemen, sit. May I assume you will be working with Inspector Lester, was it?"

"Lestrade," Holmes mumbled loud enough to be heard before he and Watson settled into easy chairs facing Penelope Stockton and Alfred Thompkins from opposite ends of the low table they remembered from their earlier visit, now with a large cut glass vase filled with a careful mix of white and yellow daffodils placed strategically over the reminder of a cigarette smoker's visit. Watson took a notebook and pencil from his waistcoat as surreptitiously as he could, the eyes of the two people whose words he would be recording nonetheless following his every movement. Holmes settled himself against his chair's back cushion, and, in a voice made to sound as solicitous as the facial expression he had adopted, he began the interview.

"Mrs. Stockton, Dr. Watson and I want to extend our profound condolences on your loss. It is our desire to bring to justice—as expeditiously as possible—the person or persons responsible for this tragedy. It is that desire, and that desire alone, that leads us to interrupt your period of mourning." Penelope Stockton gave a small nod signaling her understanding and permission for Holmes to continue.

"Am I correct it was you who discovered your husband's body, Mrs. Stockton?"

Another small nod as she now began to strangle the handkerchief she had been holding in her lap.

"How did that come about?"

"I thought I should go looking for Roger when he didn't come back from his morning walk." Not knowing the extent of Holmes's familiarity with her husband's habits, she provided a small explanation. "Roger took a walk every morning; his 'daily constitutional' he called it. He'd go along the roadway up to the woods, then tramp through the woods for a time before returning. It was the exercise for his pressure worked out for him by Dr. Montgomery when Roger insisted he didn't have time for exercise.

"Anyway, he was always back by half six. When he wasn't back by nearly seven, I took the buggy to the edge of the woods and went looking for him." Her face contorted at the painful memory. "It was terrible, Mr. Holmes. I hope never to see its like again. There was all that blood and Roger's eyes were open wide like he was trying to understand what was happening." She gave a small shudder and leaned a little closer to Alfred Thompkins who, Watson would later say, seemed torn between offering greater support and the propriety of doing so in front of himself and Holmes.

Holmes gave her time to collect herself. She responded with a small shake before straightening to nearly the position she held before describing her husband's body. "And after that terrible discovery, what did you do, Mrs. Stockton?"

34

"It's something of a blur, Mr. Holmes. I know I took the buggy back to the house, although I believe it was more the horse following a familiar path than any of my doing." She touched the much-abused handkerchief to her cheek. Watson noted the cloth remained dry throughout its travels. "I gathered the children in this room, and I told them. All of them were terribly brave." She managed a sad smile remembering their courage. "It was then I think—hearing myself telling the children about Roger's death—that I broke down, I'm afraid. I don't know for how long. It might have been an hour; it might have been two. Anyway, I finally got myself together and contacted the police. When they came, I asked if I could have time to recover and speak to them tomorrow, and they were good enough to agree. It was only then I learned that Joy and Jonathan were more upset than I realized and had run off to see Mr. Cody. I can tell you I was frantic until I heard from him. I'm feeling better now and felt I should see you after all you've done for our family."

Holmes allowed a brief smile in acknowledgment of her words before attempting to clarify Alfred Thompkins's role in her life. "And, Mr. Thompkins, I understand from what you say that you are a friend of the family; can you tell me how you happen to be here?"

In spite of Holmes's question, it was Penelope who responded. "I did leave that out, Mr. Holmes. Alfred *is* an old friend and I called him after the children went missing and I couldn't reach my brother."

"And, of course, I came right away." He shared a comforting smile with Penelope which she missed as she turned again to throttling the handkerchief in her lap. He transferred the smile to Holmes and Watson who stared blankly back to him, neither one being in need of comforting.

As tactfully as he could, Watson followed up on Holmes's query with a somewhat more pointed question. "I wonder if you could tell us something more of your relation to the Stockton family."

"It's really no great mystery. Mrs. Stockton's brother, Percy, and I are long-time friends. We go back to before I even knew Penelope. Of course, she was Penelope Dickson then." Thompkins put on a tentative smile and did his best to share it with Penelope, but it was all for naught as she continued to take interest only in the events occurring in her lap. Now, without benefit of the smile, Thompkins resumed answering Watson.

"Anyway, somewhere along the way the three of us—Percy, Penelope and me—got to be great friends. That was all, just friends if you're thinking anything else. Of course, all that was before Priscilla, her older sister, died. That's when Penelope married Stockton. She felt it was her duty to help raise her sister's child, especially with the child being a girl. I don't mind telling you I was against the marriage and told Penelope so. I know this isn't the best time to say such things, but it's not as if I'm saying them for the first or probably the hundredth time. I felt she was throwing away her own chance for happiness, her own life and I told her so." Thompkins looked hesitantly to Penelope, having shared with strangers the still painful conversations they had had years ago. Penelope's face alone showed the emotion Thompkins's words had stirred as she continued to maintain her silence.

. Unable to elicit the words he hoped to hear, Thompkins brought to a close the history of his involvement with Penelope and the Stocktons. "Of course, everything changed after the marriage. For a while we'd still see each other from time to time, but Stockton didn't like it, so we'd get together less and less, and only when I had to come by for bank business with Mr. Stockton senior or sometimes when Roger had to be in London or wherever."

Alfred Thompkins swallowed hard, aware of the easy misinterpretation of his words. "I want to make clear that Penelope and I have nothing to reproach ourselves for. In fact, we were almost never alone together. Percy was with us virtually every time in our reunions of old friends." Satisfied with having established their thorough-going innocence, he gave himself a deep nod of approval.

Watson grimaced his way to a small smile of acceptance and Holmes waved away any thought of impropriety. Both men were aware that the cloak of respectability covered actions, not feelings.

"Just as a matter of course, Mr. Thompkins, can you tell me where you were this morning?" Holmes asked.

"I was in my flat of course. It's my custom to rise at seven, have breakfast and ready myself for my position at the bank. Normally, I would leave for work at about half-eight, but I got the call from Penelope shortly before that and went straight to the

Stockton farm, only stopping to call the bank and explain the situation." Alfred Thompkins looked to Holmes for some evidence of contrition for what he was certain Holmes had been thinking. He got only an undecipherable grunt from the detective.

Watson, meanwhile, found his curiosity piqued by something in Thompkins's response and decided to pursue it at the risk of digressing briefly from the course of Holmes's questions. "Are you by any chance employed at the bank at which Mr. Stockton conducted his business?"

"As a matter of fact, I am."

"And does your position involve you with Mr. Stockton or with his account?"

"Good heavens, no. I hope to rise in my situation, but for now I have somewhat lesser responsibilities than you're suggesting. I do make occasional deliveries of papers to Mr. Stockton senior since he's been invalided, but as an important customer, Roger Stockton would have his finances managed by Mr. Murchison—he's the bank president. Anyway, that's the way it was up until a little more than two weeks ago. Which is when the two of them got into a set-to like I never heard before. It got so loud you could hear them hollering at each other all the way to the bank floor. I couldn't make out what it was all about, but at the last, when Mr. Stockton came stomping out of Mr. Murchison's office, you could hear him, clear as a bell, calling back to Mr. Murchison, 'now it's over, there's no good reason for our doing any more business.' And, next thing you know, Mr. Stockton transferred all his money and business to the Barontella Bank and Trust. It's not something that gets talked about, but I thought you might want to know about it in light of all that's happened."

"Thank you, Mr. Thompkins, you're absolutely right. That is definitely something that's important for us to know." Watson said nothing further allowing a somewhat perplexed Holmes to again focus his questions on Mr. Stockton and the morning's events. "Mrs. Stockton, did you feel your husband to be out of sorts last night or this morning? Did there seem to be anything troubling him?"

"No, there was nothing like that," Penelope replied.

Holmes screwed his face in concentration before posing the question that would likely set the course for much of their investigation. "I wonder, Mrs. Stockton, would you say your husband had enemies?" There was an involuntary snort from Thompkins, causing Holmes to wonder if Thompkins might not be the richer source of information about the enemies of his rival—as Roger Stockton clearly was.

"The truth, Mr. Holmes, is that my husband was not an easy man. He had enemies—probably more enemies than friends. But they were, all of them, long-standing. He simply had a way of rubbing people the wrong way, but it didn't lead to violence; it led to people staying out of his way."

"Can you tell us, Mrs. Stockton, who were some of his more … pronounced enemies?"

"Well, I was for one," Thompkins sounded pride in his status. "Penelope is understandably measured in what she says, but I can tell you he treated people shamefully and none more so than his own family. I felt his actions unforgivable, and I was far from alone." Having said his piece, Thompkins clamped his lips together as though certain there was nothing more to be said on the subject. Holmes was aware there was not only a great deal more to be said on the subject, but that Thompkins was anxious to tell it. Accordingly, Holmes now directed his questioning to him.

"You must realize, Mr. Thompkins, this is a murder inquiry, and we'll need more than generalities if we are to do our work. Again, permit me to inquire who are some of the people beside yourself who resented his behaviors—or saw themselves as mistreated by Mr. Stockton?"

Thompkins again looked to Penelope Stockton, hopeful of a word or look of support but she looked steadily and silently to the hands in her lap. He shrugged and unclamped his lips. "I suppose it's nothing you won't find out anyway." He laid the index finger of one hand across the pinky of the other and began what gave every indication of being the start of a lengthy count.

"There's first of all Penelope's brother, Percy. This goes back to when Priscilla, Penelope's older sister, was married to Stockton. There was this one time Priscilla went to see Percy in tears over the way Stockton had been treating her. That led Percy to go see Stockton. As it was told to me, Percy just planned to talk to Stockton and see if they couldn't come to an understanding. Well, Stockton wanted none of that. He told him what went on between him and his wife was no concern of Percy's and if he couldn't stay out of his—meaning Stockton's—business, he shouldn't come around anymore. It just grew from there until he finally told Percy he wasn't welcome in his house again. And that's the way it's been ever since. Penelope can say if it's different."

Penelope, however, remained silent, nor did she transfer attention from the hands in her lap. Thompkins nodded the affirmation Penelope denied him and continued his report. "I can tell you that Percy would like to see his niece, Olivia, and get to know Joy and Jonathan—at least get to know them a lot better than he does now. And, of course, he'd like to see his sister without having to go all around the barn to do it."

Having now warmed to the task of recounting the people he believed had reason to kill Stockton, he laid an index finger across the ring finger of his other hand. "Then there's old man Olyphant and his son, Benjamin. Olivia is sweet on the Olyphant boy, and Stockton did everything he could to break them up. He was convinced it was all a plot cooked up by Olyphant to get his farm."

"They *are* young to be thinking about marriage, Alfred." The words were spoken in a small voice that nonetheless commanded everyone's attention.

"You're right, of course, they are young, Penelope, and that's certainly a legitimate concern. All I'm saying is I don't think that was Roger's concern." Thompkins paused, uncertain of the impact of his mild disagreement but having come this far there was no turning back.

"The fact is Stockton and Olyphant never got along. For one thing, they've been arguing for as long as anyone can remember about the woods where Stockton was shot. Olyphant may be as hard-headed as Stockton on that one. Both men claim the woods—at least a large part of it as belonging to them and both say they've got papers to prove it. It's bound to end up in court—at least it was while Stockton was alive. I don't know how it'll get worked out now. Truth is, there's more than enough woods for both families to use without getting in each other's way. There's even a rough cabin in there someplace that some old tramp uses."

The eyes of both questioners widened on learning of a mystery man living in the woods in which Stockton was shot. Reluctantly, they put aside for the moment the questions his presence raised in the interest of maintaining focus on the dead man's enemies. "Mrs. Stockton, what can you tell me about your brother, Percy, and how he got along with your husband?"

As seemed her way when pressed, she didn't look to her questioner, didn't look to anyone, fidgeted for the moment, then spoke mainly to the hands in her lap. "I knew, of course, that my brother and my husband did not get along. Roger told me it was between the two of them and I was not to ask about it. I respected his wishes and never discussed it with either him or Percy. There was gossip, of course, but there is always gossip." Penelope paused, inhaling deeply before continuing. "I did disobey Roger's wishes in one area. As Mr. Thompkins says, I continued to see Percy when Roger was away on business—not that Roger directed me to give up seeing my brother, but I knew he disapproved." With that, she raised her eyes from her lap to look to Holmes and Watson before speaking with unexpected conviction. "There is one thing you must understand, regardless of his feelings, Percy could never do anything like this."

Both Holmes and Watson discounted a sister's estimate of her brother's willingness to use violence but said nothing.

Alfred Thompkins, meanwhile, had grown restless as he believed time was slipping away without his making clear the depths of Roger Stockton's character. He was determined to correct that situation. He first lightly touched Penelope's arm as if to alert her to his intent, then began a final unveiling of the Roger Stockton he knew.

"Penelope is a lady and tries to see the best in everyone. Frankly, Roger didn't deserve her." With that, he looked to Penelope with a fierce determination. "It's bound to come out, Penelope. It may as well be here, now."

Without waiting for her response, he revealed to Holmes and Watson what was bound to come out. "Simply put, Mr. Holmes, Roger Stockton was a bully. Especially with women. You've already heard about the situation with Olivia. That's part of it, but only part."

He gave a final glance to Penelope, made a final apology, and then blurted out the charge he had long been holding back.

"The truth is Roger was an abusive husband. I don't mean physically ... I don't know about that, although nothing about Roger would surprise me. But yelling, belittling, controlling every movement, and demanding total obedience to whatever requirement occurred to him. Percy called him on it—threatened him—which is the real reason he was no longer welcome in this house. We had some back and forth as well, and it's likely I would have been barred except for my job at the bank. Roger wanted to stay on good terms with the bank."

With Thompkins's revelation complete, all eyes turned to Penelope, then quickly away as each man was aware of the terrible intrusion being made into her private life. When she finally spoke, it was haltingly, each word either carefully chosen or painful to express, maybe both.

"Roger wasn't like that at first—with me I mean—As I say, I heard things, really gossip about him and Priscilla. She didn't share with me and I had a sense she didn't want me to ask. I knew Percy had stopped visiting the farm, but, as I was saying, I didn't know why—at least not all of it. And you should know that whatever else was happening, he would never strike the children. For that matter, he only struck me one time, maybe two, maybe more I can't be sure but nothing so bad as to make me have to see Dr. Montgomery or for me to tell you about, Alfred. I'm not making an apology for Roger. Living with him was difficult at times. It was as if he had demons he couldn't control. And when it was over, when the yelling and hurtful things were done and he was himself again, he always felt terrible and looked for ways to make it up to me."

An uncomfortable silence followed Penelope's admission. Holmes felt certain that further questioning about the Stockton marriage would lead to further pain without generating significant new information. And besides, there were still other people he and Watson were pledged to interview. And now there was the man in the woods as well.

"Thank you for sharing with us things that I know are difficult to talk about. Let me ask you about Mr. Stockton's father. I understand he is staying with you."

41

"Grandpa Stockton has been here since long before we were married. This is his farm after all."

"Am I correct that he's bed-ridden?"

"He is, except for being helped to his chair, but he never leaves his room. In fact, it's near time I should be getting him his lunch and medicine."

Holmes ignored Penelope's sudden concern about her father-in-law's care. "How long has he been bed-ridden?"

Penelope Stockton gave a fleeting glance to the door and the escape it promised, then turned back to the task at hand. "More than seven years. He was an active man, still doing farm work right up until the day of his accident. It's really very sad. He was such a vigorous man and now he needs help with everything and, of course, he's terribly alone. There's only me and the children to spend any time with him and I have to admit we get so busy with our own things that we don't always remember, or we don't stay with him as long as we probably should. Of course, Alfred makes it a point to visit with Grandpa Stockton whenever he comes to deliver papers to Roger or get his signature on something. I know Grandpa appreciated that." She paused and showed Thompkins a warm smile that caused him to sit up that much straighter. "And Dr. Montgomery was here regularly, but that was business, and besides Grandpa always wanted me to be in his room at the same time to take notes on whatever the doctor said or recommended, not that there was ever anything much for me to write down."

Holmes nodded his understanding, then moved the questioning to the people Penelope had not catalogued as among Stockton senior's visitors. "And I believe you have servants who live on the farm. What can you tell us about them?"

"The Fiddlemans. I don't know what there is to tell, Mr. Holmes. They're an older couple who have always lived on the farm—certainly since long before I or Priscilla came here. But they live above the stables, not in the house. And, of course, they see Grandpa Stockton as well, to bring him his meals, help him get to his chair—whatever needs doing."

"And may I assume they were here this morning?"

"Yes, they are on duty from six to seven at night. The time after seven is theirs—all except Sunday when they work a half-day."

Having reminded herself that her servants had a right to control at least a part of their lives, Penelope now acted as forcefully as she dared to assert that right for herself. "I hope what I've shared will be helpful to you in your investigation, Mr. Holmes, Dr. Watson. I must ask you now to give me some time to myself. I'm still trying to cope with all that's happened."

Alfred Thompkins came quickly to the widow's defense. "I think we can agree Penelope has been very giving of herself and her time. It might be well to leave additional questions to a later time." He rose as he spoke the last, inviting Holmes and Watson to do the same. Both grimaced their acknowledgment of the request that was not a request as they pushed off their chairs. Each of them thought about the man in the woods and the need to learn who he was and how he came to be there—a need of which they were bound to be reminded by Mrs. Hudson. For now, however, they knew they had already overstayed what small welcome they had been given and to press an additional issue would jeopardize the cooperation they would want later.

"You have been most gracious with your time, Mrs. Stockton," Holmes gave a small bow, "and permit me again to express condolences on behalf of Dr. Watson and myself. You've been very brave in the face of this terrible ordeal."

Penelope Stockton continued sitting but gave Holmes a small smile. Watson was certain it was as much to see the backs of the two of them as for his colleague's words. Thompkins led them to the front door. After first scrawling out Percy Dickson's address in response to Watson's request, Thompkins bade the visitors a somber good day, holding Holmes's hand the moment longer it took for him to hiss a last message, "Go talk to that damn Olyphant."

The ride to the Olyphant farm was not long but was sufficient to allow for an exchange of ideas about the murdered man. While both held the same low opinion of Roger Stockton, they had different reactions to what they had heard.

"How terrible, Holmes, to go to one's grave friendless and alone even while surrounded by family," Watson resumed a headshaking he had only briefly halted.

"I would contend his behavior toward his wife—wives, apparently—merits exactly such isolation," Holmes countered. "After all, he appears to have been intent on isolating himself from the human race. It seems only appropriate that the human race should return the favor."

"I'll not defend the man, Holmes, far from it. I just find it sad that he could not recognize the benefits to be derived from a caring family and friends, and now has gone to his grave with no one to regret his passing or remember his life."

The two friends lapsed into silence for the rest of their journey. Later, in the solitude of their bedchambers, each would consider what might be said of him when his time came and how he might be remembered through the succeeding years. Sleep, when it came, would prove fitful.

The Olyphant farmhouse looked the economy version of the Stockton's. No arch with the owner's name emblazoned within it greeted visitors. The path to the farmhouse was not as wide and was devoid of boxwood hedges. There was, however, a sudden profusion of red and white posies as one neared the milk-white painted farmhouse.

They parked their carriage a little before the porch, mounted the steps, and were about to make use of the ring in the lion's open mouth to summon whoever was at home when a call to them made it unnecessary.

"What can I do for you?"

It was not, as it sounded, a disembodied voice from behind the door. Rather, the voice came from a lanky man with grizzled hair and trim beard who had emerged from the side of the house. He was promptly joined by three boys varying in height and age, the older two carrying shovels, and all three dirty, sweaty and dressed in mud splattered overalls. Holmes and Watson recognized the tallest, oldest and dirtiest of the three as Benjamin Olyphant. The lanky man repeated his question.

"What can I do for you?"

"Mr. Olyphant, my name is Sherlock Holmes, and this is my colleague, Dr. Watson. We've already had the pleasure of meeting Benjamin." The young man's face did not suggest that Holmes's pleasure was widely shared. He ignored Holmes and Watson and spoke only to his father.

"These are the men I told you about, dad—the ones who came for the horse in Stockton's stable."

The senior Olyphant's face creased into a grin as he added to his son's narrative. "The horse from the Wild West Show." The grin broadened. "The horse the Stockton kids *borrowed*." He looked to Holmes and Watson in hopes of seeing his amused disbelief reflected in their faces but found them as somber as his son. He shrugged and responded in kind.

"I imagine you're here about Stockton's death. We can talk on the porch. Hannah wouldn't hear of me dragging dirt through the house, and I can answer your questions as well outside the house as I can inside." His sons, delighted with the unexpected excuse to abandon the work assigned them, followed him to the porch steps where he put an end to their short-lived jubilation. "You people continue with your digging. Your mother wants flower beds and a garden. It's the least you can do in exchange for all the cooking, washing, and cleaning she does for you." Olyphant's brow furrowed in association with a sudden thought.

"Benjamin, I suppose they'll have questions for you as well. You might come along. Timothy and Christopher, you keep right on working." He looked hard at two dark-haired youngsters Watson would later record as being about fifteen and thirteen, both of whom, with only a glance to each other of mirrored disgust, reversed course and headed back around the building.

Holmes and Watson seated themselves on a settee that looked to have been relegated to porch furniture after exhausting its use as inside furniture. Olyphant moved a rocking chair closer to the settee. The rocker and the settee being the full complement of porch furniture, Benjamin sat on the top step of the porch using a post as a wholly inadequate cushion for his back.

"My name is Olyphant as you already know. Daniel Olyphant. And I may as well tell you right off Roger Stockton and me never got along. Not even as boys. I didn't like him, and best as I can tell, he didn't like anybody. But not liking is one thing, killing is another. And I didn't kill him. I thought about it often enough, but you can't punish a man for what he thinks." Olyphant sniffed, set his jaw, and waited comment. It appeared to the men from Baker Street that Olyphant likely made a more than worthy opponent for Stockton.

Holmes nodded his understanding of Olyphant's position and began his questioning. "When did you learn of Stockton's death?"

"Midmorning I'd say. We were already well into the day's chores. Maybe ten, maybe a little later." Turning to his son, he asked, "Is that when the police carriages arrived?"

"About then," Benjamin answered.

"Did you go see Olivia, Benjamin? Did she tell you anything it would be useful for us to know?"

Daniel Olyphant answered for his son. "He wanted to go, but he had chores. Besides which, it seemed to me a time for a girl to be with her mother. I figured there'd be time for comforting from outside the family—if comforting was needed—later on." Watson took careful note of Benjamin. If the youngster disagreed with his father, he gave no sign of it.

"You say you were already into your work. Were you out earlier for any reason?"

"I was. We both were, Benjamin and me. We were in the woods—our side of the woods—hoping to get a rabbit for dinner. Anyway, we didn't get one."

Holmes postponed for the moment a question about the guns the men carried into the woods and asked about an expression used by Olyphant that he found curious. "What do you mean 'your side of the woods'?"

"Just saying what is, Stockton claims … claimed part of the woods and we claim part. Of course, to hear him tell it, Stockton's part is close to all of it. Word was that Stockton was looking to sell off his share for rights to the timber. That way he'd have all the money in the world instead of just most of it like he does now." Olyphant paused long enough to stare hard at first to Holmes, then to Watson, before giving the clarification his remark demanded. "Have you seen his place? Do you know he's got the biggest farm in the area, which means he's got the most crops and the biggest yield, which gets back to his having most all the money in the world or at least most all the money around here."

Watson ignored Olyphant's brief diatribe to pose a question about his earlier statement. "Do I take it from what you say that you argued about boundaries?"

"If you dealt with Stockton, you argued about everything. But you're right we argued about property lines."

Holmes cleared his throat by way of drawing attention back to himself, then returned the conversation to issues he thought more central to the investigation. "Getting back to the events of the morning, did you see anybody, did you hear anything when you were in the woods?"

"I heard shots, but I didn't see anybody. I never got off a shot myself, I believe my son did." He turned to Benjamin who looked clearly unhappy at having to describe limitations in his shooting skills for at least the second time that day.

"I got off a couple of shots, but I missed my rabbit," Benjamin said. "I didn't see anybody either," he quickly added.

"Do I understand the two of you separate when you go hunting?" Holmes asked.

Olyphant senior shrugged. "We double our chances of coming home with dinner that way. Benjamin follows one path and I follow another. Of course, he's usually a better shot than he was this time." Stockton chuckled; his son did not.

"And could there have been other farmers or other hunters in the woods?" Watson asked.

"Oh sure," Olyphant shrugged his response. "It's a good size woods not far from the city. Me and Stockton post signs but there's no way to control people's comings and goings. The truth is there are all the time strangers in the woods. Then, of course, there's our tramp who's been living in what passes for a cabin far back in the woods for the last month. The old tramp is probably the only thing Stockton and me ever agreed about. It took some doing but he agreed the tramp probably couldn't hurt anything and, as long as he stayed far back in the woods, he guessed it would be alright."

"Especially with him being sick he needed a place to stay," Benjamin added, which was followed by his father's affirming nod.

Holmes and Watson were determined not to lose the opportunity to ask about the man in the woods a second time. In their haste to make up for the earlier oversight, they overlapped each other with their questions.

"What can you tell us about the man? Where did he come from?"

Olyphant threw up his hands in response. His frustration was not caused by the sudden bombardment of questions but to the impossibility of his providing satisfactory answers. "You understand it's not like we have him over for tea. Mostly, he stays out of our way and we stay out of his. Did you tell me his name was Aaron?" Olyphant directed the question to his son. After Benjamin nodded his agreement, he explained the rationale for seeking his son's confirmation.

"He's more likely to talk to my boys than to me. I judge he's more comfortable around young people.

"As to your questions, first of all he just sort of appeared three, maybe four weeks ago without a clue as to why or where he come from." He looked to Benjamin who shook off any claim to such knowledge. "He's probably … what would you say, Benjamin … maybe somewhere in his middle forties?"

"Older than that, I think."

Olyphant grinned. "Never ask a young person to guess the age of someone over forty. Anybody that old is seen as cemetery material." He chuckled appreciation of his own observation, then looked to see if his guests showed a similar appreciation. He was rewarded with weak smiles that did nothing to dampen his enthusiasm.

Watson gave the senior Olyphant a moment to recover before raising his next question.

"How does he get by—I mean with him being alone in the woods and having some kind of health problems?"

"There's game, of course. And the boys tell me he's a good shot in spite of his problems. Besides, there's berries and stuff that grows wild if you know how to find it, and if you can tell the difference between the stuff that can kill you and the stuff that's safe to eat. And then there's Hannah—that's my wife—who will have the boys take him some of her baking and sometimes some of the food out of our larder—which she thinks I don't know about. And I understand Mrs. Stockton does the same thing through Olivia and her two young ones. It must of drove Stockton crazy." The image of a crazed Stockton stimulated another round of chuckling from Olyphant and a return to weak smiles from Holmes and Watson.

"What about this sickness he has?" Watson asked. "What is that like?"

Olyphant scratched his beard, then turned to his son. "You see him a lot more than I do, Benjamin, how would you describe it?"

Benjamin's face creased into a look of fierce concentration. "It's mostly the shakes you notice, that and the problem he has walking. It can look like his legs have a mind of their own. But, like dad says, none of that keeps him from being a good shot. And there's nothing really wrong with how he talks or what he says. He can just be a little slow getting his words out."

"Do you think he'd talk to Dr. Watson and me?" Holmes asked.

"It would be better if you went with me and Olivia or with my brothers, or with Joy and Jonathan. He's okay with us, but probably not so much with strangers. And he might do better with a woman than a man. I think he does better with Olivia and Joy than with me or any of the boys."

"We can see what we want to do about that, but one of us will want to talk with him and would appreciate the help," Holmes said.

"Well then, let's leave it at that for now," Benjamin's father interjected. "The boy's still got chores to get done and he'll need to clean up before he even thinks about dinner." Holmes and Watson took the less than subtle hint and rose to go. Without another word, Benjamin left to join his brothers. Daniel Olyphant walked down the porch steps with Holmes and Watson, waited while they climbed into their carriage, and nodded good-bye as they drove away. All knew the conversation between them had only been paused.

Chapter 3. Sudden Thunder and Jane Morrison

Mrs. Hudson still had the last of the breakfast dishes in her tub when the couple passed her window, turned at the entrance to 221B and momentarily disappeared from view. She'd only caught a glimpse, but it was enough to make clear she was about to provide Baker Street a spectacle that would make for hushed expressions of wonder that morning and material for spirited dinner conversations that evening. With that in mind, she started for the door before the chime sounded in hopes of forestalling the inevitable. Unsurprisingly, the open door revealed that the inevitable had already occurred. On both sides of Baker Street passers-by who did not slow their walk as they passed 221B, stood frozen, staring in often open-mouthed wonder at the couple on her doorstep.

The woman, if alone, might have excited a second look, nothing more. She was well into her thirties, and with large brown eyes, slightly upturned nose, and small chin, she was more likely to be described as cute than pretty, but it was her outfit not her features that drew attention. Her fringed leather jacket, high crowned hat, and the boots visible beneath her skirt all marked her as a member of Colonel Cody's Wild West Show.

And still, if passers-by briefly took note of the woman, they couldn't take their eyes from the man at her side. He looked to be fortyish, was hatless, clean shaven with finely chiseled features and had long dark hair pulled back into two braids that hung nearly to his waist. Beneath the braids, a breastplate of symmetrically placed small bones covered the chest of his loosely fitted blouse. His buckskin trousers and leathered moccasins were nearly ordinary, but no one in his rapidly gathering audience got beyond the braids and his breastplate.

Neither of Mrs. Hudson's visitors seemed concerned about the attention they had excited; likely, she thought, because the exciting of attention was far from a novel experience for the two of them. The man took responsibility for explaining their appearance at 221B.

50

"My name is Sudden Thunder. The woman is Jane Morrison. We're here to see you if your name is Hudson."

Mrs. Hudson was rarely surprised by her visitors or their requests. This marked one of those rare occasions. Typically, the only people who came to the door of 221B seeking her out were the very ordinary looking Andre, the butcher's boy; Mrs. Anderson, the char; and one or another boy to clean the chimney. Under normal circumstances, Mrs. Hudson would have any unexpected visitors state their business and she would then decide if they should gain entry or if their business could be conducted on the front step. These were not, however, ordinary circumstances as the still gathering crowd of observers made clear. There was a need for extraordinary action.

"I am Mrs. Hudson. We can meet in my parlor." With that, she stepped back to admit the man and woman, leaving those more knowledgeable about the residents of 221B to wonder what in the world Sherlock Holmes could be up to now, and the remaining members of the crowd simply to wonder.

While she, too, had much to learn about her exotic visitors, some things were known to her. It was, of course, obvious that her visitors were part of the colonel's Wild West Show. It was obvious as well that they had sought out Mrs. Hudson at the suggestion—or perhaps the urging – of the colonel himself. No one else from the show could have made any such recommendation for the simple reason she knew no one else in the show. They had not come to discuss anything of a criminal nature. Such a concern would have called for the expertise of Mr. Holmes, at least so Colonel Cody would have thought. The colonel would have referred them to Mrs. Hudson—to a once married woman—to work out a relationship problem, a problem of a romantic nature. That they arrived together with no evidence of rancor or conflict indicated that the problem was not between the two of them but almost certainly involved the way others related to them as what would be described as a mixed couple. That the colonel had referred the two of them to someone outside the Wild West Show indicated his concern that whatever it was could affect the functioning of the show and his hope therefore to get it resolved before it could surface as an issue.

In truth, the existence of a romantic relationship required no special skills of observation. There was, first of all, the way they stood close beside each other while they waited on her doorstep, close enough to hold hands had the setting been different, close enough to draw strength, each from the other, in this setting. Then, too, there was the smile of relief they shared when she invited them into her parlor. It was only for a moment, but it suggested a degree of shared understanding that recalled for Mrs. Hudson her own marriage, her own private communications with Tobias. It occurred to her that tea and a generous serving of baked goods might make their conversation flow more freely.

"Please sit. I'll put up some tea. And maybe you'd like some scones. They're fresh made."

Her visitors chose the settee where they could sit together and apart, while she went to her kitchen to prepare the promised refreshments. On her return, she found Jane Morrison sitting bolt upright as if in a ladderback chair rather than on soft cushions; Sudden Thunder was leaning into the cushion at his back, his studied relaxation undone by piercing eyes that followed her every move. She set down her tray of tea, scones, and a pot brimming with strawberry jam. Amid an oppressive silence, she poured tea for her guests and herself, then took the easy chair opposite the settee.

She pointed to the plate of baked goods. "I do hope you like the scones. They're quite popular over 'ere."

Jane Morrison chose a scone, then held it at some distance from her, studying it as if to determine what part of it, if any, it would be safe to bite into. Deciding at last, she began nibbling cautiously on a corner. Sudden Thunder took no such risk and left the several remaining scones untouched. Their continuing silence made clear that the couple was in her parlor at the urging, if not insistence of Colonel Cody, and that neither of them felt comfortable beginning a description of the problem they had come across town to share.

Mrs. Hudson decided finally she would have to force the issue if she was to learn about their problem before it became time to prepare dinner.

"What is it that brings you to Baker Street, Miss Morrison, Mr. ...." Mrs. Hudson suddenly became aware that addressing her visitor as Mr. Thunder did not sound quite right and Mr. Sudden

52

Thunder provided no appreciable improvement. For the moment at least she would forgo a use of names. "Why is it you want to see me?"

"Colonel Cody has told us you're a plain woman and you could be a help to us."

Jane Morrison smiled softly and laid a hand on a corner of Sudden Thunder's cushion nearly touching his hand as she did so. "He means you speak plainly and will say what you think."

Mrs. Hudson nodded her recognition of the compliment and appreciation for its clarification. "And 'ow might I be a 'elp to the two of you?" Mrs. Hudson looked from one to the other. Sudden Thunder spoke for them both.

"First, I need to tell you who we are. I mean more than just names." There was a fleeting glance to Jane Morrison and a warm smile in return. With a curt nod, he plunged ahead.

"I am Oglala of the Lakota people. Jane is not Indian. We are both with Colonel Cody and his Western Show. We are with him for some time. I am what's called 'a trick rider,' Jane is a horse trainer. She is a very good horse trainer." He spoke the last without change of expression, nor did he see Jane Morrison's smile broaden.

"That's how we met—through the horses. Now we want to marry. That is decided." He set his jaw and looked for a long moment to Mrs. Hudson. She maintained what she imagined to be a supportive look and wondered about the number of people who had tried to talk them out of marriage. She wondered as well whether her first assumption about Colonel Cody's sympathies was in error and he was, in fact, one of those counseling separation. And was that his thinking in describing her as plain talking? Even as she considered what others wanted of her, Sudden Thunder began to make clear what he and Jane Morrison wanted of her.

"We must learn what is the best place to live. We already know America would be a hard place. If we go to the reservation at Pine Ridge where my people live, it would be bad for Jane. My people are not her people, their ways are not her ways, even their language is different. And a great many would be angry to have a white woman there, and angry at me for bringing a white woman. And if we go where the white people live, we would also have problems. I speak the American language, but I have my own beliefs and traditions which Jane understands and can accept, but others cannot. And Indians do not move easily into the Americans' world. The people who know Jane would not be happy. Not that we need to make others happy, but neither do we want to live all the time with people angry at us." With that, he turned from Mrs. Hudson to his presumptive bride, his face softening as he did; Jane Morrison had never lost her soft smile and Mrs. Hudson was again struck by the bond that might yet carry them through the adversity they so clearly were about to face.

When she spoke, Jane Morrison's words did nothing to lessen Mrs. Hudson's cautious optimism. "We do know the problems, Mrs. Hudson, and have thought about solutions. We know how to live and work while keeping a distance from people. We mean to raise horses; we both know horses and horses don't care if you're white or Indian. We can use the money we've made with the Wild West Show to buy a spread in Wyoming." Seeing Mrs. Hudson's blank look, she sought to clarify her statement.

"Wyoming is a state in America—a new one." The blank look did not altogether disappear.

"A spread is what we call a ranch—a place for cattle and horses." She was about to clarify the word "cattle" when Mrs. Hudson's face cleared and there appeared no need.

"Anyway, that's what we were planning. We thought it was the best we could hope for, but then Colonel Cody told us about horse farms in England, and that it might be easier for us to live here than in America. He said we should talk to you about it—that we should hear from you how people in your country would act toward us."

Sudden Thunder reentered the conversation with his own version of Cody's suggestion to them. "Colonel Cody says you are sensible woman. He says you have feet on the ground and would know what ordinary people think. He also says not to ask your Mr. Holmes or Dr. Watson, that they are not ordinary people."

Mrs. Hudson took a long drink of tea before responding. One puzzle had been answered. Cody had not sent Sudden Thunder and Jane Morrison to be talked out of marriage. For that, at least, she was grateful since it was not her intention to try to do so. If one weight had been lifted, it had been replaced by a second of comparable tonnage. What she said and how she said it might well shape the course of the two lives the colonel had entrusted to her care.

"It's first of all a great compliment Colonel Cody pays me, as you do, in comin' to see me and askin' my opinion about such an important decision. To begin with, 'owever, I 'ave to tell you I only know about the troubles that go on between the Indian people and the white people in America from what's printed in the London papers from time to time. And, of course, I know nothin' about this Wyoming place or raisin' 'orses.

"I do know somethin' about family and friends. And you'll be givin' up both if you leave your 'ome in America. Are you comfortable doin' that?"

"We'd really be giving up very little when it comes to that, Mrs. Hudson," Jane Morrison said with a wry smile. "My parents passed away some time ago. I have a brother in Minnesota, but I haven't seen or heard from him in years. Thunder is the only friend I have or need." Sudden Thunder vigorously nodded his agreement, then spoke to that agreement.

"I have the same feelings as Jane. I mean about needing only one friend. Besides, as I said before, my family could never accept Jane. There's too much history of the Lakota with white people and not enough history of my people with Jane. The way things are I believe there never could be. They see she is white and nothing more. It's the same with others on the reservation. There are too many memories and too little time. Even here, even with people we know—or thought we knew—there are some who learned of our plans and now act like we are strangers and will no longer speak to us, and others who argue with us about our plans to be together. Not everyone, but enough."

The room became silent as Sudden Thunder and Jane Morrison waited a respectful moment to allow Mrs. Hudson to absorb the depth of their feelings and the extent of the dilemma they faced. When he deemed that understanding to have been achieved, Sudden Thunder pressed the issue.

"We see great difficulty going back to America. We don't know what it would be like if we stayed here. We never thought about it until Colonel Cody said. Now we need to know what it would be like if we stayed here."

Mrs. Hudson looked her most thoughtful and nodded once, twice, then a third time for good measure. Had Holmes been present, he would have felt it overdone but Holmes wasn't present. When she spoke, it was to take them down an unexpected path.

"Your situation puts me in mind of a man who 'as a shop on Marylebone Road. 'E's a cobbler who can make you a fine pair of shoes. 'E 'as a nice shop, loyal customers, and a lovely family. 'Is name is Khalil … Khalil Salam. Khalil is Arabic. 'E came 'ere from somewhere in that part of the world when 'e was a young man and is in 'is fifties now. There's things 'e 'ad to think about that may be 'elpful to you in decidin' whether to live in America or 'ere in England.

"Khalil had to make a decision about where in London 'e wanted to live and set up shop. The natural thing would 'ave been to go to the East End which is where most of the folks who are comin' from other countries go—includin' I'm sure people who came from the same part of the world as Khalil. As I 'eard it, Khalil thought about doin' just that, but 'e finally decided to lease a shop not far from 'ere where 'e could work during the day and above which 'e 'ad a flat for after.

"Well, of course, Khalil stood out like a sore thumb from all the other shopkeepers and from all the people livin' around 'im. 'E was asked about that, about why 'e chose to live away from the people 'e knew. And what 'e said was that first of all 'e got a good price on the shop and 'e'd be the only cobbler for several streets. But also 'e reasoned that bein' that he'd be the only businessman lookin' like 'im, 'e'd likely be seen as exotic or at least as interestin'. What 'e wouldn't be seen as is bein' part of a group that could take over the neighborhood with their different ways. Instead, there bein' just the one Khalil, they could slowly get to know 'im and get comfortable with 'is ways. Which is, in fact, exactly what 'appened.

"Now, I don't know enough about things in America to talk about that, but I do know there aren't a lot of … Oglala was it?" She got two affirmative nods. "of Oglala in London or anyplace else in England. There's somethin' else you can think about—maybe two things. There's first of all that we English 'ave a kind of soft spot in our 'earts for Americans, 'avin' pretty much gotten over the unpleasantness of a 'undred years ago."

Jane Morrison smiled. For the first time, her smile to Mrs. Hudson was neither forced nor polite.

Content with that response, Mrs. Hudson continued. "There's also that you're theater people. Nobody expects theater people to be normal. Probably nobody wants them to be."

Mrs. Hudson watched as Jane Morrison carefully chose a second scone and Sudden Thunder absently reached for his first. She judged it was time to share what else she had to say about Khalil. She now sounded a tone as ominous as the words she spoke.

"There's other things you should know about Khalil."

With eyebrows raised, her audience waited to hear what else there was to know about Khalil Salam. She began with the most innocuous part of what she had to share.

"Khalil was … is a worker—a very 'ard worker. The English respect 'ard work and anyone willin' to commit themselves to it. Neither one of you strikes me as bein' a layabout and you'll just 'ave to let people see that. There's another part though and it might be more of a problem for you." She turned to Sudden Thunder and never took her eyes from him for the rest of her talk about Khalil Salam. "Khalil decided that for business, and for every day livin', e'd 'ave to be just a little bit English."

At the last, Sudden Thunder voiced his confusion. "What does that mean 'just a little bit English'?"

"Khalil said that he had to find a place between making no change in 'ow 'e dressed and looked, and 'ow 'e kept 'is customs, and completely changin' all those things. It was, he said, a matter of makin' some changes to fit in while still feelin' good about who you are. It's somethin' everyone's got to work out for themselves—at least that's 'ow Khalil saw it."

"What did Khalil give up and what did he keep?" Jane asked.

Mrs. Hudson gave the question a good deal of thought before responding. "It's a while back, but the answer would lie in Khalil's talk about an outer man and an inner man. 'E said the outer man could give up some things in terms of dress and groomin', but the inner man stayed the same in terms of family and beliefs and 'is ways of lookin' at the world. That way 'e said 'e could still stay Khalil but look to others like 'e was in some ways one of them."

There was a lengthy pause while consideration was given to Khalil's ideas about the problem they shared and his solution to that problem. When she felt it appropriate, Jane Morrison put a question to a deeply pensive Sudden Thunder. "That doesn't sound too hard, does it, darling?"

In reply, the pensive look deepened at first as he considered how much his outer man was a reflection of his inner man and might not be as easily separated as was the case with Khalil. Looking to Jane's hopeful smile, his own expression softened, and his words reflected that softening.

"We must see. These are important ideas. Important wherever we decide to live. The colonel was right to have us see you. Now, we must think about what you say about inner and outer man— you and your friend Khalil. It is important to Jane ... and to me, so I mean to think about it hard. We will also talk together on what you say about where we can live with the smallest problems. If there is need, can we talk again about these things?"

"It would be very important to us." Jane Morrison added as she now clasped the hand of Sudden Thunder. There was no longer any point to pretending they were anything less to each other than they were. Mrs. Hudson smiled at the display of honest feeling and at the flattery of their words.

"Of course, you may come at any time."

"And might we also visit with your friend, Khalil?" Jane Morrison added.

Mrs. Hudson's eyelids fluttered for a moment. "We might see about that later, but sadly Khalil 'asn't been well for a while and is not in 'is shop on any regular basis."

Jane Morrison nodded her regrets while Sudden Thunder stared straight ahead. With a final squeeze of a hand by one of the other (Mrs. Hudson found it impossible to tell whose hand was squeezed and who did the squeezing), the two of them worked their way from the settee and waited while Mrs. Hudson did the same from her easy chair. Sudden Thunder bowed his head deeply and Jane Morrison extended a hand while her face took on a broad smile. "We've taken up more of your time than is fair. Again, we thank you most sincerely. This has been very helpful."

When her guests had left and she'd given them a suitable interval to be on their way, Mrs. Hudson changed to her traveling dress, fitted her hat with the ostrich feather over her grey coils and went in search of the tram that would take her to the Marylebone Cemetery where Tobias would be waiting. It was not yet time for her regular fortnightly visit, but it was a trip she felt to be necessary. There were things she had to share, things she couldn't tell anyone but Tobias. He would understand about there being no Khalil—at least no one Khalil. There was instead an amalgam of Khalils she had known from China, India, and Russia. From pretty much everywhere except Arabia as she now thought about it.

And she knew full well Tobias would approve of her small lie—under the circumstances—and even be amused. Moreover, she would take the opportunity of her visit to share with Tobias the story of England's littlest horse thieves, and, far more seriously, of the murder of Roger Stockton. She would tell him all she knew and would not be surprised if, when she got home afterward, she suddenly had a new way of seeing things, what Dr. Watson called "an epiphany."

Chapter 4. The Man in the Woods

That evening Mrs. Hudson surprised her colleagues with a dish never before seen at 221B. Ever since their trip to Kettner's and sampling its unexpectedly mouth-watering dishes, Mrs. Hudson had grown increasingly experimental with her cooking. Tonight, it was beef a la rossine, having first been assured by "The Good Cook," the food writer for the Sunday *Standard*, that the dish was "simple to prepare and will be a sure hit with guests or family." On seeing those words, it occurred to her that Mr. Holmes and Dr. Watson had started life at Baker Street as guests and were now more akin to family—and more particularly to her family. Indeed, if she was honest about her feelings, only her beloved Tobias occupied a more central place in her life—as he always would.

It turned out The Good Cook was only half right. Mrs. Hudson's beef a la rossine received an enthusiastic welcome when set before her colleagues which only grew with each mouthful taken. Its preparation, however, had presented challenges that made a mockery of the phrase, "simple to prepare," challenges of which The Good Cook was either unaware (which seemed to her unlikely) or chose to ignore (which seemed to her very likely). In any event, the dish more than served the purpose of putting her colleagues in a positive frame of mind for the work she intended following dinner. Indeed, it led to such good feeling that she feared it imperiled rather than assured the sober recounting of the day's events and, still more ominously, threatened the careful planning of the next day's activities based on that recounting.

The beef a la rossine was only indirectly to blame. Immediately upon its presentation Watson declared the dish to be incomplete without its being paired with a suitably fine claret. Watson revealed the happy coincidence of knowing where just such a bottle could be found and proceeded to the lumber room and its carefully maintained cache of wine for special occasions—such occasions being subject to liberal interpretation by Holmes and Watson. As it turned out, on his way to the lumber room, or shortly after his arrival there, his estimate of the quantity of wine appropriate to the size of the steaks doubled and he rejoined his colleagues with a bottle of claret in each hand, much to Holmes's delight and Mrs. Hudson's trepidation.

As she feared, the steaks, while much appreciated, were consumed ever more slowly in association with a series of toasts made to each member of the consulting agency, to the culinary skills of Mrs. Hudson, and the singular achievement of the unknown vintner. Before Holmes could complete a toast celebrating Inspector Lestrade's heretofore unheralded deductive skills, Mrs. Hudson loudly announced the need to finish eating the beef a la rossine before them while moderating their liquid intake or risk missing out on the special dessert she had prepared. She looked hard to each of them, making clear she had no intention of making her baking available to people who were past a capacity to appreciate it. They looked to her doubtfully, skeptical that any dessert could convince them to refrain from making their assault on the second bottle of claret. The reasonableness of Mrs. Hudson's argument only became clear with her revelation that the special dessert she had prepared was egg custard. It was well established at 221B that egg custard was second only to scones among Mrs. Hudson's culinary achievements and was far less frequently available.

A short time later, after a last scraping of dessert bowls, Mrs. Hudson called to order the meeting of the Baker Street consulting detective agency and asked for a report of findings from her colleagues' visits to the crime scene and to the Stocktons and Olyphants. Watson pulled the accounts book from his waistcoat pocket, smoothed down the appropriate page and began.

He described the thick woods between farms in which Roger Stockton took the early morning walks prescribed by his physician and the welcome happenstance of finding Lestrade at the murder scene as the Yard's lead detective in the case. Holmes cleared his throat by way of interrupting Watson, then reported at length on the carriage and buggy traffic he was able to identify on the roadway leading to the wooded area. Watson fidgeted as Holmes went on, certain his colleague was most largely intent on hearing how the material for his next monograph would sound.

When Holmes had finished, Watson described his findings with regard to the murder victim. He told how the murderer had shot his victim in the back, then turned him over to shoot him a second time in the very center of his heart to make certain of his death. Watson noted that he had shared his thinking about the murder with the family's physician, a Dr. Aloysius Montgomery, whom he described as a sallow looking older man "well past the time he should have turned the reins over to a younger man." He went on to tell of having to wait for Montgomery to recover from his late-night visit to a scarlet fever case patient as evidence of his age-related difficulties. Watson told of their leaving shortly after Montgomery's arrival to make certain there would be time to interview Penelope Stockton and Daniel Olyphant. "Besides which, we could be certain Watson had discovered whatever there was to learn from the body," Holmes added, causing Watson to silently forgive his colleague's fascination with carriage tracks.

In response to a question from Mrs. Hudson, Watson explained that the body was found no more than thirty yards from the roadway although he added, "the woods are dense enough the murder could have occurred thirty feet from the roadway for all anyone could have seen." A soft groan told Watson that Mrs. Hudson had processed the information and he was to move on. Accordingly, he turned his attention to the visit to the Stockton farm.

He described his surprise at finding a very solicitous Alfred Thompkins with Mrs. Stockton. He reported that Thompkins described himself as a family friend, but it was his judgment that Thompkins aspired to a good deal more than friendship with one member of the Stockton family.

"What I found unclear, however," Watson continued, "was the extent to which Penelope reciprocated those feelings, if she did at all." Watson paused to invite a comment from his colleague. "Is there anything you'd like to add, Holmes?"

Holmes had been occupied filling his briar with the shag tobacco he favored in anticipation of the last pipe of the day he would later share with Watson, and now paused his efforts to answer Watson's query. "First of all, Watson, I agree with you entirely about Thompkins's feelings. He's clearly smitten with Mrs. Stockton. As to Penelope Stockton's feelings for Thompkins, I admit to being out of my depth, Watson. Indeed, if the once married man amongst us is uncertain, any among us lacking such experience would be foolish to venture an opinion."

Having declared his ignorance in the one area, Holmes fingered the now full bowl of his pipe while venturing his opinion in an area in which he felt more confident. "Of course, Thompkins's feelings for Penelope Stockton give him ample reason for wanting Roger Stockton dead, although it must also be said that it appears Stockton did not lack for enemies, which likely means we won't lack for suspects." A deep frown accompanied Holmes's words as he turned to his colleague. "I am certain your notes will be informative in that regard, Watson."

Watson nodded acknowledgment of Holmes's words before smoothing a second page in his accounts book. "It is the case that Thompkins appeared to have a list of people in mind as Holmes suggests, but only shared two of them with us."

Watson went on to describe the men in the order Thompkins had placed them. He portrayed Percy Dickson as the aggrieved brother of both Stockton wives, reprising in that regard Thompkins's account of Stockton's verbal abuse—as well as Penelope's minimization of Stockton's physical abuse—and Dickson being barred from the house where his sisters, nephew and nieces lived, in association with his confronting Stockton about his behaviors.

Watson went on to detail Stockton's conflict with Daniel Olyphant over land, specifically the woods in which Stockton was murdered. He described Olyphant and his son carrying shotguns into the woods around the time of the murder, noting they had only Olyphant's word that his gun hadn't been fired. Watson went on to report Olyphant's comment about the Stockton farm being the largest and most prosperous in the area. He was about to describe that as a rationale for Olyphant or his son, or both, wanting to remove Stockton as an obstacle to the romance between Benjamin and Olivia and the resulting joining of properties, when Mrs. Hudson interrupted him, indicating she was already aware of that romance, and agreed it provided motive. Instead, she encouraged his detailing the persons who were known to be at the Stockton farm, or in the area of the farm the morning of the killing.

Watson's face creased in concentration as he pocketed the notes that were no longer of help to him. "There's family, of course.

Mrs. Stockton and the children, Olivia, Joy and Jonathan. Then there's Mr. Stockton senior, Roger Stockton's father. We were told he's virtually bedridden and has been confined to his room for some time. However, Holmes and I did not have opportunity to see him on this visit. Still, even apart from his physical state, it's hard to imagine a father killing his son." Watson looked to Mrs. Hudson for concurrence but found only a blank stare and continued with his face now creased by a few additional lines.

"There's also the Fiddlemans, the housekeeper and caretaker, who live above the stables. They've been with the Stockton family a long time—since before Roger Stockton's first marriage. We didn't see them either; however, Lestrade had, and he was of the opinion they showed remarkably little distress about the death of their long-time employer and were, in fact, planning on leaving shortly. Nonetheless, even if the servants had little sympathy for Stockton, it would still seem a long way from not caring to committing murder."

Mrs. Hudson nodded her appreciation for Watson's report, then added her own comment. "There's also the question of why the Fiddlemans would wait until now if they 'ad a grievance with Mr. Stockton. Which is the same question we 'ave for Mr. Dickson or whoever else we see as a suspect. Roger Stockton appears to 'ave made enemies 'and over fist, but all of them are long-standing. What suddenly triggered Mr. Stockton's killing? If we knew that we'd know our murderer." Mrs. Hudson took a deep breath before continuing. "Is there anything else, Doctor?"

"There is one thing, Mrs. Hudson." It was the moment both Watson and Holmes had been building towards, a finding that would startle even Mrs. Hudson.

"We also learned there's a man living in the woods. It seems there's a cabin of some sort well back in the woods where he lives. He's got some physical problems that put me in mind of palsy as the Olyphant boy describes them. Maybe because of that both Olyphant and Stockton have agreed to let him stay—apparently in spite of Stockton's expressed interest in selling a part of the woods for timber.

And, according to the Olyphants, this mystery man gets along better with children—which is to say the Stockton and Olyphant children—than he does with adults and, according to Benjamin, he does better with a woman than a man—although I'm not sure Benjamin has seen him with either. In any event, it would likely be well for one or more of the children to accompany whoever intends to question him. And there's one more thing to know about him. He carries a shotgun and is a good enough shot to provide game for himself in spite of his infirmity."

The bewildered look that greeted his description of the man in the woods pleased Watson more than he felt it should have and delighted Holmes exactly as much as he hoped it would have. Nonetheless, neither man was surprised by the speed with which Mrs. Hudson recovered her composure and lent direction to the course of the next stage in the investigation.

"Thank you, Doctor. That was very thorough and points up some of the additional people we need to talk to and the things we need to ask them." Watson readied his pencil for the assignments he knew were coming; Holmes assumed his best world-weary look knowing he could rely on Watson's notetaking to learn his upcoming tasks.

"There's first of all the Fiddlemans. I'd particularly like to know why they're in a 'urry to move away from what's been their 'ome for a great many years. Besides which, with all those years in service, they'll know the family secrets, some one of which may help us understand Roger Stockton's murder. You might take the Fiddlemans as your responsibility, Dr. Watson.

"We'll also need to question Percy Dickson. We 'ave Mr. Thompkins sayin' Mr. Dickson got understandably exercised about Mr. Stockton bullyin' both his wives, which is to say Mr. Dickson's sisters. We'll want to get the truth of that from Mr. Dickson and to know where 'e was the mornin' of the murder I'll ask you to see about that, Mr. 'Olmes.

"I'll be the one to talk to this man in the woods." Mrs. Hudson looked to Watson. "I'll need you to take me with you when you go to see the Fiddlemans. I'll get with Joy and Jonathan, who, from what you say, might be best able to introduce me to 'im. And I suspect Benjamin is right, that a woman will be less threatenin' to 'im than either of you. Anyway, I'll see what I can find out about where 'e comes from and what 'e's doin' in the woods between the farms. We'll need to be sure we account for everybody with an axe to grind with Mr. Stockton. There seems to be no shortage of axes to go around.

"And before you go up for your last pipes of the day, I need to tell you about a visit I 'ad from a Mr. Sudden Thunder and his fiancée, a Miss Jane Morrison." Holmes and Watson had been halfway out of their chairs, eager to enjoy their pipes and the fellowship that accompanied them, when Mrs. Hudson made mention of her exotic sounding guests. Looking to their bewilderment, she was pleased to see she had gotten some of her own back after their surprising her with their tale of the man in the woods. Still looking bemused, the two men settled back in their seats, pipes and fellowship briefly put on hold, as they waited to hear how two such different names had come to be linked.

When she was done, Watson shook his head in sympathy with the couple's plight, stating his belief that the two of them would almost certainly encounter difficulties, whether they made their home in England or America. It was Holmes's opinion they would encounter difficulties long before they tried making a home for themselves, and as soon as their plans became known. He expressed the hope that neither he nor Watson would be drawn into it as they already had a murder to solve. Watson grunted his agreement; Mrs. Hudson only smiled.

The following morning, after gaining the strength needed for the day from platefuls of smoked kippers, scrambled eggs, strips of bacon, and a small mound of toast, all of it washed down with the contents of Mrs. Hudson's bottomless tea kettle, each member of the Baker Street trio set about the task outlined the prior evening. Holmes left first, directing the hansom driver to the address for Percy Dickson he had gotten from Alfred Thompkins. Watson and Mrs. Hudson stayed behind long enough for the agency's head to tend to the morning dishes while Watson read the *Morning Standard*. When both were done, they left for the Stockton farm in the buggy the doctor had rented.

Penelope Stockton's lukewarm greeting made clear her disappointment at finding Watson so soon again on her doorstep, now, for some unknown reason, accompanied by his housekeeper. In deference to Watson, she invited him to conduct his questioning in the parlor and steered Watson to the room he and Holmes had been in twice before. She then went to fetch Mrs.Fiddleman, who was sent in turn to fetch Mr. Fiddleman for the two of them to meet with Watson. She went herself to find Joy and Jonathan and directed them to meet with Mrs. Hudson in the hall downstairs. On learning that Joy and Jonathan would be introducing the housekeeper to their friend, Aaron, she put together a basket of small cakes, an apple and an orange without instruction to her children, knowing they would be aware of its ultimate recipient. With that done, she expressed a concern to no one in particular about things needing her attention in the sewing room. She was not heard from again until it was time for her guests to leave.

In marked contrast to their mother, Joy and Jonathan were delighted to see their old friend and were only disappointed that she had brought none of her baked goods with her. Once outside they walked and danced their way along the path to the woods.

Watson, meanwhile, commandeered the same easy chair he had taken the day before. He thought it likely the Fiddlemans would want the sofa opposite to allow the two of them to be together. They did stay together but not as Watson had anticipated. After a series of apologies for being late, Mrs. Fiddleman settled herself through a succession of wiggles on the edge of a cushion to one side of the sofa while Mr. Fiddleman rejected the available seating and elected instead to stand sentry beside his wife. Seeing their discomfort at being in the residence for purposes other than serving or cleaning, Watson was regretting acceptance of Mrs. Stockton's well-meaning invitation. He judged the couple to be in their mid-sixties and, having worked for one family all their lives, were likely to be at pains to be protective of that family, all the more so when asked to talk about them in their parlor. Watson anticipated a difficult interview.

"As you may know," he began, "Mr. Sherlock Holmes and I have been asked to look into the death of Mr. Stockton. It's in that regard I've summoned you to learn whatever you can tell me that might help us capture his murderer." Watson paused to allow either of the Fiddlemans to make comment. Neither did. Instead, they both adopted looks of grave concern and slowly nodded their understanding.

After a suitable pause, under the guise of sharing information, Mr. Fiddleman attempted to draw the interview to a close before it began. "You may be unaware, Dr. Watson, that we were questioned earlier by another policeman—the man from Scotland Yard."

"Yes, we've spoken to Inspector Lestrade. He told Mr. Holmes and me he'd had only limited time to question you and urged us to talk with you as well. We will, of course, share what we learn from you with the people at Scotland Yard." Having established that Lestrade, and all of Scotland Yard were as one with Holmes and himself, and having witnessed Fiddleman's small effort at obstruction, Watson judged that a more imperious approach was not only warranted but was the only one likely to lead to success. He pulled the accounts book from his waistcoat together with a sharpened Eagle Number 2 pencil and turned to a blank page. "Suppose we start with your full names. Mr. Fiddleman, Mrs. Fiddleman." The words sounded a suggestion. The tone did not. Nor did the Fiddlemans take it as such.

"It's Charlie, Charles Fiddleman. There's no middle name. And the wife's name is Molly Fiddleman. Her maiden name was Jackson, but that's some time back."

"How long have the two of you been married and did you meet while in service?"

Whether or not intended by Watson, the question seemed to lighten somewhat the room's leaden atmosphere.

"It'll be forty-five years this September," Charlie Fiddleman offered. "Am I right, love?"

"Forty-six," she corrected him without a hint of disapproval.

"The wife would have it right," Fiddleman agreed. "Forty-six of the best years a man could hope for." The Fiddlemans looked briefly to each other, seemingly on the verge of sharing a secret smile.

"I was in service to the Stocktons when Mrs. Stockton—that would be the wife of Mr. Stockton senior—was in confinement waiting on the baby. Knowing she would be needing help—female help—the master hired Mrs. Fiddleman. Of course, she was Miss Jackson then and stayed Miss Jackson for the better part of a year after young Mr. Stockton was born. It was then we got married, and we've been with the Stocktons ever since."

"Well then, you've both known Roger Stockton his whole life. Would you say he was a man for making enemies?"

68

Any trace of a marginally brighter atmosphere disappeared with Watson's question. Charlie Fiddleman made clear the difficulty, in the process confirming Watson's supposition of his dedication to their role in service. "You understand, Doctor, we are in service to the Stockton family. People in service do not deal in tittle tattle. Not if they're proper staff." Unseen by her husband, Mrs. Fiddleman gave his comment a brisk nod of approval.

"I appreciate your concern, Mr. Fiddleman, but I would remind you that one of your masters is dead and for all we know other family members may be at risk, I'm not interested in idle gossip. Mr. Holmes and I are concerned with capturing the man ... or woman ... responsible for Mr. Stockton's death and making certain all in the family remain safe. Let me ask again, do you know of any enemies Mr. Roger Stockton had made."

Watson looked to the standing Mr. Fiddleman and the seated Mrs. Fiddleman. Neither of them looked to him. At last, Mr. Fiddleman spoke.

"I'll not speak to the situation with family. However, I can say it's well known that the master had words with the neighbor, Mr. Olyphant, from time to time."

"And what was that all about?"

"I'm afraid the master did not confide in me, Doctor."

Watson wondered whether he was dealing with a paragon among servants or someone with something to hide. Regardless of which—or both—there was nothing to do except to keep slogging doggedly in the hope that Fiddleman would grow tired of his obstructionism or perhaps even see the wisdom of cooperation. "I know something of the difficulties with the Olyphants. Were there others?"

"May I suggest you direct such questioning to Mrs. Stockton. She is likely to be far better informed than Mrs. Fiddleman or myself."

Watson looked hard at Fiddleman; Fiddleman appeared to search the room for something out of place. Watson decided to take another tack for the moment. "Thank you, perhaps I shall. What then can you tell me of the visitors the Stocktons received? I understand the two Mrs. Stocktons have a brother. Did he visit often?"

"That would be Mr. Percival Dickson. He was here on occasion. I wouldn't say he was here often."

"I've been told he only visited when Mr. Stockton was away? Is that true?"

"I believe that's accurate."

"Was there anyone else who only visited when Mr. Stockton was away?"

The Fiddlemans looked to each other; what communication passed between them was lost on Watson, but it led to a grudging revelation from Fiddleman. "I suppose it's no secret that the banker, Mr. Thompkins, sometimes visited on those occasions."

Watson was by now determined to induce greater speech from Mrs. Fiddleman than correcting her husband as to their years married. In part, he was hoping she might be more forthcoming than her husband; in part, he was responding to the challenge he set for himself of hearing from another Fiddleman. Shifting slightly in his chair to face Mrs. Fiddleman more directly, he opened up a new line of inquiry he felt more likely to allow for her contribution. It did not meet with initial success.

"Am I correct that your workday begins at six in the morning?"

"Yes, sir. That would be when Mrs. Fiddleman lights the fires and gets the breakfast on. I'll be looking to the pigs and to Abigail—she's the milk cow."

Watson now placed a particular emphasis on the name of his desired respondent. "And, *Mrs. Fiddleman*, is that when Mr. Stockton would have his breakfast?"

"I believe that's right, isn't it, my dear?"

There was a guttural sound from the woman, which, in spite of its being indecipherable, gave Watson hope.

Watson again directed his question as unambiguously as he thought possible to Mrs. Fiddleman. "Did you serve Mr. Stockton his breakfast that morning, Mrs. Fiddleman?"

Mrs. Fiddleman looked to her husband with eyebrows raised. He shrugged defeat, only squeezing her shoulder in a show of continuing support. She waited another few seconds before speaking in a small clear voice. "The master went for his daily walk— 'constitutional,' he called it—before I got to the kitchen. He would be

70

back at half six when I was expected to have his breakfast ready. It has been that way for as long as I can remember."

Before Watson could respond or Mrs. Fiddleman continue, Mr. Fiddleman interrupted with a new concern. "I need to inform you, doctor. We've our chores still to get to. This talk about breakfast reminds me there's Mr. Stockton senior's midday meal to prepare. He has a special diet Mrs. Fiddleman needs to prepare and he's got to be fed on time."

Watson grunted acknowledgment of Fiddleman's concern, then proceeded to ignore it.

"Mr. Fiddleman, I'm sure you were out early what with all there is to do on a large farm. Did you see or hear anything or anyone while you were out? Could there have been a carriage go by for example?"

Fiddleman spent no time searching his memory before grimacing his rejection of the idea and shaking his head. "You know, Doctor, we're a ways from the roadway, but the answer is, no, I saw no carriage and I heard no carriage."

"Did you hear anything that sounded like a gunshot?"

This time Fiddleman took a moment, either to search his memory or think how to frame his response. "Could've been. In truth I wouldn't have noticed. The Olyphants out hunting or somebody else trying to bag a rabbit wouldn't have made much of an impression."

"Did you hear or see anything, Mrs. Fiddleman?"

Fortified by another squeeze of her shoulder, she responded to Watson's query. "No, but I was inside the house the whole time."

Watson nodded and turned back to her husband. "Do you own a shotgun, Mr. Fiddleman?"

"Certainly, I do—this is the country, Dr. Watson. Every male over fourteen and most women own a shotgun."

"And has your shotgun been fired recently?"

There was a sharp intake of breath by Fiddleman before answering. "I ain't saying yes and I ain't saying no. There's a fox been chasing after our chickens and I been chasing after him the last few nights—yes, and night to morning come to that. Night to morning when the Mister was killed to answer your next question. But I was back and in bed before the Mister went for his morning walk as Mrs.

Fiddleman can tell you. It's a fox I'm after and only a fox if you're thinking it could be something else."

Fiddleman's look to Watson suggested more than a fox might be in danger if encountered on a sufficiently dark night. The brief relinquishing of the reserve he'd shown earlier convinced Watson that beyond the deferential façade was a man who, for all his years, could prove an unpleasant, perhaps dangerous adversary.

Watson resumed his questioning, now following another line of inquiry. "As I understand it, you suggested to Inspector Lestrade that you might well be moving from the Stockton farm. I couldn't help but wonder why you would be thinking of moving at a time when Mrs. Stockton is likely to have greater need for your services than at any time earlier."

While Mr. Fiddleman shrugged his unconcern, Mrs. Fiddleman's sudden difficulty finding a comfortable position on the sofa's cushion suggested to Watson he had stumbled onto a rare instance of marital disharmony. Fiddleman felt obliged to state his side of the disagreement.

"You must understand, Mrs. Fiddleman and myself was hired by Mr. Stockton senior and his missus. It was fine working for the two misters, and it's nothing against the current Mrs. Stockton, she's simply not why we've been here all these years. And now there's going to be new people to get used to. Mrs. Stockton will need to marry to keep up the farm—except if it's that Thompkins bloke she'll be with someone who knows less about farming than Master Jonathan. Before you know it, Mrs. Fiddleman and me will be asked to take on more chores, and with the two of us getting on in years, this seems like a good time for us to stop taking care of others and start in to taking care of ourselves. Besides which, we got to ask ourselves do we want to stay here with a killer on the loose. I don't think so. Mrs. Fiddleman has got family in Yorkshire who are quite tolerable, and we are thinking of taking a cottage near to them—as soon as things here get sorted."

Fiddleman seemed to gather himself as if preparing to stand prior to leaving, the effect substantially diminished by the fact that he was already standing. "Now, if there's no more questions, Doctor, Mrs. Fiddleman and me do have chores."

"Just one more. Do I understand correctly that Mr. Stockton senior is bedridden?"

"He's mostly bedridden. He'll dress himself part way and things like that, but it's not like he can go up and down the stairs anymore." Fiddleman swallowed hard. "It's a bloody shame— begging your pardon. He was a wonderful independent man in his time."

"How did he respond to the news of his son's death?"

While Fiddleman was still considering his response, there came the soft clear voice rarely heard during the last half hour.

"He were, of course, terrible upset. He weren't exactly himself and his words and thoughts seemed to go off in all directions. He said he didn't understand the why of it, why there had to be a killing and what was it going to accomplish. But then he talked about when Mr. Stockton junior was a boy and the things he'd done. Like riding the milk cow because he thought the exercise would make her give more milk and things like that that were funny and sad. And then he'd talk about how it was a dangerous world and all of us had to take care of ourselves. And he didn't take lunch that day nor dinner neither."

Her report complete, Mrs. Fiddleman looked to her husband with a questioning smile and received yet another squeeze of her shoulder for response.

Watson finished writing and closed his accounts book.

"Thank you. I don't have any more questions for now although I may want to see you later or Mr. Holmes might. Thank you for your time. I'll let you get on with your day."

With that, the Fiddlemans nodded their exits, leaving as quickly as a concern for propriety allowed. Watson went to pay his respects to Mrs. Stockton who appeared shortly after her servants had left. He ignored her quizzical look and made his way to the front door before the look could give rise to the questions behind it.

Holmes exited the hansom at 630 Rugby Road in Paddington in front of the second in a row of eight red-brick terraced houses. The two-story houses marked a clear triumph of function over style. White framed windows were set on either side of a white paneled door on the ground floor; white-framed windows were set on either side of a small unadorned window above the door on the second floor. The contrast of white frames with red brick was the builder's sole concession to aesthetics, a consequence of either limited funds or imagination. Beneath each ground floor window there was a small patch of earth in which a variety of flowers flourished in accord with the tastes, budgets, and gardening abilities of the different homeowners. The single exception to the display of horticultural skills was the owner of the home Holmes now approached whose patch of dirt was unsullied by flowers.

At his knock the door was opened just far enough to expose the better part of a balding man of moderate height, clean shaven with tired brown eyes that looked suspiciously at Holmes. "Is there something I can do for you?"

"I believe there is. I am Sherlock Holmes. I have been asked to investigate the death of Roger Stockton. I know you are the brother of the two Mrs. Stocktons who were his wives."

The door widened somewhat allowing the two men to be face to face with each other. "I've been expecting you, Mr. Holmes. My sister sent word you'd be calling. I'll tell you two things right out, same as I told the man from Scotland Yard. I'm not surprised by Roger's death, and I'm not going to pretend I'm broken up about it— but I didn't do it. I guess that's three things. Anyway, I figure if I don't tell you how I feel, you'll figure it out regardless—if you haven't already. But let's take this inside. It's not something to be talking about on my front step and maybe needs a drink besides."

He led Holmes to a room cheerless enough to be a match for the house's exterior. In one corner there was a table with pen and ink, a blotter and three or four piles of paper heaped on it, thereby establishing it as Dickson's desk and the corner to be his study. Near to the back wall two armed easy chairs stood on one side of a low table and one armless easy chair stood on its other side. No two pieces matched and while all could be said to have seen better days, none could be said to have seen better days recently. The single piece that still awaited the ravages of age was an oaken sideboard that held a tea service at its one end and, at its other, glasses and bottles of drinks chosen to satisfy those with stronger tastes. Holmes waved away his host's offer of each with a small smile and a murmured, "No, thank you." He added a sociable addendum, "But don't let me keep you from getting something for yourself," which turned out to be wholly unnecessary as Dickson was well on his way to the sidebar before Holmes had gotten to "keep you." Without direction, he took the single chair on one side of the low table, then waited for Dickson to fill a glass and join him.

"I need to ask you first where you were last morning?"

"You mean when Stockton was killed?'

Holmes gave a long nod to Dickson's query. "We need to know where people were the morning in question."

"You say 'we'. Does that mean you're one of a team of investigators, Mr. Holmes?

Holmes shifted position, suddenly finding the easy chair less comfortable than it had first appeared. "Hardly a team, Mr. Dickson. There is myself and my colleague, Dr. Watson, and, quite separately, there is Detective Inspector Lestrade of Scotland Yard who is conducting his own investigation. Now, I ask you again, where were you yesterday morning?"

"Yesterday morning," Dickson mused, as if hearing the question for the first time. "That's the morning I got back quite late and slept in. I don't think I got up before eleven."

"When you say you got back late, what time did you, in fact, get home?"

"I didn't look at my pocket watch, but I'd guess it was about six in the morning, possibly half six."

"And can anyone vouch for your movements?"

With a deeply furrowed brow Dickson stood and made his way to the mantel over the still fireplace to shake a cigarette from the pack he found there. He held the pack out to Holmes with a questioning look and was met with a brusque headshake as Holmes waited an answer to his question. With a cigarette lit and an initial stream of smoke expelled, Dickson was finally ready to respond.

"I'll tell you how I spent that morning and the night before that morning, and I'll depend on your discretion. I assure you my movements during the time you're asking about have nothing at all to do with Stockton or his death."

"And I can assure you that I have no use for tittle tattle. If what you have to say is unrelated to the Stockton murder, I see no reason for it to be shared with others."

Dickson nodded his appreciation for Holmes's promise, but his eyes lost none of their suspiciousness. "As I've told you, I'm innocent of murder. That doesn't mean I have nothing to hide, however. I frequently make use of a form of relaxation not everyone would approve of, Mr. Holmes, and I was taking that relaxation the early part of the morning you ask about as well as the evening before. It was the end of my work week." Dickson took a long drag on his cigarette. "I have colleagues who spend that time drinking themselves into a stupor, becoming so terribly sick they need what they call 'the hair of the dog' and find themselves pretty much useless at the start of the work week. I spend the time they're drinking themselves sick smoking opium in a place I know in the East End. There is stupor to be sure, but not sickness and I can be fully recovered in time for the Monday workday."

Holmes was about to request the address, with the intent of verifying Dickson's story as one but perhaps not his only motive, when Dickson appeared to presume his question. "It's no good my giving you the address, they'd only deny knowing me or ever seeing me. And as for witnesses, there are several, many from Soho and some from Whitehall—quite a few with names you'd recognize. Of course, they're not names I can share just as they would not give you my name in similar circumstances. I'm afraid you have only my word for where I was when Stockton was killed but I swear what I tell you is the God's honest truth." Dickson punctuated his refusal by forcibly grinding the remainder of his half-smoked cigarette in the ashtray on the mantel where he had remained standing. His position stated and underlined, he returned to the chair he had earlier deserted and looked defiantly to his questioner, daring Holmes to challenge either his truthfulness or his lifestyle.

With a small smile Holmes accepted one part of the challenge.

"It's all very well for you to insist I believe you and your silent witnesses, but you remain a man with a powerful motive for wanting to see Stockton in his grave and you now say you cannot or will not produce corroboration for the movements you claim. I can assure you that your word alone will not carry the day. If you will tell me the location of the place you ... attend, I will see to it that it stays secret and you suffer no consequences for visiting it." Holmes removed a paper and pencil from a coat pocket. "Write the address on this paper, fold it and hand it back to me. I will destroy the paper after visiting the location and confirming it to be as you describe."

Dickson shook his head and started to explain to Holmes that the nature of the business conducted inside the establishment would not be apparent from its outside, but Holmes held up a hand urging him to allay any such concerns.

"I assure you I have ways of finding out such things." He did not explain that he was not entirely a stranger to such places of business and would go to whatever length necessary to determine its activities. Nor, for the moment, would he share this aspect of the investigation with Mrs. Hudson or Watson. For now, he accepted the folded piece of paper from a resigned Percy Dickson and made his way back onto the London street.

The gleefulness exhibited by Joy and Jonathan as they hurried along the roadway to the woods contrasted dramatically with the somber journey of Holmes and Watson over the same road a day earlier. After enduring what they viewed as an interminable delay waiting for Mrs. Hudson to catch up to them at the entrance to the woods, they moderated their speed so as to keep reasonably close to Mrs. Hudson's pace. As they traipsed along, they told her of their discovery of the man they knew as Aaron when he just suddenly appeared one day when they were playing explorers. He showed them where he lived in what their father called "a rundown shack." Mrs. Hudson was glad they stayed close to her as it was clear the path they followed, while seemingly well known to them, consisted of not much more than the beaten down grass of repeated footfalls and sometimes not even that. After they had gone a short distance, they began calling their friend's name. They only used his first name, partly because they didn't know his last name—or if he had a last name—but mainly because he wasn't like other adults they knew. He was their friend and you called friends by their first names. They would call three or four times, then stop and listen. When they were satisfied there would be no response, they would plod on a short distance, then repeat the same practice. They did not speak of it, but their walk was taking them ever deeper into the woods.

The object of their search appeared suddenly from a tangle of bushes they had already passed. Later, Joy said she saw him out of the corner of her eye before anyone else did, which Jonathan argued was not possible and was, he said, "just Joy showing off." Regardless, the man's arrival was greeted with ear to ear smiles and the repeated calling of his name, now in joyous recognition of their search being over. She judged him to be somewhere in his mid-to late forties, but it was hard to be certain as his features were nearly obliterated by thick moustaches that merged with a dark bushy beard reaching to a barrel chest but knowing little in the way of other limits. His cleaning and grooming appeared dependent on the frequency and quantity of rainfall. His clothing, however, made it all but certain he was the best dressed tramp in these or any woods. Mrs. Hudson judged that the same women who made fruit and cakes available also provided freshly anointed hand-me-downs from the backs of their husbands' wardrobes. And still, what was most striking about the man was his gait as he came toward them. His knees turned unnaturally inward as he walked, making each step appear a labored exercise. A crudely carved walking stick that he planted with each stride gave him the support his legs could not reliably provide.

He showed a crooked smile as he neared Joy and Jonathan but maintained a wary observation of Mrs. Hudson. Jonathan took responsibility for introductions.

"Aaron, this is Mrs. Hudson. She's nice."

Joy found her brother's description somewhat lacking in substance. "Mrs. Hudson is here to find out about our father's death. They found him in the woods yesterday."

"Somebody shot him," Jonathan added.

Aaron nodded soberly and his eyes narrowed in response to the children's news. Mrs. Hudson was hard-pressed to judge whether he was shocked and confused by the information or was simply slow-witted and unable to comprehend Jonathan's statement. His halting speech did nothing to clarify his condition.

"There was a killing? In these woods?"

Joy took responsibility for offering further clarification. "That's right. It happened just yesterday. Somebody shot our father. Mrs. Hudson is helping her detective friends find out who it was that shot him."

Again, Mrs. Hudson was struck by the lack of feeling on the part of both children at the death of their parent.

"And this Mrs. Hudson is your friend?" Aaron looked from Joy to Jonathan, then back again, while asking his question about the person in front of him.

"She is," Joy affirmed and Jonathan solemnly shook his head before referencing the characteristic he found particularly salient. "She makes really good scones," and turning to Mrs. Hudson, "You should bring some next time you come."

The mention of scones reminded the children of the basket their mother had prepared. "These are for you," Joy said, handing him the basket. Aaron smiled his appreciation. He said nothing, nor did Joy or Jonathan seem to feel there was need of anything to be said. Nor did either of them feel there was reason for Aaron to share the food he had been given.

Feeling that whatever barriers had existed were now down, Mrs. Hudson decided the time was ripe to ask Aaron the questions she had been planning to put to him, at the same time learning something of his ability to comprehend and respond appropriately.

"Do you live in the woods, Mr. ... Aaron?"

Aaron screwed his face into a look of distress, looked to his still smiling friends, and taking heart from their obvious unconcern, responded to the woman's question.

"I have a little house. I live in a little house back there." He pointed in the direction of a dense area of the woods they hadn't yet reached.

Mrs. Hudson smiled appreciation for his answer.

"'Ow long 'ave you lived in your little 'ouse, Mr. Aaron?"

He shrugged his response, "I don't know exactly. I think maybe some weeks, maybe a month."

"It's a month," Joy declared. "At least," Jonathan added.

Mrs. Hudson grunted acknowledgment of their contribution before turning her attention back to Aaron. "'Ow did you 'appen to come to these woods, Mr. Aaron?"

As Aaron's face reflected the confusion Mrs. Hudson's question caused him, Joy again came to his rescue. "The Fiddlemans."

Joy's answer satisfied her still smiling brother and the again smiling Aaron, but now left Mrs. Hudson in a state of confusion. She posed a question for anyone to answer. "'Ow did Mr. and Mrs. Fiddleman cause Mr. Aaron to come to live in the woods?"

"It's what Mr. Fiddleman was talking about to our father when they thought we couldn't hear," Joy explained.

"That's what happened before Aaron came to live in the woods," Jonathan quickly added, ignoring his sister's critical stare as he did so.

"Mr. Fiddleman was saying that his cousin and his wife—they're the people who adopted Aaron way back—had to go to America, that their daughter needed them." Joy's voice became confidential as she interrupted herself to speak woman to woman to Mrs. Hudson. "Her husband left her which we weren't supposed to know." Mrs. Hudson half expected a wink and a nod from Joy, but the girl simply returned to her narrative. "Mr. Fiddleman said his cousin couldn't take Aaron with them and asked if they could leave Aaron with him and his wife, meaning with Mr. Fiddleman and his wife. Which he said they would do, except there wasn't room for Aaron in their flat but he thought he could maybe stay in the cabin in the woods where they would be able to keep an eye on him."

"It used to be a hunter's cabin but now it's not good for anything except the games we used to play when we were little," Jonathan added. For a second time, Joy found Jonathan's contribution unhelpful and, for a second time, she gave him a critical stare, which, for a second time, he ignored.

"Anyway," Joy continued, "we couldn't hear father's response, but Mr. Fiddleman said something about them having an agreement, and just a little after that Aaron moved here."

"And became our friend."

At this third interruption, Joy smiled broadly to her brother and echoed his words. "And became our friend."

Aaron matched her smile but said nothing.

"Where did you live before comin' 'ere, Mr. Aaron?" Mrs. Hudson found herself speaking slowly and enunciating carefully when she addressed the man.

The answer, however, came speedily in a voice that cared little about careful pronunciation. "He lived in Lambeth with his mother and father and the sister what went to America," Jonathan reported

Mrs. Hudson was beginning to marvel at Joy's forbearance. "Is that right, Mr. Aaron, did you live in Lambeth before comin' 'ere?"

Aaron nodded a vigorous affirmation.

"Do you know how long you lived there?"

"Since I was born."

"And when was that, Mr. Aaron? Do you know your date of birth?"

Aaron looked puzzled by the question and Mrs. Hudson regretted putting it more clumsily than she should. She made effort to simplify things. "'Ow old are you, Mr. Aaron?"

He brightened with the new query. "Forty-six. That's what mam and dad told me last birthday."

"And when was your last birthday, can you remember?"

"I don't know. I don't remember. It's different every year. I don't like this game. I want to play something else."

"Alright, let's talk about things that just 'appened a little while ago.

"Can you think back to yesterday mornin'—that would be the mornin' before this one. Did anythin' out of the ordinary 'appen that mornin'? Did you see anythin' or ear anythin' that surprised you?" Mrs. Hudson found herself struggling to find words that she thought would be clearly comprehensible without knowing Aaron's level of comprehension.

He screwed his face into a look of either deep thinking or utter confusion. After a few moments it became clear that thinking was holding sway. "I don't remember anything that wasn't like always."

"Did you 'ear gunfire, see anythin' you didn't expect to see?"

"There's always guns. They wake me up sometimes. What else did you want to know? Oh wait, I remember, did I see anything. No, it was a regular morning."

"Did you fire your gun that mornin'?"

"Maybe. I don't know. I could 'ave. I can't remember."

"Thank you, Mr. Aaron. You've been very 'elpful. I may be back with more questions later, or a Mr. 'Olmes or Dr. Watson may come to see you."

"Maybe you could bring scones next time," Jonathan again suggested. Aaron immediately brightened at the idea of a treat of whatever nature and Joy, who knew its nature, smiled broadly. Mrs. Hudson thought it wise to ally herself with Jonathan's magnanimity.

"That's a fine idea; I'll remember to do that."

Dinner that night was a good deal more somber than dinner the night before. Mrs. Hudson hadn't had time to do more than roast a chicken and prepare some very pedestrian side dishes. Neither Watson or Holmes felt the meal merited a trip to the lumber room and instead made do with a serviceable but unspectacular cabernet they found in the pantry. When the meal was done and the table cleared, each of the Baker Street trio recounted their experiences.

Watson first told of his interview with the Fiddlemans and their plans to join Mrs. Fiddleman's family in Yorkshire as soon as possible, after working for the Stockton family since before the birth of Roger Stockton. He went on to report that Fiddleman claimed to have spent the night to morning of Stockton's death in the woods with a shotgun hunting a fox that raided the farm's chickens. He said he neither saw or heard anything unusual and was in bed before Stockton went for his walk. Watson noted that Fiddleman had no one but Mrs. Fiddleman to corroborate the report of his activities at the time of Stockton's murder.

Holmes's presentation was no more upbeat than Watson's and made no effort to be otherwise. He made clear that Percy Dickson, like seemingly all the suspects, had motive, opportunity and an uncorroborated account of his whereabouts the morning in question. Holmes felt it unnecessary to share the nature of Dickson's uncorroborated whereabouts the morning in question.

Finally, Mrs. Hudson shared findings from her time with the man in the woods. She described his physical difficulty, slowed thought and speech, all of which Watson saw as likely the result of a birth defect associated with a difficult forceps delivery. She described how the children had overheard a conversation between Mr. Fiddleman and Mr. Stockton detailing that the man, whose name is Aaron, had been adopted by Mr. Fiddleman's cousin, but the adoptive parents claimed a need to go to America to care for their daughter, and could not or would not take Aaron with them. As a consequence, Mr. and Mrs. Fiddleman assumed responsibility for Aaron about a month ago, housing him in a cabin deep in the woods when they were unable to house him in their flat. She reported that Aaron claimed to have neither seen nor heard anything the morning of Mr. Stockton's murder.

After a short pause, Watson stated the dilemma they all felt. "We seem to have a surfeit of suspects—or at least of individuals who can neither be ruled out or ruled in. I do, however, believe this Aaron person can be ruled out. His limitations would seem to make very unlikely his participating in the events of the morning. Besides, what grievance could he have against a man who permits him to live on his land?"

"Indeed, we have no reason to believe he has anything to do with the Stocktons, or the Dicksons—or the Olyphants for that matter," Holmes added. Watson nodded agreement; Mrs. Hudson slowly shook her head.

"Unless 'e 'eard of the plans to sell off the woods for lumber. It doesn't seem likely but it's somethin' to keep in mind.

"Meanwhile, we've still two people to interview, and I want to make a trip to the registry office to check some things out. Mr. 'Olmes I think it would be well for you to meet with the senior Mr. Stockton, and, Dr. Watson, you might meet with Dr. Montgomery. 'E's known the family from way back and it would be good to 'ear 'is view of them, and of the enemies Mr. Stockton seems to 'ave made. One thing that still concerns me and that maybe 'e can 'elp with. It's as we've said before, none of the arguments with Mr. Stockton are new, so why would any of them lead to 'is murder now. Did one of them suddenly flare up or is there a new dispute we don't know anythin' about. I'm thinkin' an outsider who knows the family, like Dr. Montgomery, can maybe shed some light on that.

"Does anybody 'ave a question?"

Nobody did.

Chapter 5. A Trip to the Registry Office

The following morning Holmes and Watson had barely begun their onslaught on another of Mrs. Hudson's bountiful breakfasts when their attention was diverted first by the doorbell Mrs. Hudson went to answer, then by the strident tones of the boisterous woman she admitted, and finally by the appearance of that boisterous woman.

As it turned out, the strident tones that preceded her appearance left Holmes and Watson poorly prepared for their intruder. The woman looked to be in her early seventies, was at most a few inches taller than Mrs. Hudson and a good deal slimmer. Perhaps because of the latter, Mrs. Hudson trailed some distance behind the woman she was supposed to be introducing to her colleagues. What captured and held her colleagues' attention was the unexpected character of the woman's dress. From her wide brimmed hat that seemed to support a small flower garden to her shoes, barely visible beneath a high-collared gray satin gown ending inches off the ground, it was apparent their intruder was, in all but manners, a lady. She looked to Watson who held a forkful of sausage tantalizingly near his mouth, then to Holmes who was absently buttering the toast he had already buttered. Unable to decide, she posed a question.

"Which of you is Sherlock Holmes?"

Holmes responded without regard to her question. "Madam, you have barged your way into our home and interrupted our breakfast routine to what purpose?"

Unmoved by Holmes's critique, she sniffed her reply. "You must be him." With that, she took the empty chair at the table, which happened to be Mrs. Hudson's seat, and announced her purpose in coming.

"I'm Lady Agatha Dickson. I've just come from seeing my daughter, Penelope, at the Stockton farm. She told me of your involvement in the investigation of my son-in-law's death, so it's you I have to see to learn where things stand." With that, she sniffed a second time and sat back waiting for the man she took to be Holmes to fulfill her request. It was, however, Watson who replied.

"I can understand your feelings, Lady Dickson, and let me offer you our condolences on this tragic turn of events." Watson was prepared to move from sympathetic understanding to an explanation that the investigation was in its early stages, ending with his assurance that the person responsible for this heinous act would be caught and punished. However, while still engaged in the sympathetic understanding portion of his soliloquy, Lady Dickson waived off any more of his talk.

"You've got it completely upside down, Mr. whatever your name is."

Watson now interrupted Lady Dickson. Speaking in as aggrieved a tone as either Holmes or Mrs. Hudson could recall his ever using, he provided their uninvited guest the information she had not requested. "The name, madam, is Watson, Dr. John Watson."

Lady Dickson grunted acknowledgment of Watson's contribution and proceeded to explain the reason for her visit. "As I was saying you've got it completely upside down. When you find who killed Roger Stockton, I want to be there to shake his hand, thank him and then hire the finest solicitor in the land to defend him. Roger Stockton was a scoundrel pure and simple. If anyone ever deserved to be permanently removed from the sight of decent people, it was him. I will give you everything you will need to locate me when that happy time occurs and ask only to be assured that you will contact me immediately on his apprehension. I know these investigations take time; however, Inspector Lestrade speaks very highly of you and says you are definitely the person with whom I should remain in close touch."

Mrs. Hudson, who had been standing beside Watson's desk since losing her seat at the table, was becoming increasingly concerned about getting Mr. Holmes and Dr. Watson started on the work scheduled for the day. She took advantage of the fact that both of her colleagues were sitting with mouths open but not eating to work toward that end.

"You probably didn't 'ave time for a proper breakfast, Lady Dickson. Perhaps you'd like to come downstairs with me to 'ave a cup of tea and a scone, while we allow the men to finish their breakfast and get back to the work of findin' Mr. Stockton's killer. While you're 'avin' some refreshments, you can give me the information Mr. 'Olmes will need to locate you and report 'is progress." She accompanied her words with what she hoped would be seen as a welcoming smile.

"I did come away without stopping to have anything to eat. You don't happen to have raisin scones by any chance."

Mrs. Hudson's expression went from polite smile to a sly grin as she led the woman back downstairs. While Mrs. Hudson readied tea and freshly baked raisin scones, Holmes and Watson returned to the serious business of readying themselves for the tasks ahead by devouring breakfasts that would easily sustain them through the day—and some time beyond if necessary.

It was quickly apparent that Lady Dickson was unaccustomed and more than a little uncomfortable to find herself taking tea in the kitchen of a woman she thought to be the detectives' housekeeper. She looked critically to all parts of the room and became unnaturally silent until Mrs. Hudson set tea and scones in front of her. After a first cautious bite of the scone she had chosen, her eyes widened with surprise and pleasure and, after allowing a highly audible "ummm" to pass her lips, she took a far more generous bite of her scone while casting a covetous eye on the three scones remaining on the serving plate. The barrier between the women now lowered, Lady Stockton became again the formidable woman who, ten minutes earlier, had invaded Mrs. Hudson's apartments.

"These scones are delightful. You must give me the recipe to give to my cook." Mrs. Hudson did not respond to what sounded to her more demand than request. The distinction was immaterial to Mrs. Hudson. She had no intention of sharing the recipe with anyone under any circumstances short of torture—and perhaps not then. In any event, Lady Dickson had moved to a topic she found more concerning.

"I suppose you've been working for Mr. Holmes a long time."

"We've been together quite a while."

"I understand that he's very well thought of, that he has an extraordinary knack for identifying evil-doers. Do you find that to be true?"

"'E's been very successful. There's no denyin' that. I've 'eard people say it's as if 'e 'as access to some 'igher intelligence denied to most of us. Of course, I don't know about such things, and Dr. Watson's stories just talk of 'is bein' uncommonly clever."

"Well, it's really no matter. Justice has already been done as far as I'm concerned. If the man who killed the tyrant who abused my daughters is never found that will be just fine with me. But if he is caught, I meant what I said to your Mr. Holmes, I'll find him the finest solicitor in England and if we can get him off, he has a permanent home rent free at Evermore. my estate in Sussex."

Mrs. Hudson, who had, to this point, simply been intent on removing an obstacle to Holmes and Watson getting on with their days, now found herself intensely interested in this new piece of information.

"That's lovely, 'avin' land and a 'ome in Sussex. Did your children grow up there?"

"Yes, they did, but don't get the wrong idea about my estate. There is a great deal of land, but very little income. My husband left me with three beautiful children, a drafty house desperately in need of repairs, a great deal of land and an enormous number of debts. He never shared that part of our life with me, and I only found it out when the will was read, and his creditors gathered around. If it had been otherwise, my son, Percival, could have been lord of the manner instead of being holed up in his squalid flat—although I will admit he seems happy with the life he's found."

Lady Dickson was now fully involved in describing the burdens she bore—burdens she was unable to describe to anyone she knew. The housekeeper, in fact, made the perfect audience. An insignificant servant, far from her home in Sussex, someone she would almost certainly never see again. In truth, the housekeeper was not her only audience. Lady Dickson would hear in whole the fragments of her life that flitted through her mind days, and her dreams at night. She reached for a second scone and allowed the matronly woman to pour her a second cup of tea.

"They met at a party when both were visiting London—my Priscilla and Stockton. It was a match made in the nether world, and, God forgive me, I was its biggest supporter. He was attracted to my title and I was attracted to his money—or the money I thought he had. I knew he had a large farm—a very large farm—and I had a friend, who had a friend, who was informed by his banker, a man

87

named Mathewson or something like that, that it was the largest, most successful farm he knew. As I've said, I had terrible debts I saw no way of paying at the time, and so I urged Priscilla into a marriage that became a nightmare, a nightmare that was compounded when, after Priscilla's death, Penelope felt it her duty to marry Stockton to protect Priscilla's daughter, Olivia, a lovely child. Of course, I didn't know the man was a bully, not at first, and Priscilla was too ashamed to say anything. Percy knew, but he thought to spare me for as long as he could. And, on top of all of that, I never saw any evidence of the money he supposedly had. To be sure there was a fine farm that I would have thought to be prosperous, but he put me off whenever I asked about his assistance, although we had agreed on certain terms before the marriage."

Lady Dickson paused, unsettled by the latest memory stirred, and put the cup she held back on its saucer without drinking from it. Mrs. Hudson sat quietly, allowing her guest to collect herself. The brief interlude also provided opportunity for Lady Dickson to rediscover her hostess.

"I'm sorry, I had to talk to someone. Perhaps you can explain to your masters why I was in such a state earlier. Meanwhile, I will depend on you, Mrs. Hudson to get word to me when Mr. Holmes discovers who it was made certain Roger Stockton can do no further harm. I know how busy Mr. Holmes is and would not want to rely on him to remember.

"You might also let your Mr. Holmes know I won't be staying for the funeral. I'm certain that between Percival and this Thompkins fellow she'll be well supported, and at my age I can excuse myself from what some may see as a family responsibility. After Roger's killer is found and a few loose ends about Evermore are taken care of I'll be leaving the country. I managed to free the estate from debt by agreeing finally to sell off a parcel of land. It pained me to sell off any of the land that has been in the family for centuries. Nonetheless, Evermore remains one of the largest estates in Sussex. I suppose I could stay on comfortably, but there are entirely too many sad memories for me to remain in England."

"I will, of course get the word to you, Lady Dickson, as soon as the case is solved. But tell me if you would, where will you go?"

"I have family that emigrated to Canada, a city called Halifax on the country's east coast. They say the city is lovely and growing into an important metropolis. Of course, I'll have to arrange to see my son and daughter, and my grandchildren, but travel has gotten so much easier with ships regularly crossing the Atlantic in shorter and shorter times. I'm sure that can all be worked out. Indeed, I suspect leasing Evermore will prove more of a challenge."

Mrs. Hudson soberly nodded her support for Lady Dickson's plan, if not her confidence in its success. In any event, Lady Dickson was back to being Lady Dickson and was feeling out of place in a housekeeper's kitchen. She stood facing her still seated hostess and began her leave-taking.

"Now, I really must be going. I'll need to get to Victoria Station in time to get the train to Sussex. Let me just write out the information you will need to get in touch with me." Mrs. Hudson provided paper and a pencil and promised to give the information to Mr. Holmes as well. Lady Dickson thanked her for her hospitality. Her role as sounding board went unacknowledged. "I do thank you for your delicious scones and tea. I'm afraid there isn't time now to get the recipe from you but when Mister Holmes has identified the man who rid the world of Stockton, I will be back as I have promised and will get it from you then. Thank you again for allowing me to rest a while and refresh myself for the trip home." The women walked to the door where Mrs. Hudson stood watching until Lady Dickson climbed aboard one of the several carriages stopped along Baker Street and was on her way.

Holmes and Watson were delighted to see the back of Lady Dickson and to be spared any further harangue. They tacitly agreed to forgo their plans for a leisurely breakfast, having decided that the mild discomfort associated with gobbling their food was preferable to the far greater discomfort of further exposure to Lady Dickson should she tire of Mrs. Hudson's company. They crept silently down the seventeen steps leading to the street and certain freedom. At ground level they were pleased to note the pocket door to Mrs. Hudson's apartments was closed. Once outside, the two colleagues parted company, each on his own mission to better understand Roger Stockton and the Stockton family history.

On Holmes's arrival at the Stockton farm, both Mrs. Fiddleman and Penelope Stockton, expecting another barrage of questions, brightened considerably on learning he had come to see Mr. Stockton senior. Mrs. Stockton led him to the stairs to the bedrooms, explaining that her father-in-law's room was the sole bedroom left of the stairs, giving him the quiet he desired. He would be in his chair, she continued, having been helped into it by Fiddleman a few hours earlier. As they climbed the stairs, and well before they reached her father-in-law's room, she warned him in hushed tones about her father-in-law's fragile state. Holmes judged that whatever his infirmities, deafness was not one of them. His room faced front and when Penelope Stockton cautiously pressed the door open, her father-in-law could be seen seated in his chair at the window from which he had a commanding view of the carriage path and the arrival of strangers. He manipulated his invalid's chair to turn and face up close the stranger he had earlier observed from a distance. His greeting to Holmes had the sole merit of brevity. "Well, who is this then?"

The voice belonged to a figure far brawnier in appearance than his daughter-in-law's warnings had led Holmes to expect. Although some years past seventy, he looked fit enough to put in a full day in the fields—until one saw the high-backed chair with outsized wheels from which he could not rise without assistance.

Penelope Stockton performed the necessary introductions, then slipped from the room without a further word. Stockton wheeled himself away from the window to the room's center, at the same time motioning Holmes to the only chair in the room other than his own, a rocker that seemed almost too frivolous for Holmes's task. As Holmes bent to seat himself, he became aware of a shotgun beneath the bed, its stock nearest the headboard.

Stockton followed Holmes's gaze but made no effort to explain the gun's presence. He was, in fact, engaged in solving an unexpected problem. He stared hard at his guest for several seconds before brightening with sudden recognition.

"Of course, Sherlock Holmes. I've seen your name in the papers. You're that consulting detective that Scotland Yard sometimes uses."

Holmes winced noticeably before speaking. "I have had cause to work with the Yard, but in this instance, I am here on my own to explore the death of your son. And let me offer my sincere condolences for your terrible loss."

Like Lady Dickson had with Watson, Stockton waved away Holmes's expression of concern although his reason for doing so was far different. He doubted the sincerity of Holmes's concern and felt the detective's visit was pointless. "Why are you wasting time seeing me? Why aren't you out tracking down my son's killer?"

"I assure you that I and my colleagues are fully occupied with capturing the person who murdered your son. I've come to see you to learn who you believe could have so hated your son as to do this terrible thing. We've talked to Mrs. Stockton, the Fiddlemans and others. We feel you may have an awareness of the family history and a perspective no one else does, that a son might share things with his father that he wouldn't have revealed to anyone else."

Stockton's first response to Holmes's question was a look of utter incomprehension. That surprised Holmes. His second response was a largely unsuccessful attempt to stifle laughter behind the hand he held to his mouth. That left Holmes utterly confused.

Gaining a measure of control, Stockton recognized the need to explain his behavior. "It's obvious nobody has talked to you about me and my son. You should understand Roger would be more likely to share things with Joy and Jonathan than with me. We're not what you would call a close family under the best of circumstances and we didn't have the best of circumstances. Besides which, as you can see, I'm not likely to be getting involved in family activities. No, I'm afraid I can be of no help to you, Mr. Holmes."

"But this is your farm," Holmes insisted.

"Was …was my farm. It hasn't been my farm for a number of years." Stockton pursed his lips and paused a moment to be certain Holmes grasped his point. "As I've been saying, my son had long since stopped coming to me for advice, or much of anything else. None of that matters now, and whatever our relationship, I want his killer caught and brought to justice." There was another pause, longer this time, ending with Stockton making an unexpected request of Holmes.

"I wonder if you have a cigarette and a match." Holmes dug out his cigarette case and extended the open case to Stockton, then took one for himself. After lighting up and exhaling a long stream of smoke, Stockton came close to smiling and even struck a note of mock comradery.

"You're in trouble now. I'm not supposed to smoke. Dr. Montgomery's orders. Crack the window if you would. Anyone finds out we've been smoking we'll both be sent to bed without supper."

Stockton continued in his new-found spirit of cooperation. "There are some things about the family that might be worth your knowing. Background stuff. Like I sometimes wonder how different things might have been if Candace had lived." He looked to Holmes, saw the unsurprisingly puzzled look on the detective's face and proceeded to explain. "Candace was my wife, Roger's mother. She had a weak heart and died shortly after his birth. She would have been a steadying influence ... on both of us. She just had a way. She said it came from her Bible and doing things the Bible way. That's how she put it, 'doing things the Bible way.' That was her life—the Bible and family, which is why she so wanted children, lots of children. I really believe if she had her way, she'd have gone through the alphabet using names from the Bible." He exhaled another long line of smoke and watched it break apart and disappear before continuing.

"Except there was no alphabet of children; there was only Roger and him with a name that's got nothing to do with the Bible. At least she never had to deal with that."

Holmes nodded a sympathy that was not manufactured. Whatever else one believed about Stockton, it was clear he loved and still missed his wife, and likely missed the family she had envisioned.

"And your own infirmity. What happened to cause it, and would I be correct that it leaves you confined to this room?"

"You mean, could I go downstairs, crawl to the woods and murder my own son?" He raised a hand to quiet Holmes who was about to explain these were in the nature of routine questions. "I trust the rest of your investigation makes a good deal more sense. Nonetheless, I will answer your question. I had an accident. My horse fell on me—on my legs—and they haven't been right since. That was nearly eight years ago, and yes, I've hardly been out of this room since. But that doesn't mean I don't know what's going on around here. People don't think about you when you're an invalid stuck in your room all day. It's as if it's not just your legs that don't work, your mind has stopped working as well. People will say things and maybe do things they wouldn't say or do if they thought of you as a regular person." He gave Holmes a knowing look, followed by a wink and the detective wondered if he was expected to reciprocate in some fashion. Before Holmes could decide whether and how to respond, Stockton was leaning toward him, pretending to a confidentiality that was undone by their distance from each other

"You know I suppose that the Olyphant boy—the oldest one—is sweet on my granddaughter, Olivia. What you don't know is that that time when you and your friend, Dr. Watson, were here—the weekend my son and his wife were out of town, the Olyphant boy got upset about something Olivia said—most of the time she talks too soft for me to hear any of what she says—but the boy is something else again, especially when he gets hot. And I could hear him clear as a bell saying, 'if he won't give you permission to marry, he don't deserve you and maybe he don't deserve to live'. Those were his words. 'He don't deserve you and maybe he don't deserve to live.'" With that, Stockton clenched his jaw and stared meaningfully to Holmes. He only unclenched his jaw when he was moved to provide Holmes with another of the suspects already on his list.

"I'll tell you someone else who had it in for my son. Percy Dickson, my daughter-in-law's brother. He's over here every chance he gets, which is to say every time my son is away on business. He's busy poisoning my granddaughter's mind against Roger, urging her to defy her father and marry the Olyphant boy. It's true I can't say I heard him say exactly that. He knows to keep his voice down around me, but he talks to her all the time and I'm sure that's a big part of what he has to say.

"And that's not all. Far from it. I know he was urging Penelope to leave my son. I've heard snatches of those conversations. To tell you the truth I don't think Dickson can keep his voice down when he gets on that subject. He tells her Roger don't treat her right. Like it's his business what goes on between a man and his wife.

"And I'm not saying Roger is perfect ... was perfect. It's gonna take a while before I can talk about him like he's no longer here. Anyway, I'm not saying he didn't raise his voice when he got angry or fly off the handle at times, but that's something a lot of men do. And, as far as the other goes—I'm sure you were told the stories—I never heard of him actually hurting anyone. Of course, Dickson doesn't see it that way, so just maybe he takes matters into his own hands. If she won't leave like he wants, he fixes it so she doesn't have to." He looked to Holmes for some sign that the detective was finding reason in his analysis. He found none, shrugged, and put forth another name.

"Then you've got Thompkins who looks like a sick puppy whenever he's around Penelope—he's that obviously in love with her—and, of course, he can't do anything about it with Roger in the picture. He's got what you people call motive, but I don't think he's got the nerve. I'll say this for him though, he's the only one outside the family who comes up to see me whenever he's here. Except for Montgomery, of course. The doctor is up to see me regularly to see if I'm dead yet. Which is what I tell him every time, and every time he says, 'Very funny,' and goes about his business. Thompkins, on the other hand, who really has got business in terms of papers and stuff from Murchison, always gives me a big smile and lies about how good I look. You'd be surprised how even a lie can pick you up when you're stuck in a room all day. Which is what makes me feel bad about mentioning him, but the truth is the truth, and like I was saying anybody can tell he'd love to replace my son and now maybe he can. Meanwhile, as I'm also saying, Thompkins strikes me as someone who couldn't kill a fly much less a flesh and blood person."

Indeed, Holmes well remembered Thompkins's obvious feelings for Penelope Stockton and was prepared to follow that lead, seeing it as more credible than Stockton did.

"Do I take it from what you say that Mr. Thompkins was a frequent visitor?"

"I'd say he worked it out to visit as often as he could. Sometimes I wondered if he didn't collect some trivial papers to bring here so he could see Penelope. He wasn't fooling anybody although he probably thought he was. I'm sure Roger saw right through it. He probably thought it was funny. Like I said before, Thompkins wouldn't strike anyone as having the nerve to kill a man."

Holmes thought about the murderers he had known who were described by friends and family as not having the wherewithal to commit murder. He would leave that for another time.

"You haven't mentioned the Fiddlemans. Is that because you think they're above suspicion?"

Stockton shifted position in his chair, then settled back. "You do know the Fiddlemans have been with us for years. I can't imagine there being any reason for them to do away with my son. They have a suitable home, are well paid, have had work demands lightened as they've gotten older, and they've always been treated well by the family. What could they gain from my son's death that would match what they were getting from his being alive?

"I'll tell you what I'd be checking out. I mean besides Dickson, young Olyphant, and the older Olyphant—who you know had his own grievance with Roger. Have you thought about his killer being somebody without any grievance with my son who just happened to be in the wrong place at the wrong time—or maybe you'd say it was Roger who was in the wrong place at the wrong time. Anyway, I'm thinking about a hunter who was trespassing in the woods when my son was taking his walk. An inexperienced sort of hunter who thinks he sees an animal and shoots Roger, then, afraid that Roger can identify him and have him sent to prison for a good long time, he kills my son. That's a line I'd be thinking about."

"Would that include the mystery man living in your woods that I've heard about?"

Stockton seemed to recoil momentarily as if, Holmes thought, such an idea had never occurred to him. "I … I doubt that. From what I understand he's got some serious physical problems. Apart from which, you do know he's living rent-free in a cabin on our land. I can't see he'd have any reason to attack Roger."

"What, then, is one to make of the stories that your son planned to cut down the woods for the lumber he could sell, thereby putting the man out of his home?"

For a moment it appeared that Stockton might make a sudden, dramatic recovery and rise from his chair. Ultimately, he settled for his body stiffening as he remained in place.

"You've obviously been talking to Olyphant or Thompkins or one of my son's other enemies. Of course, he explored the possibility of selling some part of the woods for what the timber would bring. He'd have been a fool not to. Now, if you've no more questions, I do need to get my rest."

"Just one more. You keep a shotgun under your bed, which is to say you keep it handy should the need arise. Do you anticipate such a need?"

"My son's been killed. Maybe by a hunter like I said or maybe by Dickson or Olyphant—father or son—or by somebody else who's got some kind of problem with the family. Until you find my son's murderer, I'm taking no chances and I'll keep a shotgun under my bed. Now, I'm afraid I can't see you out, but I'm sure you can find your way."

Holmes smiled his appreciation for Stockton's time, then went downstairs to take his leave from Penelope before returning to 221B. He thanked Mrs. Stockton for the tea he refused, opting instead to have a second cigarette and wait outside for the carriage he had instructed to return and was nearly due. As it turned out, Holmes's respite from the Stocktons was brief. He had no sooner lit up then he was besieged by Joy and Jonathan and told by them of the limited time available for him to fulfill a promise made some weeks earlier, a promise he had conveniently forgotten in the wake of all that had occurred since. By the time his carriage arrived, Holmes had scheduled a date for the fulfillment of the promise, having found no honorable way to avoid its fulfillment. He was left to hope that Watson and Mrs. Hudson, who were pledged to the same action, would feel a like sense of obligation.

Watson announced himself to Dr. Aloysius Montgomery's receptionist who, on hearing the word "Doctor," looked up from the mail she was sorting and even hazarded a small smile. The two patients waiting, a balding richly moustachioed man of about fifty seated on a bench, and a slender, hatchet-faced woman in her early forties seated in a cushioned wooden chair, heard the magic word as well. It drew a disgruntled look from the bench and a soft groan from the wooden chair as both of those waiting knew it would place the owner of that title ahead of them in spite of their earlier arrival.

Watson handed the woman his card and she put aside the mail she was sorting to receive it and give it the expected cursory examination. The mail on the small desk lay near enough for him to see the top envelope was marked "Personal" and bore the embossed return address of George Thomas Beatson, MD.

It was a name well known to Watson. Both men had gotten their medical degrees in 1878 and Watson had followed the medical career of his fellow Scotsman with interest and occasional bouts of envy. While Beatson had made a name for himself in the typically thankless area of cancer treatment, Watson was known chiefly as Holmes's Boswell—when he was known at all. Still, there would be only a moment devoted to consideration of what might have been, what was was altogether too rewarding for Watson to long dwell on others' accomplishments. Rather, Beatson's private correspondence to Montgomery set him to thinking along a different track regarding the doctor's haggard appearance.

Before he faced the need to choose a chair that would place him a comfortable distance from the two waiting patients, the door to Montgomery's office and examining room opened, revealing a worried looking young woman with a child of about three or four quietly sobbing into his sleeve. Following them as far as the doorway Montgomery wore a reassuring smile and uttered empty phrases he hoped might be comforting. Watson was again struck by the harried state of the man even as he now had an alternative understanding of its origins. As his two patients left and his remaining two looked on eagerly, the receptionist explained to Dr. Montgomery that a visitor, *Dr.* Watson, had some questions for him.

Carefully avoiding eye contact with the two seated patients, Montgomery redirected his smile to Watson, broadening it as he recognized his colleague from the Stockton woods. Still smiling, he swept Watson into his office. The waiting patients could do little other than hone their skills at feigning indifference to events over which they had no control.

Montgomery took a seat in the chair behind his small desk and motioned for Watson to take the chair opposite. The only other furniture was an examining table, a tall bookcase with shelves of books visible behind its glass doors, two filing cabinets and a credenza holding a tea service with four cups. A typical, if sparsely furnished doctor's office, Watson thought. "How may I help you, Doctor? As you may know, I've given a report to the authorities."

"I haven't had opportunity to see that yet, but I wanted to ask you some questions about the family if I might. As you know, one hears stories, but I wanted to get the perspective of a more dispassionate source. In a word, we thought the family doctor would provide the most reliable information. I assure you the information is only wanted as part of our investigation and will be treated with the utmost confidentiality."

Montgomery found a pencil on the almost bare desktop and began twirling it between the thumbs and index fingers of his two hands. Finally, its role as an aid to thought complete, he set the pencil back on the desk.

"I appreciate that, Doctor, but we both know the great risk of things slipping out and becoming public. So, while I view it as my obligation to tell you anything that can be helpful to your investigation, I ask you to be mindful of the tendency for information to leak out and to be vigilant in your efforts to prevent that from happening. If that is understood and agreeable to you, we can proceed."

"Of course, that is perfectly reasonable, Watson gave a deep nod to underline his willingness to abide by Montgomery's terms before somewhat clouding the issue, "recognizing that, should the case come to trial, you will almost certainly be asked to provide testimony." Montgomery gave a deep nod of understanding and waited Watson's questioning.

"May I first ask you something about yourself? Specifically, about your health. I couldn't help but notice your color is not good. I know how easy it is to ignore your own health when you have patients to care for. Have you had someone examine you?"

Montgomery smiled his appreciation for Watson's concern. "It has been stressful of late, but I'm doing fine. Thank you for asking."

Watson was aware that he had not gotten an answer to his question but felt it fruitless to pursue it further. He'd seen old warhorses like Montgomery many times before. They would ignore limitations imposed by age or illness until they were either carried out or forced to retire—hopefully before making a dangerous miscalculation in their practice. In any event, there was no point in pressing the man for information he was unwilling to share. Watson put on a tight smile and resumed speaking.

"I know you have patients waiting so I'll try not to take up too much of your time. First, am I correct that you have known the Stockton family for a very long time?"

"That would be accurate. I've known most all the farm families in this area for a very long time."

"When did you organize your practice, Doctor?"

"I took my first patient more than forty-seven years ago. A young man showing symptoms of catarrh. I prescribed Mackenzie's Catarrh Cure and that, combined with rest, led to a speedy recovery. I doubt that any of us ever forget our first patient." Montgomery waited for Watson to respond to his cue. Watson, though tempted, stayed with the task at hand.

"Then, you would have known Roger Stockton all his life."

"Yes, that's true. I've been his doctor since he was an infant. In fact, I've now been doctor to three generations of Stocktons. Apart from the death of his wife shortly after childbirth, the most difficult in many ways has been attending to Avery Stockton, Roger's father. Such an active, vigorous man, now virtually bedridden."

This time Watson yielded briefly to temptation. "It is tragic. It's always tragic to see men struck down in the prime of their lives. I was an army surgeon and saw far too much of it." Watson's comment drew a deeply respectful nod from Montgomery acknowledging him as a brother in the more difficult aspects of their chosen profession.

"I wonder," Watson continued, "what you have observed of Roger Stockton's relations with others? He's been described as a man who easily collected enemies. Was that your observation as well? I only ask because of its obvious importance in capturing his killer."

"Of course, I understand. I'm afraid it's quite true. He was in too many ways an exaggeration of his father. Except Avery had an innate sense of how hard you could push people and knew when to stop. It often seems Roger only learned the part about pushing." Montgomery retrieved the pencil from his desk and sighed audibly before resuming. "After the accident, with Avery not there to smooth some of his roughest edges, it was just a question of how many people Roger would offend and how often he'd offend them. I imagine you've already heard about his conflict with Olyphant." He hesitated until his imaginings were confirmed by a nod from Watson. "And perhaps also of the difficulty created for Olivia and the Olyphant boy." A second confirmatory nod.

As the pencil between his fingers again began to twirl, Montgomery's thoughts began to stray to another consideration. "Odd really. The two of them trying so hard to maintain the past. Disagreeing on everything else and not recognizing the one insoluble problem they share. They can't see—or won't see—that the days of large farms as close as theirs to the city are numbered. The city keeps moving west and will swallow them up soon enough. The money will simply be too tempting. First, their neighbors and then the two of them will sell." He shook his head after hearing himself. "I guess I keep talking as if Roger was still alive. I have difficulty getting past that.

"Anyway, as to the conflict between Roger and Olyphant, I'm sure there's not much I can tell you that you haven't heard already." He returned the pencil to the desk once more, this time with the intention of making its retirement the first stage in ending the interview. Watson, however, still had an issue to pursue.

"We have heard that Stockton sometimes acted intemperately with his wife—actually, with both his wives. I wonder what you can tell me about that."

"Here, Doctor, I'm afraid we get into a sticky area. As you know, I can't inform you about injuries, real or imagined, for any of my patients, especially as they would involve a husband's actions."

"I quite understand. Let me ask you this, Doctor, did you ever see Priscilla and Penelope Stockton outside their regularly scheduled appointments?"

"I may have done."

"Did you have cause to speak to Mr. Stockton after seeing his wives?"

"Again, I may have done. Is there anything else? I really should get back to my patients."

"Just one more question? In all of this, I've heard very little of Avery Stockton's wife. Can you tell me anything about her?"

Montgomery leaned back in his chair as the ghost of a smile unexpectedly took possession of him. "She didn't belong here. She was better than any of us, better than all of us." The smile lingered as his speech sounded nearly dreamlike. "She was deeply religious, took comfort from her Bible and died far too young. She had a weak heart and it simply gave out with Roger's birth. It was a tragedy on several counts. I do believe she would have had a gentling effect on her son, and a positive impact on all who knew her. I'm certain that Avery and his son would have gotten along much better had she lived." Montgomery became silent and Watson suddenly felt himself an intruder without understanding the nature of his trespass. What he did understand was that the conversation was moving ever farther from Stockton's death, making it time for him to leave. "Thank you, Dr. Montgomery. This has been very helpful." Watson rose from his chair, pulling Montgomery to a standing position with him. Opening the door, the two patients watched his departure with relief and eagerly turned to Montgomery's receptionist as the doctor returned to his office.

Holmes, Watson, and Lady Dickson having all departed, Mrs. Hudson was preparing to make her own departure for the registry office nearest the Stockton farm when she had a second unexpected interruption to her day, this one involving a delegation of three men whose dress identified them as members of the Wild West Show. On any other day she might wonder about the attraction of Baker Street to men she recognized as American cowboys from the many posters around town. On this day she felt certain she knew. Their stern expressions, combined with a furtive study of their surroundings, made clear to Mrs. Hudson they had come about the planned nuptials of Sudden Thunder and Jane Morrison, and they had not come to ask her assistance in getting invitations. Their spokesman was the shortest and stockiest of them, and the only one, as best she could tell, who had a gold front tooth.

"May we come in, ma'am, if you're Mrs. Hudson we'd like to chat with you." All three looked to her expectantly.

"Certainly, won't you come into my parlor. Can I offer you tea and there's some freshly baked scones ...."

The group's spokesman cut off Mrs. Hudson before she could describe their raisin filling. "No, thank you, ma'am, we don't expect to take up that much of your time." With that, the three men arranged themselves on the room's settee and one of the two armed easy chairs while Mrs. Hudson made use of the other.

Without pausing for introductions, the group's designated spokesman came to the point of their visit. "It's our understanding, ma'am, that you've met with Miss Morrison and her Indian friend and that the three of you talked about a wedding." Again, all three looked to her expectantly.

"There's no secret I 'ad a talk with Miss Morrison and Mr. Sudden Thunder. What we talked about is our business."

"I don't think you understand, ma'am, there's laws against Indians and white people marrying where we come from, and there's a many of us would be quite put out over such a marriage being talked about. We figure you couldn't know any of that, what with your being English and all. So, we're willing to let it go this one time being as you was ignorant of the situation." He took a deep breath before getting into the explanation he thought certain to make everything come clear. "See, we're against mongrelizing the races. By that I mean mixing the races, which can only serve to weaken the white race." He paused to allow for a response from Mrs. Hudson and, after a few seconds, he got one.

"Of course, I understand. I understand you believe you have a right to stand in the way of two people's 'appiness because of the prejudice you feel toward one of them. And you want me to stand against, or, at least, apart from the two of them, neither of which I'll do. I won't stand in the way of any two people who love each other and are willin' to face any challenge to their bein' together, even the challenge of livin' in a place that's got people like the three of you in it. I can only 'ope that sometime in the future there'll be a loving couple in your country that will prove once and for all that people 'ave a right to choose who they want for their partners." With that Mrs. Hudson stood, stretching herself to her full, if unimpressive height. "But now I'll thank you to leave this 'ouse before I call Constable Chase to show you out."

The men rose from their seats slowly in a last act of ineffectual defiance. As they crossed to the door, the leader turned back to Mrs. Hudson and growled a last warning. "You're making a mistake—a big mistake." It was meant to sound as a threat, and it did.

An emphatic shrug, several spirited walks around her flat and two cups of tea later, Mrs. Hudson was prepared to undertake the task she had set for herself the evening before. She had first determined which registry office was nearest the Stockton farm, and then had Mr. Holmes contact Inspector Lestrade to make an appointment for her. In accord with her instructions to Holmes, the people at the registry office were told that Mrs. Hudson was acting as an agent for Sherlock Holmes (Lestrade was to add "the renowned detective" if he thought it advisable), who was helping Scotland Yard with their investigation, and that he would appreciate the registry office staff giving her their full cooperation. Lestrade had wondered about the task being assigned to the landlady but had been assured by Holmes that the task was a simple clerical one, that he and Watson were involved with other parts of the investigation, and that Mrs. Hudson had long expressed an interest in learning what she could of detective work "to improve herself." The first two rationales had been suggested by Mrs. Hudson, the third was Holmes's own invention and had not been shared with his ambitious landlady.

Stepping from 221B, she first searched the street for any sign of the three men from the Wild West Show. Seeing none, she walked to the hansom parked nearest to the lodgings. When she told him her destination, a great smile wreathed his face as he asked, "Is it that we're gettin' married then?"

Mrs. Hudson replied, "Is it that you're askin' then?"

The smile grew into a broad grin and a hearty laugh, but the coachman made no further response and stayed silent for the rest of the journey. His silence, duly noted, earned him a half crown for the ride.

Her first thought on seeing the registry office was that it would be a dreadfully grim place for a wedding. There were four buildings of dun colored stone, each of them seemingly inexpertly joined to another such that the four jutted in and out from a theoretical center. One was three stories high, two were two stories and the fourth, much narrower than the other three and sandwiched between two of them, rose well above all the rest. Each building had a set of tall narrow windows on each level except for the tallest building which had only a single window high above the entry door to the registry office. All in all, the structure put Mrs. Hudson in mind of a castle whose builder either had a problem with alcohol or possessed a grim sense of humor.

The building's mundane exterior left her wholly unprepared for the opulence of its interior. White columns, eight feet high were set at ten-foot intervals lining the path to the entrance hall while high above a crystal chandelier dangled from a long chain to light the way across the oak wood flooring. As she traveled that path, she was aware of voices coming from a room to her right that became distinct finally when she came to an open door. She could see rows of chairs and the voices made it clear that a negotiation was in progress to work out the date and details for a future wedding. A second, smaller room off to the left appeared designed to serve the same purpose for a more modest ceremony. Mrs. Hudson was so caught up in a study of her surroundings—and the happy memories they stirred—that she only became aware that she was not alone in the hall when a voice sounded behind her.

"Is there something I can do for you, ma'am?"

She turned to face a neatly dressed man of fifty or a few years more whose severe posture and small limp suggested an earlier military career cut short by injury, the suggestion confirmed by the red, blue and orange ribbon he wore in his lapel marking him a veteran of the First Boer War. His tone and manner made clear to Mrs. Hudson both his administrative responsibilities and his belief that, whatever her issues, the registry office was not the place to address them—at least he hoped it wasn't.

"My name is Mrs. 'Udson. I believe you were contacted by Inspector Lestrade that I would be visitin'."

Her incredulous host looked to Mrs. Hudson as if his worst fears were about to be realized. "Did you say *H*udson?"

"That's right. 'Udson."

"I see." Allowing a brief "excuse me" to escape his lips, he went to close the door to the room in which the wedding planning was underway. He returned with something bordering on a smile as he ushered her toward the stairs beyond the smaller of the wedding venues. "My name is Carruthers. I'm the superintendent registrar at this registry office. Do I understand correctly that you work for Mr.

Sherlock Holmes and are here today on his behalf?" He made no effort to hide his continuing disbelief.

Mrs. Hudson pursed her lips before confirming that his worst fears had indeed been realized. "I do work with Mr. 'Olmes, yes. Would it be possible, Mr. Carruthers, for me to get started on the work I need to get done?"

"Yes indeed, if you'll follow me. I have your materials all neatly laid out on a desk upstairs. I've organized it so you'll have the office to yourself for as long as necessary." He drew in a breath unrelated to his exertion climbing the flight of stairs. "Have you some idea as to how long that might be, Mrs. Hudson? We do have people coming."

"I think not long, but I won't really know until I see the materials you've gotten ready for me. Who might I contact if I 'ave a question?"

Carruthers pursed his lips. He hadn't considered the possibility of questions. "I suppose you can check with Mrs. Leaphart. She's two offices down; you'll hear her typing." They stood outside the office assigned to Mrs. Hudson. "Now, you must excuse me. I have urgent business downstairs." There was again the plastic smile and then he was gone. Mrs. Hudson sat down at the desk and began her attack on the papers that had been gathered for her. She removed a small pad from her purse and set the desk's pen and ink conveniently nearer to her. An hour and a half later she had finished her work. For the first and only time she then stopped in to see Mrs. Leaphart. Introducing herself to the typist, she found that Carruthers's plastic smile might well be a condition of employment. She announced that she had completed her work, asked her to thank Mr. Carruthers for his assistance, then proceeded down the stairs past the pillars and back onto the London street.

Dinner that night was a comparatively simple affair of lentil soup, roast pork loin with potatoes and applesauce, followed by Stilton cheese. It was properly filling but little more than that. It merited only the measured consumption of a clearly pedestrian wine and an easily maintained sobriety throughout the meal. Praise for the cook was equally measured which Mrs. Hudson found a fair exchange for her colleagues' clear-headedness.

With little to hold them at the table and with a long day behind them, Holmes and Watson were anxious to have a leisurely pipe and prolonged period of relaxation before taking to bed. To hurry things along Holmes and Watson began their summaries of the day's activities as soon as they had seated themselves at the table. They spent the first several minutes in competition with each other to provide outlandish descriptions of Lady Dickson's outlandish behavior. Watson drew on his clinical expertise, placing a particular emphasis on hysteria as his guiding theme. Lacking Watson's medical background, Holmes made use of more traditional descriptors such as "flighty, ill-mannered" and "bizarre," repeating bizarre several times in the course of his reporting. Both men were surprised to hear Mrs. Hudson express her belief that the woman could prove extremely useful at some later time. After opinions about Lady Dickson had been fully vented, and between spoonfuls of lentil soup "lest it get cold," Holmes began to share findings from his visit with Avery Stockton.

"It should first be understood that the man is unable to walk on his own and is confined to an upstairs room. If it was even conceivable that a father would kill his own son, Stockton is clearly incapable of doing so. He made a strong case for his belief that young Olyphant is particularly suspect in light of his wish to marry Olivia and Roger Stockton's commitment to keep that from ever happening. What appears particularly incriminating was the conversation he reported overhearing between Benjamin Olyphant and Olivia—or, at any rate that part of the conversation he could hear clearly. I wrote down what Stockton said because of its obvious significance." Holmes paused to pull from his pocket a somewhat battered piece of paper. "According to Stockton, Benjamin Olyphant said to Olivia the man 'didn't deserve to live if he tried to block our marriage.'" Holmes refolded the paper, replacing it in his pocket. "Stockton only mentioned Olyphant senior in passing, but it seems unlikely the son could pull off anything like this without the assistance of the father and we know Daniel Olyphant had his own grievances with Roger Stockton." Holmes paused to make a quick check of his audience and found Watson nodding his respects and Mrs. Hudson's face screwed in concentration. He took a deep breath and continued.

"He spoke of Percy Dickson as a kind of busybody who was urging Penelope Stockton to leave Roger, and of Thompkins as being what he called "a love-sick puppy" with strong feelings for Mrs. Stockton but lacking the nerve to do anything about it. I must say, after our session with Thompkins, I'm inclined to agree.

"He spoke very highly of his own wife, Candace, who died not long after giving birth to Roger. He saw her death as a terrible loss to the family, which I judge from what you were telling me earlier, Watson, is what you heard from Dr. Montgomery as well." There followed a deep nod from Watson.

"He described her as a deeply religious woman. In fact, according to Stockton his wife's desire was to go as far as she could through the alphabet giving Biblical names to a houseful of children. In that regard, it's not clear how their son came by the name Roger although I suppose with her death, she would have had no role in the naming.

"There's one more thing to report from my meeting with Stockton. And this is so far-fetched I only report it in the interest of giving a complete account of my interview. He seemed much taken with the notion that the killer might be a hunter whose errant shot wounded Stockton making it necessary for him to finish the job to avoid having Stockton name his assailant. When I asked if his statement meant that he thought the stranger living in the woods should be regarded as a suspect, he was instantly dismissive of the idea. It wasn't clear why. It is clear that he sees some unspecified danger to himself. He now keeps a shotgun under his bed for protection.

"In that regard, his bedroom is right off the stairs on the left; every other bedroom is on the right. His concern could be seen as justified I suppose. If someone could get in the house, he could very possibly get to Stockton's bedroom without being heard.

"Nonetheless, considering everything, I believe quite a good case can be made for seeing Benjamin Olyphant as our murderer. He was in the woods with a shotgun the morning of the murder, his gun was fired twice by his own admission, and we have only his word that he missed a rabbit at which he was aiming. You'll remember that his father told Watson and me that his son was quite a good shot. Combine that with the threat that Stockton overheard." Holmes sniffed approval of his own reasoning and sat back in his chair to await his colleagues' applause.

Applause was not, however, immediately forthcoming.

"All very neat, Mr. 'Olmes, but 'ow do you imagine the bride would feel about a groom who's shot 'er father?"

Holmes sank a little in his chair before recovering sufficiently to register a response. "I don't think we can discount the impetuosity of youth, Mrs. Hudson. Young people will often act on the spur of the moment. They lack the self-control that comes with age and maturity. Moreover, in the heat of the moment who knows what a young man in love might do to any man he sees as denying him his sweetheart." Holmes sat a little straighter in his chair; Mrs. Hudson's position was unchanged.

Watson thought this a good time to provide a summary of his meeting with Dr. Montgomery. Accordingly, he smoothed the relevant page of his accounts book and after clearing his throat, he began. "As you know, I met with Dr. Montgomery at the same time Holmes was meeting with Stockton. Montgomery was circumspect as, I have to say, was appropriate to his position as the family doctor. Nonetheless, what he was able to tell me may prove useful if only because he's known Roger Stockton all the younger Stockton's life. In fact, his practice appears to date to a little before the time of Roger's birth.

"As Holmes reported, Montgomery, like the senior Stockton, spoke of Candace Stockton's death as a great tragedy. Indeed, I'd say he very nearly deifies the woman. He believes the father and son would not only have gotten along better but would have been better people if she had lived. And, like Stockton senior, Montgomery, too, emphasized the importance of religion in Mrs. Stockton's life."

Watson paused to scan his notes, finding what he was searching for, he resumed speaking. "I tried to draw Montgomery out about the allegations of misbehavior by Roger Stockton toward his wives, but Montgomery refused to commit himself. We can only say he did not deny the allegations."

Watson closed his accounts book, but his worried look indicated he still had more to say. As the book disappeared into his waistcoat pocket, he spoke to his concern. "There is something else I need to share. As a physician I couldn't help but be aware of how unwell Montgomery appears. He had on his desk—really, on his receptionist's desk—a letter marked private from Dr. George Thomas Beatson. Beatson is perhaps the physician most knowledgeable about cancer, a particularly pernicious disease. That diagnosis would be consistent with the characteristics we've observed. Of course, the fact that he's pushing himself well beyond what's wise at his age doesn't help. He may be having difficulty finding a successor willing to take on a largely rural practice—it would be very demanding—but between his age and disease, the poor man is almost certainly working himself into an earlier than necessary grave." Watson looked grimly to his colleagues, who both did their best to show with sympathetic expressions their appreciation for Watson's unsurprising sensitivity to a colleague's difficulties.

After a suitable pause, Mrs. Hudson pulled together her notes from her trip to the registry office and prepared to give a report of her day's activities. She considered and quickly rejected sharing her morning visit from the three members of Colonel Cody's Wild West Show. Really, she reasoned, it had nothing to do with Roger Stockton's murder and it would, moreover, at the very least lead to a lengthy digression, and could even result in a call to action. Besides, time was slipping away, and she had important news to report—news that could lead to a breakthrough in the case.

"I discovered some surprising things at the registry office." As she anticipated, her brief statement was sufficient to cause Watson to retrieve his accounts book, smooth a blank page and hold a pencil in readiness while Holmes leaned back in his chair, a raised eyebrow his only concession to the curiosity he shared with Watson.

"There's first of all Mr. Stockton's Christian name. It's not Roger. It's Balthasar, a Bible name like Mrs. Stockton would 'ave wanted, and we now know 'er wish was obeyed. We can also understand why 'is middle name, Roger, was used by people early on and, of course, was used by 'im when 'e came of age. And if you're wonderin' where Balthasar comes from, 'e was one of the three Magi who visited the baby Jesus.

"Now, just think of where that takes us. Mr. Stockton senior told Mr. 'Olmes that 'is wife would 'ave gone through the alphabet givin' all 'er children Bible names. Except the birth records signed by Dr. Montgomery as their doctor, start with Balthasar, and there's no record of a child with a name startin' with A. But we do know of someone who says 'e's forty-six, or so 'e told me—the same age as Balthasar, or Roger, Stockton—whose name starts with A and who was conveniently taken in by a cousin of Mr. Fiddleman accordin' to what Joy and Jonathan say they over'eard.

"It's all pointin' to Aaron, the man in the woods, bein' Roger's undeclared older twin brother. We can judge that Aaron was born with somethin' terribly wrong with 'im which explains 'is troubles today. The senior Mr. Stockton didn't see a need to break 'is word to 'is wife in givin' the first born a Bible name startin' with A because 'e was already arrangin' for the boy to be growin' up somewheres in a family well away from 'ere, and there'd be no rhyme or reason for anybody to put the two families together. Mr. Stockton made a promise about the name, but 'e didn't say anythin' about who was goin' to inherit the farm, and what with all the work 'e and 'is father before 'im 'ad put in to make it a success, 'e wasn't about to turn it over to someone who 'e could see was goin' to be some kind of cripple.

"Of course, 'e felt a responsibility to provide for his son and we'd probably find that 'e was sending money regularly through Mr. Murchison, the banker, to the family that was carin' for Aaron. When the family decided they had to go to America and couldn't take Aaron with them, it was worked out for Aaron to use the abandoned cabin in the woods with Roger Stockton givin' up on 'is plan to sell off 'is part of the woods for the timber—at least for the moment—and the Fiddlemans takin' first responsibility for makin' sure Aaron was bein' taken care of." Mrs. Hudson paused to allow herself and her audience to catch their breath. After she and they had, Watson spoke.

"If what you say is true, it means the Fiddlemans were—are—complicit in this deception."

"And I'm bettin' that not only was money goin' to Mr. Fiddleman's cousin for the care of Aaron, but money was also goin' to the Fiddlemans to keep their mouths shut almost certainly in the form of wages lots 'igher than their positions would suggest. That's why they were ready to leave without waitin' for the readin' of the will. They figured they'd already gotten all they were goin' to get. Think about what Mr. Olyphant said which, by the way, goes along with what Lady Dickson told me. 'E believed that the Stocktons had the most successful farm in the area, meaning the Stocktons were the richest—or should 'ave been. But remember the insides of their 'ouse. The furniture was all chipped or worse and there was nothin' as fancy as you'd expect from the most successful farm in the area. Maybe they didn't want to spend a lot on the inside but just 'ave it so the outside would impress people, or maybe they didn't 'ave a whole lot of money for the inside because of what they were payin' out both to care for Aaron and to make sure the things they wanted to keep secret stayed secret."

"Even if the Fiddlemans were being paid exorbitant wages, the money could still be seen as legitimate income, and as to whatever part they played in a cover up about the births, the Fiddlemans could claim to be following their master's direction. But what of Dr. Montgomery?" Watson asked. "He could have been ruined if it was learned that he was falsifying records. Why would he take that chance?"

"It could be any of a bunch of reasons. Bein' a new doctor just settin' up 'is first practice, 'e might 'ave thought 'e was 'elpin' a family in need with no 'arm to anyone, or, at the other extreme 'e might 'ave been paid by the family to stay silent, or anythin' in between."

"Or it could be that a young doctor makes a dreadful mistake in the course of one of his first deliveries and it's determined to be in everyone's interest to cover it up," suggested a somber Dr. Watson.

Mrs. Hudson nodded acknowledgment of Watson's addition, then softened his assessment. "Or there's a medical accident where nobody wants to make things worse by puttin' the blame on someone doin' the best 'e could under what could 'ave been difficult conditions. Likely, we'll never know the truth of what 'appened all those years ago."

"Regardless, Mrs. Hudson, what we're saying is that we have an elaborate conspiracy." Watson's tone sounded the incredulity his words expressed. "There' the two Stocktons—but not the women—the Fiddlemans, Fiddleman's cousin, and Dr. Montgomery."

"And very possibly Murchison at the bank," Holmes added, receiving a groan of support from Watson and a nod from Mrs. Hudson. Thus confirmed, Holmes continued.

"It's all interesting speculation—most ingenious speculation." Holmes bowed his head to Mrs. Hudson, thereby astounding both her and Watson. "But does it get us any closer to finding our killer? I don't see how—not unless you're proposing that Aaron reasoned things out as you have and killed Roger Stockton to get his rightful inheritance."

"I'm not proposin' anything about our murderer just yet, Mr. 'Olmes. I'm only sayin' Roger Stockton's death may be tied up in this conspiracy of silence to deny Aaron his birthright. As you say, Mr. 'Olmes, it can only be seen as speculation right now—although ingenious speculation I'm told—and we need to get beyond that. To do that, we're goin' to need the assistance of Mr. Thompkins since we'll 'ave to break into the bank to get at the Stocktons' bank records. We can talk about all that tomorrow. For now, we'll need our rest, or, at any rate, I need mine. I believe we 'ave Inspector Lestrade comin' for a visit after breakfast tomorrow. I suggest we discuss our plans directly after 'e's gone. For now, while you gentlemen have a pipe, I'll tend to the dishes and then get to bed. I'll be needin' to be up especially early to get fresh scones made for the inspector."

"There is one more thing Mrs. Hudson, Watson," Holmes had kept his seat and now waited until his colleagues resumed theirs. "The Stockton children—that is, Joy and Jonathan, sort of cornered me at the end of my visit to the Stockton farm today. They pointed out that the Wild West Show will be leaving for the continent shortly and that we had promised to take them to see a performance. I thought it important we be seen as keeping our word." Holmes fondled the pipe he hoped to be enjoying soon. "In a word, I got Mrs. Stockton's approval for us to take the children to tomorrow afternoon's show. Of course, you don't have to go, Mrs. Hudson, if you believe it would be too taxing."

Mrs. Hudson resisted her initial response to Holmes's muddled invitation and went with her second, and far more genial response.

"I would be delighted to see Colonel Cody's Wild West Show. And there's no good reason we shouldn't take a 'alf day out for some relaxation. I'm glad the children suggested it. For now, I'll be wantin' to get my work done and take my rest. I suggest we all do the same."

In spite of her pronouncement, Mrs. Hudson was sorely tempted to leave the dishes soaking in the tub at the kitchen sink and was only dissuaded by the knowledge that they would still be there when she awoke the next morning. By the time she had washed out the tub with soap and washing soda, she would have been ready for bed even if she didn't have to get up by half five to get breakfast and prepare the raisin scones that were the inspector's favorite.

Chapter 6. The Wild West

Holmes and Watson were well into breakfast when there came two staccato doorbell rings, followed by a single knock, indicating Detective Inspector Lestrade had arrived. A smiling Mrs. Hudson went to admit him.

"Good morning, Mrs. Hudson. May I assume Mr. Holmes and Dr. Watson are at home?"

"They are, indeed, Inspector. They're just finishin' breakfast. I could set another plate for you. I'm sure there's enough for you to share."

"Just tell me, Mrs. Hudson, have they eaten all the scones?"

"I've 'ad some 'idden away until you got 'ere. There 'ave been questions so I'm that glad to see you."

Lestrade chuckled and started in the direction of the stairs. A short time later Lestrade was in an armed easy chair, and Mrs. Hudson was setting out a platter of scones, a pot of strawberry jam, three plates and a teacup and saucer for the inspector. As she turned to leave, the inspector was speaking. "Before I take action, Mr. Holmes, I wanted you to hear from me the Yard's plans. I believe you are owed that much." Lestrade paused, knowing that what he had to say would not be welcomed by his sometime colleague.

"I think you should know, Mr. Holmes that, based on the available evidence, it is my intention to go to the Olyphant farm later this morning to arrest Benjamin Olyphant and charge him with the murder of Roger Stockton."

With eyebrows at full staff, Holmes and Watson for the moment held off ladling the proper amount of jam on their scones while Mrs. Hudson let out a small startled cry from where she stood at the sitting room door.

The inspector counted himself as especially sensitive to the feelings of the woman he regarded as Holmes's devoted landlady and housekeeper.

He affected a gentle smile and spoke of the inevitable disappointments one experienced in the course of a lifetime of criminal investigation. "I'm sorry, Mrs. Hudson, I didn't see you

114

there. I know you knew the boy. I'm afraid this is the nature of the work Mr. Holmes and I do. At the end of an investigation you can find yourself accusing people you previously thought well of, maybe even liked, of the most awful crimes. I suspect Mr. Holmes has kept from you some of those more distressing aspects of his work." Lestrade looked to Holmes for the supportive word or nod that would affirm his comment.

Unfortunately, at the precise moment of the inspector's request, Holmes found himself overtaken by a sudden fit of coughing. Watson, who seemed to the inspector strangely amused by his colleague's difficulties, went for water. Mrs. Hudson urged the inspector to clap Mr. Holmes on the back repeatedly and with vigor, something she understood to be helpful in such situations. Holmes glared at Mrs. Hudson while the inspector administered the prescribed treatment in accord with his own rather generous understanding of vigor. The water and the multiple slaps to his back finally seemed to do the trick. Mrs. Hudson smiled her satisfaction with the results of the action she had suggested and left for downstairs.

Holmes, now largely recovered, raised the questions that had been directed to him when he came to the same conclusion as Lestrade.

"I wonder, Lestrade, I appreciate the boy's strong feelings for Miss Stockton, but could the young lady be expected to have positive feelings for the boy who murdered her father? Wouldn't that discourage Benjamin from taking such action?"

Lestrade answered Holmes's objection with the argument Holmes had used earlier to refute it, that argument sounding to him suddenly rational all over again. "I think you're forgetting the hot passion of youth, Mr. Holmes. We believe the Olyphant boy acted impulsively as young people will do rather than rationally as he might have done if he were older."

His core logic framed, Lestrade began to methodically tick off items in the Yard's case against Benjamin Olyphant, each of them remarkably similar to those considered around Mrs. Hudson's table a short time earlier.

"We know the boy was in the woods at the time of Stockton's death; he admits to firing his gun twice while claiming to have missed his rabbit; he was blocked by Stockton from marrying the girl he loved; and, most important, he was overheard by Stockton's father threatening the life of Roger Stockton. It all fits perfectly, Mr. Holmes. Means, motive, opportunity. They're all there. I'm betting that, a short time after we start the questioning, he'll trip himself up and we'll get a confession. In any event, I mean to have him in a cell at the Bow Street Station by this afternoon."

Setting her tray down in her kitchen, Mrs. Hudson was also thinking of the Scotland Yard questioning of Benjamin Olyphant but viewing it quite differently than the inspector. Tobias had referred to such questioning as "grilling" and that, combined with the days, and especially the nights, the boy would spend in a cell at the Bow Street Station, could break the resolve of a youngster without any experience of such treatment. In due time he might well confess to anything of which they accused him. She now regretted the time she would spend at the Wild West Show but had no intention of reneging on Mr. Holmes's promise. She was so absorbed in her thinking about all there was still to do she did not hear Inspector Lestrade's calling out to her as he exited 221B.

"Thank you, Mrs. Hudson. The scones were again delicious." He waited a moment for her usual cheery response. When he got none, he put it down to her being busy cleaning up after his visit. He was more right than he knew.

The remainder of the morning went more quickly than she expected. She had errands to run to the greengrocer and post office as well as needing to place an order at the butcher's while Dr. Watson was absorbed in updating his journal, making additions and corrections to a case he would name *The Adventure of the Body in the Woods*. Holmes, meanwhile, could finally return to his microscope and slides, and the study he was making of the chemical composition of tears. Thus far, he had been almost entirely dependent on his own ability to produce specimens for analysis. He had finally coaxed a few drops from Watson notwithstanding the doctor's insistence on his inability to cry at will, and he remained hopeful about Mrs. Hudson. She had expressed a rather vehement "no" the last time he approached her, but it seemed to him slightly less vehement than the time before.

116

At five minutes to one, Mrs. Hudson carefully fitted her hat with the single ostrich feather over her grey coils, and promptly at one o'clock the Baker Street trio haled a carriage and directed the driver to take them to the Stockton farm, where they added to the carriage first a hyperexcited Jonathan, then a determinedly nonchalant Joy. After being told by each passenger and then by the coachman to "please sit," the movement of the horses finally accomplished what none of the humans could and Jonathan sat.

As all knew from Joy's and Jonathan's horse stealing days, the Earl's Court exhibition grounds were a short distance from the farm, and they arrived well before the show was to start. On taking note of all there was to see, they decided it was well they had. In an encampment that adjoined the exhibition grounds, a collection of teepees identified the area as an Indian village. Smiling faces and words of welcome made clear these were friendly Indians. Led by an exuberant Jonathan and an increasingly animated Joy, they watched Indian women making what they called frybread and were even offered some by one woman which they nibbled at tentatively before devouring it voraciously. An Indian man with two feathers angled into the hair at the back of his head and a hatchet in hand, asked them if they liked frybread. As Joy said later, if they didn't like it—which, in fact, they did—they would have said they liked it to avoid any chance of being scalped. The man was telling them that he belonged to the tribe of Indians known as the Lakota when there took place one of the most remarkable things that had ever happened in the lives of Joy and Jonathan. An Indian man with long dark braids and a breastplate of small bones he wore over a white blouse called out as he came toward them, "Hello, Mrs. Hudson. I'm glad to see you again."

And if that wasn't enough of a surprise, Mrs. Hudson answered him, hoping as she did, she had chosen a proper mode of address. "It's lovely to see you again, Mr. Sudden Thunder. I hope you and Jane are well."

"We are, and we are thinking very hard about what you told us. We again thank you very much." Sudden Thunder then turned to the man who had asked them about frybread, speaking to him in a language they did not understand, which led to his nodding somberly to the group and then walking hurriedly away.

117

Stunned surprise was no longer the province of Joy and Jonathan alone although for Holmes and Watson it was relatively short-lived as both remembered Mrs. Hudson speaking of being visited by Sudden Thunder and Jane Morrison. Introductions and handshakes followed. While Sudden Thunder maintained a properly solemn pose, the people to whom he was introduced ranged in expression from sober but friendly to wide-eyed astonishment. Watson then pointed out it was getting near time for the show, and Sudden Thunder agreed, indicating it was time for him to get ready as well. Fortified by a storm of good wishes, Sudden Thunder turned back to the Indian encampment and all the rest headed for the entrance to the exhibition grounds.

Holmes gave the ticket-taker the complimentary passes given them by Colonel Cody and received a spirited welcome to Buffalo Bill's 1903 Wild West Show in exchange. They were then escorted by a most ingratiating usher to seats in the first row of the stadium immediately behind the low barrier that ran nearly the circumference of the huge oval. Once again, Jonathan was encouraged to sit, once again, he resisted all human entreaties and, without the availability of equine intervention, he continued, as Joy succinctly put it, "being a pest." Only the promise of cherry phosphates was able to bring Jonathan under a modicum of control and their arrival put him finally in his seat.

Holmes had purchased a lavishly decorated program on whose cover was a picture of King Edward when, as the Duke of Wales, he had earlier attended the Wild West Show. Reading from the program, Holmes announced they would first see the entrance of Wild West performers. Moments later each of several groups made their entrance. American cowboys entered the exhibition grounds on high-spirited steeds, whooping and hollering with Stetson hats sometimes on heads, more often in hands and waving to the crowd. Then came Indians in war paint and feathered bonnets clutching their bows as they rode. Next came Mexican vaqueros in their distinctive round hats with colorful braid on their trousers, swinging lariats in wide circles above their heads, and then Cossacks in fur hats showing off the riding skills that had made them the most famous horsemen in Europe. When the riders had been to all parts of the oval and bathed in the shouts and continuing applause of an enthralled

118

audience, they formed ranks facing the entrance, quieted their horses, and to the surprise of no one and the delight of everyone, waving his Stetson to the crowd allowing his long locks to flow in the breeze of his own creation, Buffalo Bill Cody galloped to the center of the oval, welcoming a crowd, now giddy with applause, to the Congress of Rough Riders of the World. For the next two hours the audience was alternately entertained and enlightened by performances from the colonel's collection of showmen and women.

There came first a race around the oval featuring representatives of all the cultures joined in the show. A cowboy, an Indian, a Mexican vaquero and a Cossack rode in a competition that had no clear winner as the audience loudly cheered for all the riders.

Cowboy sharpshooters then arrived to amaze the crowd with feats of marksmanship with pistol and rifle. It was two years since Annie Oakley and her one-time competitor and present day husband, Frank Butler, commanded center stage among the sharpshooters, but the audience was more than thrilled to see Buffalo Bill close out that segment of the program riding across the arena rifle in hand, shooting apart glass balls thrown into the air by a rider galloping in front of him.

There next came a reenactment of Custer's last stand at the Little Big Horn with a mournful Colonel Cody arriving too late to save the day. That was followed by a display of horsemanship in which Indian, Cossack and cowboy riders impossibly managed to stay mounted in spite of the multiplicity of tricks they performed on their horses. Mrs. Hudson and the others recognized Sudden Thunder among the riders, but he was far too occupied twirling his body all around the back of his horse to spot, let alone acknowledge them.

After that, came a different display of horsemanship in which riders demonstrated the technique and speed of mounting, dismounting and changing horses, as was done, the properly breathless announcer reported, by Pony Express riders carrying the mail from St. Joseph, Missouri to Sacramento, California. And while few in the audience had any idea where those places were, all were impressed with the riders' skills, wherever it was they were going to or coming from.

An intermission allowed the audience as well as the performers to catch their breath. It allowed Watson to wait on a rather long line at a concession stand to get popcorn for everyone and another round of phosphates for Jonathan and Joy. For once, Jonathan was speechless, thunderstruck by the performances. However, the second phosphate appeared to remove all impediments to speech, and he became his old self only a good deal more so as he reviewed for anyone who'd listen—as well as all those who wouldn't—all the events they had just witnessed. This time, however, Joy had given up her small pretense of dispassion and eagerly joined his reprise adding elements she felt he'd missed.

Watson broke in on the children's reporting long enough to raise a question to Holmes about their leader and landlady, "Where has Mrs. Hudson gotten to?"

Holmes swallowed a mouthful of popcorn before answering Watson, "While you were off getting refreshments, one of the cowboys came by to tell her that Jane Morrison wanted to see her if she could spare the time. They both went off a little while ago. I trust she'll be back soon."

All were barely in their seats when the Deadwood Coach came racing onto the exhibition grounds, filled with passengers drawn from the audience, and being chased by a group of marauding Indians. As the coach traveled the oval in an effort to outrun the attackers, a band of cowboys entered the scene led by Colonel Cody, rescuing the coach and its passengers in the nick of time.

Before the dust of the coach and the men had settled, it was stirred again by the appearance of cowboys, Indians, Mexican vaqueros and Cossacks riding bareback on horses that repeatedly kicked high in the air as they covered a good part of the oval. Several of the men fell off the horses, which Holmes explained were called "bucking broncos" in the program. Those who fell tried, almost always unsuccessfully, to remount their horses before finally quitting and leaving the arena. It was left to other riders on far more cooperative horses to chase down the bucking horses which they did with artfully thrown lassos much to the delight of the audience who applauded them as vigorously as they had the men who rode or tried to ride the animals they were catching.

It was finally time for the show's finale and there was still no sign of Mrs. Hudson. Her absence went unnoticed by Joy and

Jonathan but had become a cause of some concern to Holmes and Watson.

"This isn't like her, Holmes. This isn't at all like her."

Holmes gave a tight-lipped nod but said nothing.

The program indicated that the last performance in the show involved the attack on a settler's cabin by a band of hostile Indians.

The cabin was rolled out to the center of the exhibition grounds and the attack began. Indians with flaming arrows sped on horseback toward the unprotected cabin. Had Mrs. Hudson been with Holmes and Watson, she would have noticed that one of the Indians wearing a war bonnet and decorated with warpaint had one gold tooth. What Holmes and Watson did notice was that in the supposedly unoccupied cabin a hat with a single ostrich feather was visible at one window.

To the surprise of everyone but Watson, a figure in morning coat and striped slacks vaulted over the barrier separating the audience from the performers, and the son of a country squire mounted a horse standing idle waiting its later use in repulsing the invaders. Just as remarkably, he was joined by an Indian who had been one of the trick riders in an earlier event, now making an assault on what were presumably his tribal allies.

The spectators were not alone in their confusion about what they were seeing. They assumed it was some aspect of the show whose meaning would be revealed in good time. Colonel Bill Cody knew better. He had no idea what was happening, but every cell in his showman's body was telling him that he had to *appear* to know exactly what was happening and, accordingly, to demonstrate for all to see that he was in total control. Three things would guide his action. First, the Indians could not be seen as victorious in their attack on the settler's cabin. Second, whatever the reason, the Indians attacking the settler's cabin were not Indians. War paint was misapplied, and the bonnets worn by most were inappropriate to the situation. Indeed, the only genuine Indian taking part in the attack was Sudden Thunder and he was attacking the fake Indians. And third, most importantly, he couldn't imagine a rationale whereby Sherlock Holmes would have reason to become a participant in his Wild West Show unless something was seriously amiss. He didn't know what that something was, but he knew whose side to be on if he was to find out. With a wave of his arm to the cowboys, vaqueros and Cossacks waiting to repel the attack on the settler's cabin, and with the roar of the crowd as encouragement, he set his sights and the course of his riders on capturing the fake Indians allowing Holmes and Sudden Thunder to pursue whatever objective they had chosen for themselves.

Lassos whirling in the troop the colonel led, the several cowboys masquerading as Indians were quickly captured while Holmes and Sudden Thunder battered in the cabin's locked door freeing up what all assumed was a mother and daughter captured and bound by bloodthirsty savages. Although the marauders were white and an Indian came to the women's rescue, the escapade fed the audience's assumption of Indian villainy, Sudden Thunder being the exception to a rule of which they were certain.

Whatever the audience thought they were seeing, they were delighted by it. They had seen the cowboys reign supreme with the assistance of their very own Sherlock Holmes as the show's announcer proclaimed with glee and utter bewilderment.

For Joy and Jonathan, there was only glee. They gave voice to their delight and excitement throughout the closing ceremony and final parade of cowboys, Indians, Mexican vaqueros and Cossacks, over the course of the carriage ride taking them home, and—the Baker Street trio were certain—throughout the rest of the day if not well beyond.

The gold-toothed cowboy and his cohorts were brought before Colonel Cody's hastily assembled tribunal, at which he presided as judge, jury, and as necessary, prosecuting attorney. The counterfeit Indians insisted they meant only to discourage the marriage between "that Indian" and Jane Morrison—that they were hoping to shock Miss Morrison into an awareness of the fate that awaited her and to discourage Mrs. Hudson from ever again meddling in affairs she didn't understand. Nothing they said made the least impression on Colonel Cody other than to harden his resolve to rid his show and his sight of the presence of the gold-toothed cowboy and those who had shared in his actions. They were provided their earnings, tickets on the next liner to America and 24 hours to clear out their belongings and separate themselves forever from the Wild West Show. Cody let it be known that any others who had not participated in the attack on the settlers cabin, but shared the thinking of those who had, should come forward to make themselves known to him. None did.

After giving prodigious thanks to both her saviors, Mrs. Hudson's mood turned uncharacteristically somber. It was not, she knew, the consequence of being kidnapped, bound, and then locked in a cabin that was subjected to fiery attack, although she granted the reasonableness of such thinking. It was rather that she had become still more aware that time was slipping away, and that just as others had come to her rescue, it was up to her to come to the rescue of Benjamin Olyphant as he waited his fate at the Bow Street Station.

Chapter 7. A Bank Withdrawal

Mrs. Hudson knew that Mr. Holmes was right. All she had was speculation about the Stockton family and its history, about Roger—or Balthasar—and Aaron. And still she was certain she was right about that history, and equally certain that that history was somehow connected to the murder of Roger Stockton. There were simply too many coincidences for things to be coincidental. Proof for her speculation, she was certain, could be found at the Wilberforce Bank and Trust where Mr. Murchison was the branch manager, proof that would have to be found when Mr. Murchison was at home and asleep. To enter the bank and access its records after business hours would, however, require skills customarily possessed by the people she and her colleagues were pursuing, rather than people like themselves. Holmes claimed to know exactly the right person for one part of the job who, he said, would be delighted to join them. The second person needed promised to be far more difficult to attract to the work of the evening.

The more agreeable of the nominees was Thomas Wiggins, historically one of the area's more resourceful petty thieves and leader of the group Mr. Holmes called the Baker Street Irregulars, more recently the page boy at 221B, and currently printer's apprentice at Lewin and Sons Custom Printers—the "and Sons" a fabrication created by Mrs. Lewin to assure her husband's customers of the stability of his business. Wiggins's name drew Mrs. Hudson's instant support much to the surprise of both Watson and Holmes until she reminded them of Wiggins's substantial contributions to solutions of the cases of the Irish Invincibles and the murder of the boxer, Sailor Mackenzie. She did, however, voice concern about the skills Holmes reported Wiggins as having added to his repertoire, useful as those skills promised to be in the evening's assault on the Wilberforce Bank and Trust. It was agreed that Holmes would get Wiggins to promise never to use those new-found skills for criminal purposes—cross his heart and hope to die, an addendum that had been found significant to Wiggins. Mrs. Hudson was well aware that Wiggins would swear to anything for the chance to work with

124

Holmes again. Nonetheless, if less than wholly satisfactory, it was as much of a commitment as she could hope to get.

The skill in question was lockpicking. It was not, Wiggins had assured Holmes, that he was thinking of a career change. Not at this time was the unstated remainder of his response. There were, in fact, clear attractions to his current position. Most particularly, he found the reliable receipt of wages a desirable change from the unpredictability of reward from his earlier endeavors although, at the same time, lacking the excitement that accompanied those endeavors. Moreover, he found his employer reasonable in his demands, and ready to reward his industry with increases in both responsibility and salary—which latter went a long way to making his employer appear reasonable. Nonetheless, it had been Wiggins's experience that life was ever changing, at least his life was. Good times had a tendency to give way to deeply difficult times. Under those circumstances he had felt it wise to develop a fallback position in the event the rewards of virtuous living proved ephemeral. He understood from several of his earlier acquaintances that picking locks could provide a relatively consistent income although there was always the risk of interruptions in the pursuit of one's career to spend unplanned and indeterminate periods as a guest of His Majesty. It was this possibility that kept lockpicking a decidedly secondary career option. That and Mr. Lewin's dark-haired, blue-eyed, curvaceous daughter whose smile could light his windowless workroom with constant sunshine.

Alfred Thompkins was the other person whose assistance would be needed, and, unlike Wiggins, his cooperation was far from guaranteed. Thompkins was a by the book man whereas Wiggins had never felt the need to consult the book if he even knew of its existence. It would take some doing to convince Thompkins to break into his own bank. And Thompkins was necessary to let them into the bank quickly given the suspicion that people milling outside a bank at two in the morning would surely arouse. He was needed, as well, to show them where the materials they wanted were located once they were in the bank. Mrs. Hudson's plan to convince Thompkins of the appropriateness of this otherwise inappropriate behavior involved making full use of the influence of Penelope and Olivia Stockton, that influence still to be engaged. To begin the process, telegrams were sent to the two of them requesting a meeting with Mr. Holmes at the Stockton farm midmorning the next day for unspecified discussion.

Midmorning saw Holmes and Watson welcomed to the Stockton home with great excitement by Joy and Jonathan, modest enthusiasm by Olivia, and polite reserve by Penelope Stockton and Alfred Thompkins, the latter taking a rare half day of leave grudgingly provided by Mr. Murchison, the bank manager. Mrs. Fiddleman gave them no greeting at all but set out tea for the four adults, then took a disappointed Joy and Jonathan back to the kitchen with her, their disappointment significantly relieved by the sight of the bag of scones Mrs. Hudson had had the foresight to place in Mrs. Fiddleman's very temporary possession. After a brief exchange it was decided to allow Olivia to stay, nominally in recognition of her relationship to Benjamin Olyphant, more accurately, in recognition of her unwillingness to leave because of her relationship to Benjamin Olyphant. With everyone assembled, Thompkins cautiously challenged the need for their assembly.

"It was my understanding we had already answered all your questions, Mr. Holmes. We certainly want to be helpful, but I just don't see what more we can do." In deference to Olivia, he did not say what he was thinking—that the authorities were confident they had taken into custody the person responsible for Roger Stockton's murder and he saw no reason to question their judgment. Holmes shared neither Thompkins's hesitancy about speaking of Benjamin's capture, nor his confidence in the wisdom of Benjamin's captors.

"I believe that Scotland Yard has moved too quickly in this instance. To put it most simply, I am convinced they have made an error and that we therefore have a special responsibility to set things right—to capture the real murderer and to see to it that Benjamin Olyphant is freed from the Bow Street Station as soon as possible."

After Penelope and Thompkins had each caught their breath, they glanced to Olivia who appeared to be having difficulty staying in her chair as she beamed her appreciation to Holmes. As Mrs. Hudson had predicted, with Holmes's strong statement of support for Benjamin—in the presence of Olivia—it became impossible for Thompkins to refuse serious consideration of whatever it was Holmes was proposing. To do so would not only appear to be denying any possibility of Benjamin's innocence; it would appear to be denying, as well, any possibility of Olivia's happiness. Thompkins gave voice to the inevitable.

"Of course, if there's still more to be done, I'm sure we all want to do what we can." He paused for the moment before adding, "And, of course, that means doing all we can for Benjamin." His face drawn in sympathy, he looked to Olivia a moment before turning back to Holmes. Olivia kept her focus on Holmes the whole time.

"But tell me, Mr. Holmes, what more do you suppose we can do?"

"There is, in fact, something only you can do to aid the investigation and bring the killer to justice. You see, Mr. Thompkins, we have good reason to believe that a clue to understanding the circumstances leading to the murder are contained in the financial activities of Roger Stockton, activities that involved Stockton and Murchison and will be apparent from their financial transactions. In a word, Thompkins, we need to see the bank records of the two of them and likely one other."

The banker fell back against the cushion of the sofa, mouth open but saying nothing. It was as if Holmes had suggested the unthinkable and was about to call for the unconscionable, which was, in fact, precisely what was occurring.

"You can't mean it. You don't know what you're proposing," Thompkins said to the man who knew exactly what he was proposing.

"I do. I am proposing that we break into the bank after hours. That we do it this weekend. Indeed, that we do it tonight." Watson winced slightly. He would have preferred for Holmes to have led up to his call for Thompkins to break several laws with greater discretion and less drama, but he was also aware that, throughout their long association, discretion rarely triumphed over drama. For his part, for the second time in a very few minutes, Thompkins again sat open-mouthed and speechless. This time, Penelope Stockton did a very passable imitation of Thompkins's response while Olivia warily watched the two of them. To allow his audience a moment for its recovery, Holmes took a sip of tea and nodded his satisfaction to his hostess.

"You must give my compliments to Mrs. Fiddleman. The tea is excellent."

Thompkins at last found his voice, although he found it nearly a half octave higher than where he had left it. "You can't be serious?"

"About the tea?"

"About breaking into the bank."

"I am most serious. Nor do I make the suggestion lightly. I fully appreciate what's involved in taking that action. But I also know what's involved in inaction. I assure you I wouldn't be asking this if it wasn't critical to getting us closer to identifying the murderer of Mr. Stockton."

And then another voice was heard from. It was the voice for which Holmes and Watson had been waiting, the voice that would set them in a direction from which there would be no turning.

"It has to be your decision, Alfred, but I would say one thing. It doesn't seem to me that you'd be breaking into the bank. Not exactly. You do work at the bank and it's not as if you'd be taking money or anything that doesn't belong to you. And if being in the bank after hours can help to set things right as Mr. Holmes says ...." Penelope Stockton let her voice trail off and relied on a look of determination to complete her thought.

Holmes gave several small nods before adding to Penelope's comment. "I believe it can or I wouldn't suggest this admittedly unorthodox action. Indeed, I believe that the information we can gain will be critical to resolving this problem. My only concern is with acting quickly before those responsible can get access to the materials and pilfer or perhaps even destroy them."

Having done all he could, Holmes paused, allowing all eyes to fall on an increasingly fidgety and now wholly isolated Thompkins. With visions of constables dragging him off to Newgate Prison, he chose the one course that would allow him continued access to the Stockton farm and the companionship of Penelope Stockton.

"Of course, I'll do what I can to help solve Roger's murder and to see justice is done for Benjamin. I do wish you would permit me to contact Mr. Murchison and enlist his help in all this. I'm sure you're wrong about the possibility of his being involved in any kind of wrongdoing." He paused to scan his audience for support, found none and resumed his capitulation. "But we'll do it your way. What is it you want me to do?"

Holmes outlined the plan that would be put into play at half two the next morning. Everyone was cautioned, several times, to maintain secrecy, that the evening's success depended on it. At the last, Holmes informed the group that one other colleague, in whom he had the greatest confidence, would be joining them. He was identified as Thomas Wiggins, an expert with locks. At that point Watson thought it wise to add a note of reassurance for the newly shaken Thompkins.

"You must understand, Mr. Holmes's sometimes imaginative investigative strategies are well known to Scotland Yard and, for the most part, are well respected."

In answer to Thompkins's follow-up query, Holmes assured him that Inspector Lestrade was indeed familiar with Thomas Wiggins. Holmes thought it best not to elaborate on the point.

Promptly at half two a tall, slender man and a short, stocky youngster emerged from the dark shadows of a cobbler's doorway onto the street newly, if only partially illuminated through the efforts of the City of London Electric Lighting Company. They were met by a third man who gave them a spiritless greeting after making the last of his several searches of the empty streets above and below them. All three had come to the site of the rendezvous by keeping to parts of the street beyond the reach of the electric lights whenever possible and making liberal use of darkened recesses between buildings, and shopkeepers' shadowy doorways whenever necessary. Holmes had had his coachman take him to Mycroft's apartments much earlier in the evening thereby avoiding a coachman's question about his interest in being taken to Wilberforce Bank and Trust at two in the morning—a question the coachman might later repeat to the local constabulary. Instead, he was able to have a pleasant dinner with Mycroft at his Diogenes Club and still be within easy walking distance of the bank from Mycroft's Pall Mall lodgings to which they had repaired later for a pipe and conversation.

Wiggins, too, had no concerns about a curious coachman. The print shop, where he had a small room, was, in the light of day, a pleasant stroll to the bank. He spent the evening leading up to his becoming an accessory before and during the act, arranging and rearranging his collection of picks, studying each as he did so. When that was done, he went over in his mind the action involved in opening doors and filing cabinets. At one in the morning, he declared himself ready; at two he bid goodbye to the print shop cat, chucking it gently under an ear, eliciting a soft purr of contentment, before getting on his way.

Holmes contained his curiosity and didn't ask Thompkins where he had spent the earlier part of his evening. It was enough for Holmes that he was there, since he hadn't felt at all certain that would be the case. It was quickly decided to forgo an immediate use of Wiggins's expertise and instead make use of Thompkins's key to gain a more traditional entrance to the bank. It was explained to Wiggins, who regarded the decision as showing some lack of confidence in his ability, that there was a need to get them all off the street as quickly as possible lest they be seen loitering outside the bank by a curious passer-by or an efficient constable.

Once inside, the banker first made certain the heavy curtains were drawn across the windows, nearly jerking one from its bolster in his rush to get it done. Holmes urged him to sit for a moment to gather himself, assuring him everything would work out and asking him only to be directed to the door leading to Murchison's office. In the dark he stumbled in the direction Thompkins pointed, found at last the electric lamp nearest that door and nodded to the third member of the team. Wiggins gave a long slow nod in return. It was finally time to undertake the practicum that marked the end of his academic studies.

He pulled from a trouser pocket a set of picks that elicited a look of dread in Thompkins and of delight in Holmes.

"I had no idea you'd come that well prepared, Thomas."

"Yes, well, I've been setting myself for this moment, Mr. Holmes, so I brought everything I thought I might need. I'll get started on the door now. It shouldn't take me too long."

Wiggins's face took on an expression Holmes had never seen before. A brow, that was routinely devoid of care, was now deeply furrowed, lips that heretofore regularly curved their way into an easy smile were now drawn in a tight line, and eyes, that typically sought to capture every item in a room that was not nailed down, were now focused narrowly on the lock temporarily denying access to Murchison's office. Having assessed the lock, he looked to his supply of picks, chose one, and began to work that tool in the lock amidst a background series of frequent groans, occasional sighs, and an infrequent "aha." Watching the youngster at work, all of Thompkins's innumerable misgivings about the exercise reasserted themselves. He was certain the face, now contorted in concentration on his task, was well known to all members of the Metropolitan Police, no doubt making superfluous its appearance on the wanted posters he imagined adorning the walls of every police station in London and several nearby communities. In response, Thompkins began what would become his routine response to the anxiety their late-night escapade was causing him. He began pacing all through the bank's reception area, wringing his hands as he walked, sometimes berating himself for his involvement, sometimes berating others for his involvement, and sometimes calling on Divine Providence to rescue him from his involvement.

Holmes, in contrast, appeared wholly unruffled. He sat on a desk several feet from Wiggins, watching with a bemused smile the efforts of his one-time protégé to break into the office of the branch manager. And then, after one last groan, followed by a soft "aha," a click sounded, and Wiggins rose from the crouch in which he had set himself and pushed open the door to Murchison's office.

As they moved past him into the office, Holmes clapped him on the back and congratulated him warmly while Thompkins turned out the light in the outer office, mumbled something incomprehensible, and went to check the drawn curtains in Murchison's office before attending to the light. The curtains in Murchison's office were not the thick cotton of the curtains in the public area they had just left. That troubled Holmes for the moment, but things were too far along for it to be a concern for long.

"Which do you want me to work on first, Mr. Holmes, the desk or the filing cabinets?"

The two oaken filing cabinets were set side by side in the corner of the room away from the windows. Each cabinet had three deep drawers that allowed for large documents to be set in place without folding, a characteristic that explained the popularity of the newly developed vertical file cabinets. A lock at the top of each cabinet guaranteed the user the security of his files. Every drawer had a label holder at its center, and every label of the bank's drawers showed a range of letters of the alphabet. Holmes judged that the filing cabinets held the details of each customer's activities with the Wilberforce Bank and Trust, and Thompkins confirmed his judgment.

Holmes thought the desk offered the greatest potential for significant discovery. It was, he reasoned, the more private of the two choices, the one of the two more largely under Murchison's control. "The desk, Thomas, let's start with the desk."

Wiggins set himself atop the cushion on Murchison's swivel chair, and after first testing the swivel in both directions, he once again set his face in grim concentration, made careful choice from the picks he had brought and began the delicate task of making available the contents of Murchison's desk. In less than ten minutes Wiggins pushed back from the desk, swiveled in his chair halfway round to face Holmes and, grinning with self-satisfaction, he pointed to the middle drawer of the desk he had pulled half-way open. It earned him a second pat on the back even as Holmes directed him to find another place to sit so that he and Thompkins could jointly review the desk's contents.

Holmes first removed the small stack of papers from the center drawer taking care to leave them cross-hatched in the same sequence he found them. With Thompkins eyeing each document as if it might suddenly burst into flame, Holmes uncovered a stack of business loan applications, a smaller stack of personal loan applications, and a still smaller stack of forms for opening savings accounts. Beneath those were menus from several area restaurants as well as a half dozen letters from someone named Julia. Holmes was prevented from reading past "My dear Tony, Missing you awfully …" in the first of them by Thompkins's threat to end the night's activity if Holmes did not replace the letters in the drawer immediately, asserting they had nothing to do with Roger Stockton's murder. Holmes attempted to argue the unpredictability of murder investigations but was unable to convince even himself of a need to see Murchison's very private correspondence. Thompkins, meanwhile, insisted he did not know any Julia and thought it must be

Mr. Murchison's niece, feeling certain that only he would know that Murchison was an only child. For his part, Holmes filed away his discovery of a Julia, thinking it might prove useful if a bargaining chip was needed in later negotiation with Murchison.

After carefully replacing everything in the middle drawer, Holmes turned his attention to the topmost of the two deep drawers to its right. He waded through wills for Murchison and his wife as well as materials related to his home ownership and insurance policies. Beneath the papers lay a picture of Murchison's wife and children, their identities confirmed by Thompkins. Holmes took note that the letters from Julia were kept in the locked center drawer and the picture of Mrs. Murchison and their children were in the unlocked side drawer, and even there it was buried beneath papers. He suspected the picture's only surfacing coincided with visits from Mrs. Murchison. For now, he put the picture back beneath the other reminders of home without further question or comment much to Thompkins's relief.

In spite of his outward calm, Holmes was beginning to worry. He had to grant, if only to himself, that Mrs. Hudson usually got these things right, and that, as the bank manager, Murchison had to be in the middle of things just as she said, but he wondered if Murchison wasn't storing sensitive materials at home to counter the risk of exactly the kind of invasion Holmes was now conducting. In any event, there was only the one drawer left and he would learn soon enough if a new strategy was required. At first blush that appeared likely. Materials in the lower drawer seemed to bear no relation to banking. Holmes lifted out a folder of travel brochures, typically involving exotic destinations, and ship schedules presumably linked to those destinations. Both Holmes and Thompkins shared the same unspoken thought. None of the destinations could be viewed as appropriate for a family vacation.

Beneath the travel brochures and ship schedules lay a slender volume titled, *Romantic Poetry: A Collection*. This time Thompkins did not discourage Holmes from examining his finding. The table of contents listed poems by Keats, Dickinson, Browning and Byron among others. Widened eyes and a crooked smile were Holmes's only concession to the surprise he felt. Thompkins lacked Holmes's capacity for self-control. He first emitted a small cry of wonder, then gave way to a series of thin coughs ending with a prolonged throat clearing. Having exhausted the entertainment value of their finding, both men made effort to retrieve the expressions of solemnity appropriate to their investigation. Holmes said only, "You never really know about people." Thompkins, still struggling to connect Julia, exotic travel, and love poems to the staid boss he knew, nodded agreement, knowing that the Carleton Murchison he had known all the days before would be gone from all the days going forward.

Holmes now looked to the filing cabinets in the hope they might yet save the day. Anxious to get started on them, he grasped the still open book of poetry by its front cover and the first several pages meaning to snap it shut and replace it in the drawer when a single page fluttered to the floor from where it had been stored between Housman and Hunt. Wiggins retrieved it for Holmes whose mood became buoyant on getting a close look at the paper. Although yellowed with age, the writing was easily legible and the purpose abundantly clear. It was a contract between Horace Fiddleman and Avery Stockton, witnessed by Carleton Murchison identified as "second teller, Wilberforce Bank and Trust." Thompkins clarified that Horace Fiddleman was Charles Fiddleman's cousin and that Mr. Murchison was second teller until Arthur Grimes, Mr. Capehart's brother-in-law, and the bank's first teller, chose to leave the banking profession. Mr. Capehart, he explained, was the branch manager at the time. When Mr. Capehart passed away, Mr. Murchison, who had by then become first teller, was promoted to the manager position. Holmes saw no reason for remembering the bank's history of personnel changes, doubted he could and so dismissed it from his mind, turning his attention instead to the contract.

The document specified that "Avery Stockton, his designee, or descendant, will make available from his account the sum of nine pounds, twelve shillings monthly for care of Dependent A so long as that dependent is living with, or being cared for by Horace Fiddleman." The money was to be transferred from the Stockton account the fifth of each month by Carleton Murchison and would include in addition to the nine pounds and twelve shillings a service charge of two pounds, six shillings payable to the Wilberforce Bank and Trust. Ignoring Thompkins's misgivings, Holmes placed the contract in a folder he took from Murchison's desk and placed the folder in the large envelope Wiggins had brought at his request, an envelope which more customarily held circulars, advertisements or print orders from Lewin and Sons.

"I take it we're done. You've seen the contract. I don't like your taking it, but now you've got what I presume you wanted describing the arrangement to move money from Stockton to Fiddleman's cousin for this A person. Isn't that enough?" Thompkins spoke with more hope than conviction.

"Not yet. We still have to see the bank accounts of Roger Stockton and Horace Fiddleman."

"Why Roger Stockton? It's his father signed the agreement."

"Yes, but it's Roger who would have assumed responsibility after his father had his accident and was incapacitated—and maybe even before that." Holmes looked to his pocket watch and scowled. He had hoped things might be further along.

"Thomas, I need you to open up the filing cabinets to allow us to get to the bank records that are almost certainly inside them. And before you object, Mr. Thompkins, let me assure you I am only interested in three records—Roger Stockton's, Horace Fiddleman's and Murchison's."

Thompkins sputtered his objection even as Wiggins began his selection of the pick appropriate to the task. "Have you no regard … none … for the law … or privacy … or simply proper behavior? What are we doing? … What are you doing?"

Holmes was curt in his response. "We need to confirm that the conditions of the agreement were met. We can only do that by seeing the bank records. How are you doing, Thomas?"

For answer, Wiggins, once again grinning broadly, opened the top drawer of the filing cabinet containing A to L records, paused a moment to allow for proper note of his achievement, then moved on to the second cabinet. Holmes nodded his appreciation to Wiggins before going to the E – H drawer he had made available. He found Horace Fiddleman's file just behind Charles Fiddleman's. As the contract he had signed stipulated, his bank records showed a deposit of nine pounds, twelve shillings added to Horace Fiddleman's account the fifth of every month for as far back as Holmes checked. The single exception was the past month marked, "Account Closed," when Horace Fiddleman would have left for America and Aaron, who was surely "Dependent A," would have moved to the Stockton woods.

By the time he had satisfied himself about Horace Fiddleman's account, Wiggins had gotten the second filing cabinet open. Only the press of time kept Holmes from examining Charles Fiddleman's account to confirm his suspicion that he and Mrs. Fiddleman were extraordinarily well-paid servants. He, instead, searched the drawer marked "M-P", found records for Morgan and Myerson but there was no Murchison between them. Holmes was disappointed but not surprised. He didn't really expect Murchison to keep his account with those of the bank's customers, but once again he had the problem of determining where Murchison did keep his account information.

Holmes took a deep breath, closed the M-P drawer and opened the Q-U drawer. He pulled from it the two Stockton folders but only looked to the Roger Stockton folder. It showed a sum of eleven pounds, eighteen shillings paid to Carleton Murchison on or before the fifth of every month except the last when Roger Stockton's account was closed. Holmes placed the two Stockton folders in Wiggins's envelope. This time Holmes's action elicited no words but instead a resigned groan from Thompkins. Holmes took no notice. He had a problem on his hands. He wanted the last piece of evidence of the conspiracy involving Murchison, Avery Stockton and his son, and Fiddleman and his cousin. He wanted to see Murchison's accounts for confirmation of his continuing role as the essential go-between for the several parties determined to keep A far from the Stockton farm. And he wondered about something else. With all the money flowing through Murchison, and with the banker's willingness to lend himself to behavior that was highly questionable, if not illegal, would there be more to learn about Murchison from a reading of his accounts. A glance to his pocket watch told Holmes that soon the first light of morning would appear. It was time to try anything, even an unlikely anything.

"Mr. Thompkins, what can you tell me about Murchison's accounts? More particularly, can you tell me where they're kept?"

"Mr. Murchison maintains his own accounts and doesn't share that information with me."

"I understand that, but those records have to be kept somewhere in the bank. Where might that be?"

Thompkins pursed his lips as if to prevent speech, but his eyes wandered about the office and Holmes followed their trail. They paused a moment on a series of four pictures on the wall behind Murchison's desk depicting the Wilberforce Bank and Trust in varying stages of construction. Holmes crossed the room to the pictures and began to search behind each. He let out a soft groan of satisfaction when he looked behind a picture showing workmen poised on steel girders well above ground level, apparently heedless of the danger obvious to any onlooker. Removal of the picture revealed a small safe that must certainly house Murchison's personal papers and account.

With a smile of relief as much as satisfaction, Holmes turned again to Wiggins, only to find his young protégé staring back at him with wide-eyed dismay.

"I'm not a cracksman, Mr. Holmes. I never said I was. It's locks I been studying not safes."

Holmes sat back in the chair previously occupied by Carleton Murchison and Thomas Wiggins. He swiveled the chair, so he was no longer facing the impregnable safe, and proceeded to stare Thompkins into speech, a defensive, pleading speech to be sure, but speech, nonetheless.

"I just don't see how you can still believe there's some irregularity in the bank's actions. You've seen the Stockton accounts and Horace Fiddleman's account—all of them perfectly in order. I admit the contract that was drawn up is a little bit unorthodox—maybe more than a little bit—but legal nonetheless. What else could there possibly be to learn?"

Holmes straightened in his chair. He now believed that Thompkins was holding back, that he knew more than he was saying about accessing Murchison's information, and that he was hoping to convince Holmes that gathering such information was unnecessary. The detective's initial response was stony silence. It was a strategy once suggested by Mrs. Hudson although such origins had been long forgotten. When he believed that silence had increased the pressure to speak sufficiently, Holmes pressed his case, making it clear that in urging him to share what he knew, he might provide the basis for absolving Murchison of any impropriety.

"The picture is still incomplete. As you say, we have what we need to know about the Stocktons and Charles and Horace Fiddleman. We need to know about Murchison's actions to get the complete picture. When we can absolve him of any wrongdoing, I promise I will no longer trouble you for anything further about your Mr. Murchison." As he hoped, dangling the prospect of Murchison's absolution encouraged Thompkins's cooperation. He gave a weak-spirited statement of cooperation. Weak-spirited or not, it was sufficient to the task.

"Alright. If that's what it will take to bring this nonsense to an end, then I will help you get into the safe. But first, I must have your word that this will be the end of it." He looked steadily to Holmes until he got the nod he sought. When it came, it was accompanied by a miserable groan from the third member of the nighttime team who was now facing an end to the most exciting evening he'd had since his last evening with Mr. Holmes.

Thompkins heard the groan and felt the young man's disappointment. He thought his distress terribly inappropriate, but nonetheless genuine, and he was therefore willing to do what he could to lift his spirits—although with some concern about encouraging Wiggins's less wholesome ambitions. "Would you like to work the dial on the safe if I give you the combination, Mr. Wiggins?"

Wiggins stood for a reverent moment, nodded his respects to his unexpected benefactor and, with great solemnity, advanced to stand beside the safe where he straightened to add what centimeters he could to his height. He then proclaimed himself ready to proceed.

Thompkins affected a comparable gravity as he announced each number. Within minutes the safe was open and Wiggins, recalling from his youthful indiscretions the precautions to be taken in association with the sudden acquisition of property, was wiping the open safe clean of fingerprints.

The safe contained a thick bundle of papers held together with strong twine. Holmes undid the simple bow and looked to the monthly entries to Murchison's account for the past half year. Each entry but the most recent showed a deposit of two pounds, six shillings in Murchison's account with no evidence of a transfer of funds to Wilberforce Bank and Trust. Holmes was not a man to say, "I told you so," but he came close to becoming such a man with the discovery that Murchison was not only complicit in denying Aaron's birthright but was profiting from his role in facilitating that denial. He pointed out his finding to Thompkins who searched for an explanation of Murchison's behavior other than that he was pocketing money that was to be paid to the bank. Finding none, Thompkins bit his lip, made a long face, and was about to share his disappointment with Holmes, when he heard the door to the street being forced open, and the voice of authority he had been dreading sound throughout the bank.

"Anybody here? Declare yourself. This is Police Constable Spencer speaking."

At Holmes's whispered direction, Wiggins stuffed several sheets from the bundle they had been reviewing into his envelope; closed the safe using the same somewhat discolored handkerchief he had used in opening it; then slipped the picture back on the nail so it again covered the safe. Thompkins, meanwhile, showing an ingenuity that Holmes thought gave promise of a career beyond banking, extinguished the lights in Murchison's office even as they could hear Constable Spencer bumping his way through the outer office while he searched for a light. Still whispering, Holmes asked Thompkins if there was another way out other than the front door. There was none. There were, however, the windows. The offices were on the first floor and the drop to the street outside would not be difficult. As the constable continued his search for a light in the outer office, Holmes directed his confederates to leave by way of the windows and for Wiggins to deliver the large envelope to Watson. He could spend the rest of the night at 221B but should arrange to be at the print shop before it opened, while Thompkins was instructed to appear at the bank later that morning acting as if nothing had happened—certainly, nothing of a criminal nature. Holmes would, meanwhile, engage the constable in conversation. So saying, he turned to go toward the light their visitor had finally located while his confederates made for the windows. The last they heard was a cheery voice calling out, "Good evening, Constable Spencer."

139

Constable Spencer had heard of Sherlock Holmes but had never met the man and was unwilling to believe that the great detective spent his evenings breaking into banks. Holmes was not of a mind to argue the point, instead agreeing to accompany the constable to the Bow Street Station to spend what remained of his evening. Holmes asked only that someone contact Detective Inspector Lestrade on his behalf at a suitable hour after the sun had risen. With that done, Holmes slept until late in the morning, total exhaustion accomplishing what the Bow Street Station's thin mattress and hard pillow could not have achieved on their own.

He was jostled awake by a beefy constable who bit off four words of direction, then repeated two of them lest his message be lost.

"Come on. Get up. Get up."

Holmes opened his eyes and for a moment was uncertain where he was. Upon recalling the events of the prior evening, he asked the officer if Inspector Lestrade had been called at which the constable became more voluble but no more amiable.

"Now, why would we call Inspector Lestrade? And why not the Commissioner? Why not Sir Edward Henry himself?"

Holmes sat on the edge of what had been his bed minutes before and pretended to stifle a yawn. "You might be right. Judging by our mutual interest in fingerprints, Sir Edward might be the more appropriate person to call."

The constable muttered something incomprehensible before going, slamming the cell door as he left.

Left to himself, Holmes recognized the heretofore unfamiliar ache of an empty stomach. The ache was accompanied by vivid recollection of the sumptuous breakfast Mrs. Hudson routinely provided. As his mind drifted from kippers to kidneys to stacks of toast and pots of marmalade, he thought he could hear familiar voices and feared his going without food, together with his missing a proper night's sleep, was creating a softening of his brain. It was only as the voices grew nearer and more clearly recognizable, he became confident that his intellect was still intact, and that rescue was at hand. He could make out the somber tone of Lestrade, disgust evident in his voice. The inspector allowed himself to be interrupted occasionally by Watson's soft reasoning but not at all by apologies from the constable who had wakened him earlier. Holmes heard the key turn in the lock and sprang to welcome two of the three men who entered his cell.

"Greetings. I'm delighted to see you both. I regret not being able to offer you refreshments."

Watson stepped forward to grasp more than shake the hand of his colleague, while Lestrade made it to half a smile before becoming again his austere self. The constable hung back at the door, poised to make his escape as soon as the situation allowed.

"We will have you out of jail very shortly, Mr. Holmes," promised Lestrade, "however, Mr. Murchison has given us to understand that he plans to press charges—which means you may only be free a short time. He's reported that a man claiming to be Sherlock Holmes broke into the Wilberforce Bank and Trust, probably with a confederate. Your purpose ... excuse me, the purpose of the man claiming to be Sherlock Holmes, is not yet known. Murchison, together with his employee, Mr. Thompkins, is checking to see if anything was removed from the bank offices. I assume you know nothing about that."

Holmes feigned a look of wide-eyed wonder but made no other response.

Lestrade accepted the look as sufficient. "That's what I thought. Of course, if they do find that documents have been stolen, the charge could be quite serious." Lestrade paused, pursing his lips for the moment to make clear the importance of what he was about to say. "However, if the Yard got word, anonymously, that the documents in question could be found at a specified location, there'd be nothing to investigate." Lestrade looked knowingly to Holmes who looked unknowingly to Lestrade.

"I appreciate your sharing that information with me, Lestrade. I'll keep it in mind should I encounter the thief."

"May I suggest we get on our way?" Watson urged. "I know that Mrs. Hudson is holding breakfast for you and is most anxious to see you."

Do you have any objections, constable?" Lestrade asked the nameless defender of the law.

The constable could barely contain his joy at the prospect of their leaving, bringing this sorry chapter in his otherwise spotless, if uneventful career to an end. "No, sir. No objection at all."

"And will you see to it that the proper paperwork is completed for Mr. Holmes's release?"

"Yes, inspector. I most certainly will.

With that the three men made their way from the sultry confinement of the Bow Street Station to the bracing freedom of London's early fall.

Murchison had closed the Wilberforce Bank and Trust for two hours for what the hastily prepared sign on the front door described as "routine maintenance." Mrs. Harrison was allowed to leave her post as receptionist/ secretary for the first time in her sixteen years of service. She was encouraged to go to the Rose and Crown Tea Room three doors down from the bank and to take Miss Franklin with her for the two hours of closure. Murchison suggested Mrs. Harrison might outline for Miss Franklin all that was expected of an employee of Wilberforce Bank and Trust. As a newly employed teller, he explained, she could benefit from time spent with an old hand like Mrs. Harrison.

After getting past being described as an "old hand," Mrs. Harrison wondered if anyone with six weeks experience as second teller could rightly be called newly employed, especially one who had been given an extensive orientation by Mr. Murchison, spanning several days, and including at least one luncheon. Nonetheless, if Mr. Murchison was willing to pay her to spend two hours drinking tea and eating biscuits, she had no complaints and she was certain neither would Miss Franklin, or Julia as she had asked to be called.

Murchison took great pride in his self-control. He thought it certain Kipling had someone like Carleton Murchison in mind when he wrote of keeping one's head when all others had misplaced theirs. He was a man in his early sixties with grizzled hair he kept at moderate length, matching the moderate length at which he kept his beard and moustache. He was more than six feet tall, and while his once trim build was beginning to give way to a small paunch, it was no more than one might expect of a man in the position of branch manager at Wilberforce Bank and Trust. It was, in a word a moderate paunch. Now, however, with only Thompkins as witness, he gave way to the rantings of an immoderate man.

"What do we have police for? They're supposed to protect us and still they let people just walk into our bank and do God knows what. I suppose we should be thankful the building is still standing. And what was Sherlock Holmes doing here?" He stopped in mid-stride to properly consider a sudden thought. "Who hired him? That's the ticket. If we knew that, we'd know what this is all about." He nodded vigorously in support of his own conclusion, then put forward a course of action. "The thing to do now is to learn if anything's been taken. If anything has, we can bring charges against Holmes, then get him to say who's paying him and what their game is. Thompkins, you look in the outer offices. I'll look to the files in my office."

Thompkins had spent the night thinking about what to say and do in almost exactly this situation. He hadn't expected to be alone with Murchison this soon and he hadn't expected Murchison to be so obviously unnerved. Thompkins held no illusions about his own courage. He was not a brave man and he knew he was not a brave man. The suggestion of a chink in Murchison's armor—a rather large chink—made it that much easier for him to do what he had to do.

"Mr. Murchison ...."

"What is it, Thompkins?"

"Mr. Murchison, I think you should know Mr. Holmes wasn't alone last night. I was with him."

Murchison turned back from entering his office to face his employee. He spoke more in wonder than anger. "You were with him. Why would you have done that?"

"The why doesn't matter now. It's what we found that matters. Mr. Holmes ... got into the files and into your safe." Thompkins had decided that, for the moment, it would be prudent to hold back on his contribution to the night's activities.

At the last, Murchison fell more than sat in Mrs. Harrison's chair. "Where are you going with this?" Then, attempting to assert the authority he once held, "You do know I could have you arrested for this. In fact, I just might."

From his position in the secretary's chair this seemed a hollow threat and it was, in any event, something Thompkins had considered on and off through much of the night. He had decided finally that Penelope was right. As an employee of Wilberforce Bank and Trust, he would be unlikely to be accused of breaking into the bank where he worked. Indeed, he had not really broken in, but simply used his key to enter. There was the matter of Holmes and Wiggins, but as he understood things both of them had a relationship with Scotland Yard.

"Mr. Murchison, I think you should know Mr. Holmes discovered your arrangement about funds being transferred from Mr. Stockton's account to Mr. Fiddleman's—Mr. Horace Fiddleman's."

"What in the world are you talking about?" But Murchison's near normal volume, combined with the hint of resignation in his voice, indicated he knew exactly what Thompkins was talking about. He showed no surprise when Thompkins confirmed it.

"For the last forty years—more than forty—you've been charging the Stocktons a monthly fee for transferring payments to Mr. Fiddleman and you've been putting that fee into your own account instead of paying it to the bank. I don't know what crime that is, but I suspect it's a lot worse than breaking and entering."

Murchison sank deeper into the chair he'd appropriated and, much to Thompkins's surprise and relief, began to reminisce. "Have you ever been in love, Thompkins? I mean really, truly, deeply in love. I was once. I thought she was the most wonderful woman on Earth. And when I proposed and she accepted, I was beside myself. It seemed like my life was complete. I had married what I thought was the girl of my dreams and I had just been made second teller at the bank. Except, as you know, a second teller doesn't make a great deal of money. And I discovered Mrs. Murchison had expensive tastes. She was the daughter of a successful draper and expected her style of life after marriage to be the same as it had been before. And what I was doing didn't seem so bad at the time. It was such a small amount. Besides, I had every intention of paying it back—anyway, at first. But then, after a while, it somehow got to be more than I could think of paying back. Besides, the bank had so much money. Who would miss it? Man to man, Thompkins, haven't you ever been tempted? I mean surrounded by all that money."

Murchison had asked the wrong man. Thompkins drew himself to his full height and found himself suddenly aware that he was looking down on the still seated branch manager. His lofty words matched the position in which he found himself.

"Not at all. Not ever."

Murchison shrugged at the response he should have expected. "Well then, consider this. If you expose me, there will be a scandal. People will take their money out of the bank and businesses will seek loans elsewhere. The truth is no one will want to do business with a suspect bank. It will be the end of Wilberforce."

In all his late night and early morning musing Thompkins had never gotten beyond accusing Murchison of a crime and receiving his admission of guilt, or, more often, his stout denial of any wrongdoing. His admission of guilt, combined with his challenge to exposure, posed an unexpected dilemma. And still he felt a strange exhilaration. He had suddenly come to control the fate of the man who, only a day before, controlled his. Emboldened by recognition of their changed relationship, he put forth a plan. To be sure, it was a plan to cede to others responsibility for further action, but it was a plan, and it was his.

"I don't see that there's anything to do except inform the Board."

"No, I didn't think you would see there was anything to do but tell the Board." His expression mirrored the contempt in his voice as he tried to reassert his authority, but Thompkins neither heard nor saw it. He was already mulling over the procedure for informing the Board and how to describe Murchison's actions while putting the best light on his own.

Murchison was meanwhile working out his own procedure relative to the Board. "Tell me, Thompkins, how soon do you have to tell them. Can you wait until tomorrow?"

"Why would I do that?"

"I'd like some time to get my things in order. At the very least I need to talk to my wife, and I want to write a proper letter of resignation. Surely, Thompkins, one more day isn't going to make any difference." He tried looking sympathetic but quickly gave it up as a lost cause and reverted to the contempt he felt.

Thompkins thought he could use a day himself to work out a proper approach to the Board, and he could see no harm in giving Murchison the day he wanted. "Alright. You can have the rest of today to do whatever it is you need to do, but only on one condition. You call and drop the charges against Mr. Holmes. You do it here where I can see you do it."

"That's fine, but who would I call to do that?"

"Have the operator connect you to the Bow Street Station."

Murchison looked to Thompkins with an eyebrow raised. He spoke to him briefly before dialing. "You're growing, Thompkins. I didn't think you had it in you. I might have put you on a managerial track if I had known you had this much spine."

Murchison dialed and gave the confused officer to whom his call was referred the information that the records he had thought were stolen had simply been in another office and that Mr. Holmes had, unbeknownst to him, been hired by his superiors to review security procedures at the bank. Moreover, he explained, the review was to take place in the evening when it wouldn't interfere with normal bank operations. He was sorry for the inconvenience created.

The following day, the initial response of the Board Chairman to whom Thompkins described Murchison's actions, was blind rage and an intent to contact the police preliminary to seeking a long prison term for Murchison. Informed by Thompkins of the likely effect of a very public accounting of the branch manager's mismanagement of funds, the chairman's second and ultimately governing response was to leave the police out of it and to deal with Murchison privately with some as yet undetermined punishment. A bank official's visit to the Murchison home early that afternoon led to the discovery that the disgraced manager had sailed the night before on the SS Miltiades bound for Sydney and Melbourne, Australia. It was subsequently learned from Mrs. Murchison and from a Miss Julia Franklin, described as an employee and friend of Murchison's, that he was traveling alone, and no one was known to have plans to join him.

The Chairman of the Wilberforce Bank and Trust, with the Board's concurrence, determined that life in Australia was not unlike penal servitude and that, as long as he remained there, no further action was to be taken against Murchison. Thompkins was named to the position of branch manager on an interim basis, the promotion based on his "ingenuity, resourcefulness and reliability," and doubtless with the hope that the promotion would induce him to stay silent about Murchison's indiscretions and the bank's long-time ignorance of those indiscretions.

Julia Franklin remained at her post for six more years before becoming the wife of Winston Oglethorpe, a successful wine merchant specializing in the emerging market of Australian vintages.

Chapter 8. Something for the Children

Following Holmes's directive, Wiggins went to 221B to deliver the envelope entrusted to him. In spite of the hour, his former employers welcomed him as if his return stirred a wealth of happy memories as indeed it did. At their request, he described in colorful detail the events that had transpired at Wilberforce Bank and Trust. He elicited looks of wonder as he told of breaking into Murchison's safe, and grimaces of disapproval as he told of their discovering the banker was regularly pocketing other people's money. He spoke at only modest length of his own contributions to the evening's activities, shrugging off their lavish praise after first giving them ample opportunity to express it. When he had finished his report, Mrs. Hudson and Watson were insistent that he get at least some sleep to which he readily agreed, only to find himself too keyed up to take advantage of their offer. After an hour he gave up trying and he left to rejoin Lewin and his nonexistent sons and reenter the comparatively humdrum world of custom printing.

Gracious as it was, the welcome given Wiggins paled in comparison to the exuberance of the reception given Holmes several hours later that same morning. Perhaps no overnight guest of the Crown was ever received more warmly on his return home than was Sherlock Holmes. Watson appeared to require substantial self-discipline to keep from embracing his friend and colleague. Mrs. Hudson said only, "It was good work, Mr. Holmes," but her words were accompanied by an uncharacteristically broad smile as she went to get Holmes's breakfast from where she had it warming in the oven.

Watson and Mrs. Hudson joined Holmes at the table taking tea for themselves and watching Holmes wolf down the breakfast to which he'd been looking forward since waking in his Bow Street cell. Watson outlined what they had heard from Wiggins. Holmes interrupted Watson and his own breakfast at strategic points to add what color he deemed essential to Watson's somewhat drab narration. When he was done and the best part of a pot of tea had been consumed, Holmes was excused to get a few hours sleep with the understanding that, when he awoke and was sufficiently recovered, plans would be laid for the next steps in unmasking Roger Stockton's killer.

Watson used the time to catch up on his journal reading. Activities of the preceding two weeks had kept him from staying abreast of *Lancet's* reporting of the latest findings in medicine. He was particularly keen to review the article titled, *The Medical Man, the Coroner, and the Pathologist.* Having skimmed it earlier, he wanted to understand more fully the argument set forth by Dr. H.H. Littlejohn questioning the competency of typical medical practitioners to conduct post-mortem examinations, and to commit to memory the refutation of that argument as propounded by *Lancet* editorial staff.

Mrs. Hudson contented herself with organizing her larder and straightening up the sitting room while Mr. Holmes slept and could offer no protest. When she was done, she took up the book she had just borrowed from the British Museum Library, the recently translated work of Dr. Karl Landsteiner describing different blood types with the resulting capacity, among other benefits, to identify and distinguish between the blood specimens of the victim and the assailant at a crime scene.

A little more than two hours after excusing himself to catch up on his sleep, and just as the clock was striking the noon hour, Holmes ventured refreshed from his bedchamber and, together with Watson, joined Mrs. Hudson in her parlor. She lost no time getting to the purpose of their meeting.

"I believe what we found in the bank records gets us that much closer to identifyin' our murderer. I'll not share my thinkin' with you just yet. It's important we don't do anythin' that would show our 'and, but I'm thinkin' we're getting' close to bein' ready to set a trap for the killer." In response to the blank looks of her colleagues, she felt a need to elaborate—but only a little.

"The bank records, in association with what we learned at the registry office, make it clear that Aaron truly is Avery Stockton's first-born son, not just somebody's 'ingenious speculation,' and that a number of people 'ave benefited from keepin' 'is identity secret with no one benefitin' more than Roger Stockton. All of which may 'ave somethin' to do with 'is murder.

"So now with all we've learned, let us take stock one final time of our suspects and where we believe things stand with them?"

Watson looked up from his notetaking to venture a name. "I can't speak to the conspiracy of silence about Aaron, but for me Percy Dickson remains a prime suspect. As we know, he had strong feelings about Stockton, believing, as he did, that his sisters were being brutalized by the man. He may even have believed his one sister, Priscilla, was helped to an early grave because of him. And it would appear he was willing to use violence where he thought he had cause. Olivia apparently witnessed his knocking Stockton down on one occasion, which may explain his being barred from the Stockton farm by Roger Stockton. Nonetheless, Dickson couldn't be barred from the road or the woods, and he likely knew about Stockton's early morning walks." Watson turned to his colleague for comment. "You interviewed the man, Holmes. What is your thinking?"

Before speaking, Holmes drew down his hands from where they were steepled in front of his chin. "All that you say is quite correct, Watson. I would only add that he could offer no satisfactory explanation for his whereabouts when Stockton was killed. I didn't go into detail earlier, but he claimed to have spent the night before Stockton was killed and much of that morning in an opium den." Seeing his colleagues' critical stares, he explained, "I saw no reason to embarrass the man at the time. In any event, he says he was virtually surrounded by a number of prominent individuals who would prove irrefutable eyewitnesses, except that not one of them will come forward and admit to having seen him lest they lose their positions in society."

Holmes pursed his lips before continuing. "What then do we make of the Olyphants? While Lestrade has arrested him, we've ruled out the boy, Benjamin—a point I made clear to the Stocktons and Thompkins when I was with them. Still, it must be admitted that Benjamin and his father each had motive, means and opportunity. Different motives perhaps, but the same means and opportunity. And even if we discount the likelihood of the boy killing his prospective father-in-law, there's still Daniel Olyphant. We have only his word that he didn't fire his shotgun while we know for certain that he is now rid of a quarrelsome neighbor and a haggling about boundaries certain to end in a lengthy and costly court battle."

After a respectful pause, Watson again weighed in. "In addition, I don't think we can discount Thompkins. I recognize that, as others have said, he doesn't look the part, but love can do funny things to a man. Especially to a man who is forced to witness the cruel abuse of the woman he loves, and who can only hope to be with that woman if the man she clearly doesn't love is removed from the scene." There was a thoughtful nod of approval from Holmes while Mrs. Hudson continued to keep her own counsel.

Emboldened by the support of half his audience, Watson went on to suppose the unthinkable. "I guess, if we're to consider the possibility of Thompkins as our murderer, we can't discount the possibility of Penelope or Olivia Stockton, alone or perhaps together with Percy Stockton or Thompkins, ridding themselves of the man standing in the way of their happiness. The two of them would have had access to shotguns at the farm and I've been told that most everyone in the countryside knows how to use them. Admittedly, we'd have to check on both those things in relation to the Stockton women. We do know the two of them had easy access to the scene of the murder and no one to say they were someplace other than the woods at the time of the shooting. I recognize you could say the same about Aaron who almost certainly was someplace in the woods at the time of the murder, but, as I said earlier, it seems terribly far-fetched to see him as sufficiently organized to commit this murder or knowing enough of his own history to want to."

"Mrs. Fiddleman may be the only person with a credible alibi for the time in question," Holmes observed, "although she would seem an unlikely murder suspect in any event. She would have been in her kitchen making breakfast when Stockton was killed. Nobody was with her, it's true, and it appears likely the family ate the evidence of her alibi, but I can't see the woman trudging out to the woods with a shotgun in hand or think of a reason why she would.

"One can't say quite the same thing for Mr. Fiddleman. He admits to being in the woods overnight, shotgun in hand, in hopes of catching the fox that raids the Stocktons' chicken coop with only his wife to support his claim that he was back and in bed before the murder. And very suspiciously I would say, he's been packing for himself and Mrs. Fiddleman to leave as soon as possible—even before the will is read. Why would he do that? You would expect loyal servants who've been with a family for many years to receive a substantial bequest and be anxious to hear the will read on that account.

"And then there's Murchison?" Holmes added. "We've heard how much at odds he's been with Stockton and how they parted on deeply unpleasant terms."

"There is something about that you wouldn't know, Holmes," Watson spoke as if he was sharing a confidence with his colleague. "While you were asleep, Lestrade sent you a message that Murchison is currently aboard a ship to Australia.

"Also," Watson continued, "it has been reasoned that Murchison was an unlikely suspect no matter what his feelings about Stockton. Everyone else we've named had opportunity to learn the time and location of Stockton's routine—specifically his early morning walks. They could know it from their own observation or from being told about it by Penelope or Olivia Stockton. Nor would Murchison have any knowledge of the Stockton farm and the nearby woods. For those reasons we had to dismiss him as a suspect." Watson didn't mention Mrs. Hudson's role in discounting Murchison. He didn't he have to. Hearing a low groan from Holmes, he thought it useful to move to a last and somewhat unlikely candidate for the role of Stockton's killer.

"I believe there's one more possibility that has to be considered, even if a somewhat dubious possibility. It's an idea that Avery Stockton suggested to me. He has this notion that the murderer could be a hunter, trespassing in the woods, who shot his son accidentally and then made certain of his death by shooting him a second time to avoid any chance of his victim identifying him. Rather unlikely I'd say but perhaps worth some consideration." Watson looked to Mrs. Hudson with eyebrows raised. Mrs. Hudson looked back to Watson with eyebrows perfectly positioned.

His report complete, Watson spoke for both men. "I believe that about sums it up, Mrs. Hudson. Is there anything more to consider?"

"I think you've covered a number of things very well—you both 'ave. The only thing you're missin' is what's been learned about Aaron and 'ow that factors into the murder of Roger Stockton because I'm sure it does. In fact, it's on account of all that's been learned that we're ready to set a trap for our murderer. To set that trap we're goin' to need Joy and Jonathan workin' with us. And to get them to work with us I'm thinkin' we might take them on a little outing. That will also give Penelope Stockton some time to 'erself which I'm sure the poor woman will appreciate. Dr. Watson and I will go to the farm tomorrow. For now, I 'ave to send a telegram to Lady Dickson. She was wantin' to be 'ere when the murderer is revealed. I 'ave to let 'er know when to come. When that's been done, I 'ave in mind to ask 'er for a small favor for our friends." With that, she edged off her chair to gather her things for a trip to the post office.

"When I get back," she said to the two still seated men, "we need to talk about the plans I 'ave in mind for tomorrow and, more importantly, tomorrow night. You'll need your rest; it will be a very busy time for the both of you." Holmes and Watson knew better than to press Mrs. Hudson for information. They would learn everything in good time, which was to say in Mrs. Hudson's time.

At the Baker Street Post Office, Mrs. Hudson handed the clerk the message that was to be sent as a telegram to Lady Agatha Dickson at Evermore in Sussex. It read:

"You wish know murderer. Suggest go Stockton farm late morning day after tomorrow."

The clerk lost his glassy look at the word "murderer" and was about to ask her to repeat herself to be sure he'd heard what he thought he'd heard when he recognized Mrs. Hudson as the telegram sender and knew he'd heard what he thought he'd heard. Aware of her famous lodger, he simply recorded her message as if it was of no greater significance than the "Happy Birthday, Eustace" telegram sent by the customer who preceded Mrs. Hudson. From prior experience with equally provocative messages, he, like Holmes and Watson, knew better than to raise questions. Regardless, he was certain his curiosity would be fully satisfied in a few days' time by a page one story in the *Morning Standard*. For now, he simply took her money and gave her the receipt she requested.

The telegram was brought to Lady Dickson by her butler, Krebs, on the silver tray reserved for that purpose. Both Lady Dickson and Krebs were intent on maintaining the conventions of the society in which both had grown. It was a losing battle but one to which they were both committed.

The telegram occasioned a broad smile and a soft-spoken, "Yes," followed by a full-throated, "Yes, indeed," that caused Krebs to raise an eyebrow, but only one and that one only partway.

"The boy wants to know if there is any reply, ma'am."

"By all means. Send to Mrs. Hudson that I'll be there with bells on."

Krebs nodded and withdrew. He told the messenger Her Ladyship's reply was that she would attend as requested. He neglected the bells or any other aspect of Lady Dickson's dress.

In the late morning the following day, Mrs. Hudson, together with Dr. Watson, took a coach to the Stockton farm where they asked the coachman to wait while they called on the lady of the house. Penelope Stockton had given the Fiddlemans the day at leisure in hopes of being that much closer to having the house to herself and made no effort to hide her disappointment at finding Watson and Mrs. Hudson on her doorstep. She did her best to hide her feelings, but they were too near the surface to stay down long.

"Dr. Watson, ma'am, is there something I can do for you?" Somewhat belatedly she recognized her hostess duties and stepped back from the doorway to allow entry into the farmhouse. "Won't you come in?" She gave the woman she knew as Holmes's and Watson's housekeeper a small nod together with an equally small smile which Mrs. Hudson returned in kind.

Recognizing the need for conversation, Penelope chose the person and subject she thought least likely to provide difficulty. "Joy and Jonathan have told me about your scones, Mrs. Hudson. They've made me quite envious of your baking skills." The smile widened and was accompanied by a small cry of pleased surprise when Mrs. Hudson took from the voluminous purse she carried, a bag of the much admired scones.

When all were seated in the parlor, Penelope offered them tea and the opportunity to share in the scones they had just presented to her. Watson demurred for himself and Mrs. Hudson and proceeded to explain the purpose of their visit.

"That's very kind, Mrs. Stockton, but we've come expressly to give you a day at rest—or, at least, the best part of a day at rest. Speaking as a doctor and, I hope, a friend, I can say you've had a dreadful shock and deserve some time to yourself to recover. In that spirit, Mrs. Hudson and I would like to take Joy and Jonathan out for the afternoon. We've a coach waiting, and with your permission, we thought we might take the children to lunch and then to the music hall where they're showing the moving picture, *A Trip to the Moon*. After that, perhaps a stop for a treat and then back home in time for dinner."

On hearing Watson's offer, Penelope was so caught off guard she was momentarily speechless. When she had again gathered herself, her words tumbled out on top of each other. "Oh my, that's extremely kind … extremely generous of you … of you both. Yes, yes, of course. I'm sure they'll be delighted."

The two extremely kind and generous people blushed slightly, themselves caught off guard by Penelope's effusive expression of gratitude for what was, in fact, nothing more than a part of Mrs. Hudson's plan to capture Roger Stockton's killer. Watson cleared his throat before acknowledging her praise. "Glad to do it." Penelope mouthed a last thank you, then hurried to get the children.

She returned moments later, some distance behind Joy and Jonathan who had sprinted ahead to confirm the afternoon's plans. Watson and Mrs. Hudson were happy to assure them of all their mother had promised. Joy then revealed there would be another person joining them.

The need for a change in plans became apparent when Penelope reentered the parlor with her older daughter at her side.

"Olivia is most anxious to go as well, there being so much talk about the moving pictures, and she can help keep an eye on her brother and sister. Besides which, it will help take her mind off … other things."

"Yes, of course, that will be delightful," Mrs. Hudson did her best to sound delighted as she began to calculate how to fit this unexpected actor to a part in the play she was even now rewriting.

"Are these scones for us?" Jonathan pointed to the open bag over which he had strategically placed himself.

"You can each take one," his mother replied, "and don't forget to thank Mrs. Hudson for bringing them."

Some version of "Thank you, Mrs. Hudson," was garbled by Joy and Jonathan during a brief break in their chewing. A more ladylike "Thank you," came from Olivia who swallowed the bite she'd been chewing before speaking.

All were directed by Penelope to go upstairs to find something suitable to wear for a trip downtown. Joy returned first. She wore a peppermint striped dress and a wide-brimmed hat, an outfit she was certain made her look years older. Jonathan came a short time later accompanied by Olivia who took obvious pride in having made him over into "a little gentleman" as she described her creation. Jonathan looked to the adults watching him descend the stairs, on alert for the first snicker that would send him scurrying back up the stairs. Instead, he received nothing but admiring oohs and aahs for his outfit of a tightly buttoned jacket over a white shirt and the dark tie Olivia had put on him in spite of waving arms and complaints of strangulation. The remainder of his outfit consisted of grey knickers topping long dark stockings. Olivia wore a light blue traveling suit, she had worn once before and believed very becoming.

"I must say," Watson began, "this is as handsome a group as I am likely ever to be seen with. Wouldn't you agree, Mrs. Hudson?"

"I would indeed, and now perhaps we shouldn't keep our coachman waitin'."

The less than subtle hint taken, they were shortly out the door and on their way to lunch before going to the two o'clock moving pictures show.

Mrs. Hudson had it in mind to overwhelm rather than merely impress Joy and Jonathan in an effort to make them as amenable as possible to the tasks she had in mind for them. Olivia's presence made the job more challenging. She appeared to have perfected the look of blasé sophistication uniquely available to young ladies of late teenage years. Countering that look required Mrs. Hudson to step up her game. Instead of lunching at a simple tearoom, Mrs. Hudson requested the coachman take them to the Langham Hotel where, she explained to her fellow passengers, they would take a light lunch in the hotel's Palm Court.

The coach came to a stop in front of the majestic four-story ocher-colored hotel. Once the grande dame of London hotels, it remained an exclusive and highly desirable address even as it faced an increasing number of aspiring upstarts. The doorman, after opening the coach's door and setting a box to enable the descent of the coach's passengers, found it suddenly necessary to step back quickly as Jonathan sought to determine whether he could jump from the top step of the coach to a place alongside an idle luggage cart some distance away. The doorman achieved only modestly greater success with his effort to assist Joy in exiting the coach in as much as she viewed the task as one that was well within her capacity. He did better with Olivia who accepted his assistance as befitting the treatment of a young lady accustomed to dining out. Watson and Mrs. Hudson proved to be more conventional guests of the hotel; however, the doorman's expression remained equally placid regardless of the visitor and their chosen strategy of egress.

The Palm Court, to which they were directed, provided a second opportunity for Olivia to be embarrassed by her brother and sister, or "the children," as she scornfully referred to them. Much to her chagrin, Jonathan insisted on lagging behind to finger each of the potted palms along the path the maître d'hotel was forging. To make matters worse, a number of the elegantly dressed diners found his behavior amusing. For her part, Joy got to the table without doing anything unseemly, but then refused any assistance in getting her chair closer to the table, insisting she could do it herself and proceeding to noisily prove she could indeed scoot her chair up to the table. It was Olivia's judgment that, whereas Dr. Watson and Mrs. Hudson should have taken steps to rein in the children's more objectionable behavior, they were, in fact, no help at all, and Olivia was belatedly beginning to rethink her decision to spend the afternoon with them when the waiter arrived to visit on her the greatest indignity yet. The man left five menus on the table—two adult and three children's menus. Before she could cry or scream, Dr. Watson loudly called the waiter back and told him "the young lady is to be given an adult menu." At that moment Olivia decided things just might work out after all.

At the waiter's return, Jonathan placed an order for a jelly sandwich and Joy vigorously nodded her desire for the same. The waiter, having already been upbraided by Watson, responded as though jelly sandwiches were all the rage at the Palm Court in spite of their never having appeared on a Palm Court menu. He proceeded to give what he intended to be colorful descriptions of the preserves he knew to be in the Palm Court larder.

"We have a tart orange marmalade as well as a rich sweet orange marmalade." Seeing the puzzled expressions that greeted his suggestion, and taking note of Watson's slowly wagging head, he modified somewhat the listing he had planned to provide. "We have orange, peach, strawberry, and pomegranate." He waited the moment they took to decide, then recorded an order of peach for Joy and strawberry for Jonathan. Olivia, after coldly watching the exchange between the waiter and the persons who were regrettably members of her family, ordered the Norwegian smoked salmon while Mrs. Hudson selected the white meat chicken salad. Watson expressed the thought that Olivia's order sounded delicious and asked for the same.

The luncheon conversation was difficult. There was some review of events at the Wild West Show, but that had largely been talked out long before. Watson was soon reduced to asking Joy and Jonathan about their school, the two children answering politely, if briefly, and with a thoroughgoing lack of enthusiasm. Olivia was solely concerned about Watson's views on the guilt or innocence of Benjamin. His response to her question that he believed it "very likely that the boy is innocent, but we'll need to find the guilty party to get him freed" did not provide the reassurance she was hoping for. She hadn't considered that Benjamin's freedom could depend on finding the real murderer and whatever that might involve.

The conversation became more spirited, if equally brief, when Mrs. Hudson called for opinions about the food at the Palm Court. They were, nonetheless, uniformly positive. So much so, in fact, that it was decided to return to the Langham Hotel for snacks after seeing the moving pictures. There followed yet another lull in the conversation ultimately interrupted by Jonathan, for the third time wondering whether they shouldn't be going, Watson and Mrs. Hudson exchanged a look that suggested it might, in fact, be time— or in any event close enough to time—to start for the music hall that had been temporarily refitted to permit the showing of the moving pictures. As it turned out, it was just as well they attended to Jonathan's concern.

The music hall had begun to fill up early as much of London had read or heard of the acquisition of Georges Melies's *A Trip to the Moon* and its London showing. They found seats three rows from the screen, where Watson and Mrs. Hudson spent the time until the show began fending off requests for the treats Joy and Jonathan saw others enjoying. Arguments of their having just eaten, it's spoiling their appetite for the return to the Palm Court, and too many sweets not being good for them, all fell on two sets of deaf ears, three if one judged by Olivia's facial expression. The argument that finally won the day was that the show was starting, at which point silence descended. It persisted until the rocket shot from Earth struck the man in the moon in the eye leading to cries of wonder from every quarter of the music hall including theirs. After nearly fifteen minutes, and with the scientists safely returned to Earth and duly celebrated, it was time for their own return to the Langham Hotel and its Palm Court restaurant.

The coach trip back to the Palm Court was a far cry from the earlier trip from the Palm Court. While Olivia continued to play at being too grown up to be awestruck by the moving pictures, Joy and Jonathan suffered from no such constraint and recounted scenes from the moving picture accompanied by questions as to how those scenes could possibly have been created, neither receiving nor expecting answers to their questions.

At the hotel, the doorman stepped gingerly to the side of the coach door he opened to allow Jonathan full range to display his twelve-year old athleticism. Instead, he chose an unexpectedly conventional exit from the coach, using the box provided as he skipped to the door of the hotel. After Joy, Olivia and Mrs. Hudson had also stepped down, Watson apologized for Jonathan's antics only to be told by the doorman that he had three at home and understood perfectly the lad's high spirits.

Seated at the table, there was this time no confusion about menus as Olivia was given an adult's menu without the need for Watson's intervention. Mrs. Hudson recalled reading that the Langham Hotel's Palm Court boasted that it had created afternoon tea, which the same article noted, had by now been adopted by dozens of other restaurants. Olivia and Watson nodded politely for the information they would soon forget while Joy and Jonathan continued to work their way through their menus.

Watson drew Mrs. Hudson's attention to a listing of "classic and raisin scones with Cornish clotted cream and seasonal preserves." His action was wholly unnecessary. Mrs. Hudson was already wondering about the quality of scones—classic or raisin-filled—that could not stand on their own merits but required clotted cream and preserves to render them palatable. It was true she regularly served strawberry preserves with her scones, but they were not essential to the enjoyment of her baking. Her curiosity piqued, she vowed to give the Palm Court bakers a chance to prove themselves. Watson followed suit, himself somewhat curious about the comparison to the scones that were a staple of one's diet at 221B. He was aware as he did so of the need for careful expression of his preference, indeed of the need to lie if it came to that. Olivia, meanwhile, chose an almond and English strawberry tart, and Joy and Jonathan ignored the selections on the children's menu and went instead with the Tahitian vanilla cream crunchy wafers. With the work of choosing refreshments concluded, discussion of *A Trip to the Moon* resumed.

"Do you think people will really ever go to the moon?" Olivia asked.

Watson pursed his lips as he thought about an answer. "Who can say. There's long been the hope that we could fly some day and there's been no shortage of attempts to fly. It's 1903, a new century, and no one can say what's to come. By the end of the century, we might have flying machines filling the air just as we seem on the verge of having motor cars running everywhere along the ground. I did see a story in the newspapers not so long ago about two brothers getting their flying machine off the ground for a few seconds someplace in America."

"But that's not going to the moon. Do you think that someday they'll be able to shoot a rocket out of a cannon like they do in the moving pictures?" Jonathan asked.

"I think I can pretty well guarantee that won't be the way we'll get to the moon."

"What about moving pictures?" Joy looked to Watson, her eyes widened, "Do you think they'll make any more moving pictures, or will this be the only one?"

Watson's face creased in thought before he answered Joy. "I think they will. I know there's lots of folk who think moving pictures will fade away, but I don't agree. You could see how big the crowd was at the music hall, and how much they enjoyed the moving pictures. I think as long as they keep perfecting them, they'll be here to stay. I won't be surprised if, in time, moving pictures halls come to replace music halls."

Olivia's eyes widened at Watson's prediction. "You can't mean it. How can moving pictures replace singing, or dancing, or juggling, or people being funny?"

Whatever rejoinder Watson planned was cast aside with the arrival of tea and refreshments. After first testing a naked raisin scone she pronounced acceptable, Mrs. Hudson fitted it with clotted cream. She felt the addition did little for the scone unless one was a particular fan of clotted cream which she was not. Watson diplomatically agreed with Mrs. Hudson, reporting the Palm Court's rendition acceptable but nothing more, although he appeared to deflate his argument somewhat by reaching for a second scone, justifying his seeming act of disloyalty by claiming a wish to try the orange marmalade. Joy and Jonathan expressed delight with their choices while speeding their way through them. Olivia smiled satisfaction with the strawberry tart which she savored with small well-spaced bites.

When Olivia was done, and while Joy and Jonathan shared the remaining two scones, Mrs. Hudson nodded to Watson and suggested he might proceed "in light of the time." Whether with children or adults, Mrs. Hudson was certain the intrigue she had devised would enjoy greater acceptance if presented by a man.

Watson's face and tone turned suddenly as serious as his words as he focused his attention on the three youngsters. "We need the help of all of you to capture the man who killed your father. I am asking you to follow a plan created by Mr. Sherlock Holmes, whom you all know to be a great detective—indeed, whom all the world knows to be a great detective." Watson hunched slightly forward to make clear the confidentiality of what he would say next. Everything

161

I tell you from here on must remain a secret between us, and only us, and, of course, Mr. Holmes. There are some things not even your mother can know. And you must understand there can be some danger, although I'm certain all of you can be kept safe. Any questions to here?"

"Will this help Benjamin?" Olivia looked earnestly to Watson. "More than what happened with the bank?" she added, speaking more diplomatically than she felt.

"The wisest detective I know believes the incident at the bank has gotten us closer to finding the murderer. And that same person believes this next action will finish the job and make certain the innocent go free and the guilty are punished."

"Then, I promise to do whatever has to be done." With that, Olivia stretched a hand across the table.

Joy and Jonathan had allied themselves with the cause at the words "there can be some danger," exactly as Mrs. Hudson said they would, and now stretched their hands to meet their sister's. Watson and Mrs. Hudson joined their hands to those of the Stockton children and diners at neighboring tables wondered at the agreement struck between two older adults, an adolescent girl and two children. However, strain as they might to listen for clues as to the nature of the strange bargain, the conversation was too soft to be heard other than the occasional question from one or another youngster. Thus, nearby heads turned after, "Do you think he'll bring a gun?" and later, "Shouldn't we call Scotland Yard?" but turned back, their quest unfulfilled, after being frustrated by the shushing that came from all sides following each of those questions. When the man had finished, the children spoke briefly but very earnestly to the two adults who nodded approval of what they were hearing.

When all questions had been asked and answered, Watson and Mrs. Hudson took the children back to the Stockton farm. They waited while hugs were exchanged between Penelope and her children. Joy and Jonathan then entered into a spirited competition to provide their mother something well in excess of a brief synopsis of the day's activities. Recognizing that Watson and Mrs. Hudson had made no move to leave, Penelope told her children she wanted to hear all they had to tell her, but for now she needed to speak with Dr. Watson and Mrs. Hudson. As the children disappeared into the house, Penelope invited Watson and Mrs. Hudson to join her in her parlor. Once seated, they rejected her offer of tea with thanks, explaining they could not stay long.

"Let me say first," Watson began, "we had a perfectly delightful time. Joy and Jonathan were well behaved throughout, Olivia was quite the young lady, and we thoroughly enjoyed our time with your children." He turned to Mrs. Hudson for corroboration.

"I quite agree with Dr. Watson. It was a very pleasant afternoon."

Penelope beamed. Watson judged this was the right moment to share the next part of their intrigue.

"As you know, Mrs. Stockton, we remain deeply concerned with finding your husband's murderer, not only to punish the man responsible for that dreadful crime, but to protect whoever may still be at risk. To accomplish that, we will need your cooperation and assistance in some few areas that I trust will not provide too great a strain on you or your household."

"What is it you propose, Dr. Watson?"

Hearing the hesitancy in her voice and seeing the sudden stiffness in her posture, Watson felt it wise to cite the person who, however inaccurately, would be seen as the ultimate authority for the actions he was proposing. "Let me emphasize that there has developed a need to move swiftly, and it is in that context liberties were taken without proper discussion. I apologize for that, but I assure you it was only done to better enable us to capture your husband's murderer and as a part of the master plan devised by Mr. Sherlock Holmes." Penelope gave an intense, knowing nod; Mrs. Hudson gave a nod that was less intense but more knowing.

"It's my understanding from Holmes that your father-in-law occupies the bedroom to the left of the stairs facing front." Watson received a cautious nod. "And that it's the only bedroom left of the stairs, making it quite private." A second still more cautious nod.

"Very good. In accord with his plan, Holmes wishes to arrive at the farm with me at midnight tonight to prepare for the following morning when he will reveal the identity of your husband's murderer. We will require your father-in-law's bedroom to act as a sort of staging area for the morning's activity which is to say we will need to move Mr. Stockton to another bedroom. I recognize that Mr.

Stockton will not be pleased and will resist being moved. I intend to explain to him that this small inconvenience is in the interest of capturing his son's murderer and I have every confidence that he will then prove to be quite cooperative.

"Toward that same end, Mrs. Stockton, Mr. Holmes has, himself, sent telegrams to your brother, as well as to Mr. Thompkins, and Mr. Olyphant requesting their presence here tomorrow morning at eleven. Lady Dickson has also been invited in accord with her wish to be here when the murderer is revealed. The Fiddlemans will, of course, already be here. Until that time, Mr. Holmes asks you to say nothing of his and my presence here or of your father-in-law's changed sleeping arrangements. Everything is to remain secret until Mr. Holmes is ready to act. The single exceptions are your children. With all the moving around there will be, Mrs. Hudson and I thought it prudent to share with them the plans for tonight while we were out together. Indeed, Olivia was so set on playing some part in all this—in light of her feelings for young Benjamin—that we agreed to allow her be the one to let Holmes and myself in when we arrive at your door at midnight."

Penelope, initially shaken by Watson's matter of fact description of the disruption to her home and routine, was now further taken aback to learn that the plan described had already been discussed with her children. "Don't you think it would have been appropriate to speak to me before talking to the children?"

"It would indeed, Mrs. Stockton," began Mrs. Hudson, looking a great deal more shame-faced than she felt, "and I apologize for it but knowin' as I do Miss Olivia's feelin's for Benjamin, it just seemed a kindness to let 'er know that there were things bein' done that offered some 'ope and, of course, it got said in front of the little ones as well."

Mrs. Stockton huffed her way to an acceptance of Mrs. Hudson's apology. "I suppose there's no real harm done, and I agree with you about Olivia—poor thing. I will say she seems to have some of her color back after her outing."

Watson acted to take advantage of the renewed good fellowship. Perhaps now would be a good time to move Mr. Stockton. If you'll just tell me in which bedroom you think he'd be most comfortable."

When the logistics were worked out, Watson went upstairs to confront Stockton who was predictably unsympathetic to the idea of moving. Much as Watson predicted, when he pointed out that his noncooperation would obstruct efforts to identify the person who murdered his son, and that his obstruction would quickly become common knowledge, Stockton became grudgingly agreeable to be moved.

Meanwhile, downstairs, Mrs. Hudson found herself in the awkward position of offering sympathy to a woman whom, she thought, was very likely feeling herself well out of a difficult situation. Indeed, Penelope was in an equally awkward position, pretending a despondency she was not feeling. The conversation turned back to Mrs. Hudson reaffirming how delightful the day had been, how grown-up Olivia was, what fun and how challenging Joy and Jonathan were.

In as solicitous a manner as possible, Mrs. Hudson asked Penelope if she was alright with being alone in the house with the three children. Penelope admitted to having some concerns but explained that her husband had had a telephone installed for his own use but trained Penelope and Olivia in its use "just in case." Moreover, Penelope's brother, Percy, and Mr. Thompkins both had been given keys to the farmhouse some time ago, again "just in case." Mrs. Hudson guessed the earlier "just in case" involved protection from Roger Stockton's abusive behavior.

Both women were relieved to have Joy and Jonathan return to see their mother after finding themselves unable any longer to contain their excitement about the afternoon. This time Penelope made no effort to correct them, and the children were blithely carrying on as Watson came downstairs having gotten Avery Stockton settled in his new quarters. Penelope broke away from her children's excited tales of space travel and haute cuisine long enough to see her guests to the door. Before leaving, Watson once again sought assurance from Penelope that all was understood about his and Holmes's midnight visit and the need for secrecy surrounding the evening's activity.

He continued after getting the expected solemn nod. "There is just one other thing, but it is very important. You are to leave the light over the stairs burning all night. On no account should that lamp be turned down." Watson paused to receive the second solemn nod. Satisfied finally that all was in place, they let Penelope return to the moon while they went no farther than Baker Street.

Watson's presentation of the plot of *A Trip to the Moon* was better organized but less spirited than that of the Stockton children. His audience's reaction was a mix of astonishment and repulsion with astonishment largely fueling his repulsion. As Watson told of the attack on the scientists from Earth by the insect men on the moon, Holmes threw up his hands, announcing he'd heard enough and urged Watson to put off any further discussion. "If such nonsense is the best they can come up with for this new fad, I predict it will have a very short life, and deservedly so."

At that point Mrs. Hudson, who'd been observing the exchange, thought it wise to change the subject. "And Mr. 'Olmes, were you able to get done all that 'ad to be done?"

"I did, Mrs. Hudson. I sent the telegrams asking our suspects to meet with us tomorrow at eleven. There was, however, a small snag. Lestrade cannot be with us at the Stockton farm as we planned. Constable Chase will fill in for him and knows to get to the farm in the early morning. You'll remember Chase is our local police officer and as dependable a man as we could hope to find. Both Lestrade and I have been in contact with Chase, and I am confident he understands his responsibility."

Mrs. Hudson was, in fact, well acquainted with Constable Chase and was in strong agreement with Holmes about his dependability. Unsung among his other attributes was an often-expressed appreciation for Mrs. Hudson's baking.

"It seems to me we're about as well prepared as we could be for what's to come. We might do one more run through just to be safe, but that can wait 'til later. For now, I'll leave the two of you to occupy yourselves while I see to my kitchen."

Chapter 9. Springing the Trap

Sometime after eleven, Holmes and Watson boarded a coach fitted with lanterns on its either side and directed the coachman to take them on what they hoped would be their final trip to the Stockton farm. On learning his riders' destination, and after some discussion about nighttime travel and road conditions, the coachman demanded a crown more than his usual fare. That led to a short round of spirited haggling, ending finally with agreement on an additional three shillings six pence, and the coachman's promise to return to the Stockton farm at twelve noon the next day to return them to Baker Street. When they came to the last stretch of woods before the turn that would allow the carriage lamps to be seen from the Stockton farmhouse and the stables beyond, they had the coachman rein in his horse. The Fiddlemans, like all the other suspects, were to be kept unaware of the midnight visitors. Holmes and Watson climbed down, reminded the coachman of his promise for the following day, and sent him on his way.

As they left the woods and started on the carriage path, they took note that the farmhouse, as well as the Fiddlemans's apartments above the stables were dark. That was as wanted; less desirable were the clouds that hid the half moon, making the walk slow and somewhat treacherous. A horse's whinny sounded from the stables, and they waited a moment to see if it would be repeated or picked up by the other horses or, worse yet, lead to a lamp being lit by the Fiddlemans. The moment passed without incident, and they continued to the back door of the farmhouse where Holmes rapped lightly three times in quick succession.

It was the signal worked out at the Palm Court and led to the door being opened by a somber looking Olivia Stockton. As had not been worked out at the Palm Court, Olivia was accompanied by her younger brother and sister. Before the question could be asked, Olivia explained that the three of them had worked to keep each other awake and it seemed only right to let Joy and Jonathan come with her. She left out that there was also no way to get rid of them. Holmes nodded his understanding, if not agreement, put a finger to his lips

167

and asked the three of them to lead Watson and himself upstairs. By some small miracle, even Jonathan grasped the gravity of the situation and never uttered a word as he tiptoed to the front of the group before mounting the stairs a single step at a time as opposed to his usual two. At the top of the stairs they parted company, Holmes and Watson going to the single bedroom on the left and all the Stocktons going to their bedrooms on the right.

The light at the top of the stairs, left on as Watson had requested, allowed them to see their way clearly into the room before shutting the door and becoming reliant on what glow there was through their window from the partly obscured moon. They dared not risk a lamp that would alert any would-be intruder that the house was still partially awake. In the pale light of their room, they made out a bed and the rocking chair Holmes had taken in his meeting with Stockton.

Befitting the secrecy of their mission, Holmes spoke in a voice a little above a whisper. "Given your age, Watson, it would be well for you to take the bed while I curl up in the rocker."

"I am all of a year older than you, Holmes," Watson replied in a throaty undertone, "and quite fit as well you know. Nonetheless, I will take the bed as long as you are prepared to remain vigilant for whatever develops."

"Agreed."

"And, Holmes, I think we'd do well to run through the plan one more time."

"I swear, Watson, you get more like her with each passing day."

The woman Holmes referred to was peacefully asleep in her own bed. It would have surprised him to learn that she slept so soundly because she had near perfect confidence in his ability—after observing several practice sessions—to carry out his several tasks without the smallest misstep. It was something she would have to remember to tell him when all this was done.

The house again grew silent except for the low buzz of Holmes and Watson challenging each other with questions that might follow from the execution of Mrs. Hudson's plan. The quiet held for nearly an hour.

It was shattered suddenly by piteous screams coming from Jonathan's room. Penelope rushed to her son where she was soon joined by Olivia and Joy rubbing sleep from their eyes, while Avery Stockton loudly questioned whether something couldn't be done about the boy. Only Holmes and Watson neither appeared nor were heard from.

Penelope cradled her son in her arms while Joy and Olivia stood together at the door, their faces reflecting their brother's pained expression.

"Tell me what hurts, Jonathan."

In response to his mother's question, Jonathan tried to detail his complaints.

"I feel hot, mommy. And my belly hurts something awful. It feels like I could throw up." With a great moan, he suddenly seized up, bending well forward in response to the pain he was describing.

Penelope began to rock him gently in her arms, but Jonathan remained inconsolable.

Olivia felt obliged to offer her judgment of what should be done. "Mommy, if any of us are to get any sleep tonight, we need to call Dr. Montgomery."

The wisdom of Olivia's recommendation had to be acknowledged. Moreover, it came against a background of repeated calls of "what's happening ... what's being done about the boy," from Avery Stockton that served to increase Penelope's sense of urgency about taking some sort of action. Her statement of hating "to call the doctor at this unearthly hour" was met with fresh howls from Jonathan leading to a sudden resolve on her part to follow Olivia's suggestion. Hearing the call made and learning of the doctor's promise to come, Olivia and Joy went back to their beds, Olivia stopping for a moment to tell her grandfather of Dr. Montgomery's planned visit. He grunted his acknowledgment but did not seem pleased. Penelope alone sat up with Jonathan. The worst of his pain appeared to have subsided, and Jonathan was content to writhe quietly in his mother's arms waiting on the doctor's arrival.

Dr. Montgomery made no secret of his displeasure at having to leave the comfort of a feather bed visited far too infrequently of late due, in part, to reports of dysentery-like symptoms among

169

several of his patients. In truth, he doubted the Stockton boy was exhibiting dysentery, but his mother's description was sufficient to make it necessary for him to check it out. He put a supply of Johnson's Digestive Tablets in his bag to contend with his young patient's far more likely problem of dyspepsia.

On his arrival at the Stockton farm, he was led upstairs by Penelope, who had deserted Jonathan to wait by the door for Montgomery. Neither one spoke a word beyond the briefest greeting as Montgomery went straight to work. Somewhat shamefaced, Penelope reported that Jonathan seemed to be doing a little better, his improvement, in the wake of the doctor's nighttime journey, meriting an apology.

After a brief examination, Montgomery found his diagnosis confirmed. Given his patient's age, he cut one digestive tablet in half, and had Jonathan swallow it with the glass of water provided by Olivia, who had returned with a mumbled explanation of a need to help her mother. After first promising to sit up a while with Jonathan to gauge his response to the medicine, Montgomery shooed the two women from the room, urging them to get some sleep before he had another two patients on his hands. Penelope only agreed after he promised to spend the night, fearing, she said, that she would be the cause of his collapse if he did not get some rest himself. His room, she told him would be the first one on the right just off the stairs. The light above the stairs would, she told him, be left turned up. Montgomery thanked her and apologized for the difficulty he was creating but said he looked forward to seeing everyone in the morning. A room for the night was, in fact, no less than was customarily made available for late night visits, and he would have suggested it himself if Penelope hadn't made the invitation. He relaxed in the chair he had drawn up beside Jonathan and called a "good night" to Penelope and Olivia as they left, adding he might just look in on her father-in-law "as long as I'm here anyway." At the last, Penelope started to turn back until Olivia took her mother by the arm, shouting her own "good night, Doctor," as she gently steered her mother out the door.

Within the hour Jonathan was asleep, his problems, to all appearances, relieved by a half dose of Johnson's Digestive Tablets.

The rest of the Stockton family appeared to have followed suit as sounds of sleep were again all that could be heard. The whispered exchange from the room Holmes and Watson shared had long since ceased as well. As a hedge against the risk of falling asleep, Holmes had set the rocker to face the room's lone window in hope of capturing what light would be available from the partly obscured half-moon. To guard against being surprised by an intruder, he had taken the further step of placing the rocker in position to capture whatever change in light would be created from the lamp above the stairs with the opening of the room's door.

Indeed, it was not long before Holmes's careful positioning of the rocker was rewarded. A slender shaft of light fell across the bundle of blankets curled together on the chair, alerting the detective hidden beneath them. As the door was now noiselessly shut, the bundle of blankets came sufficiently to life to monitor the sounds of the intruder as he made his way slowly across the room. Floorboards creaked ever so slightly and, as Holmes held his own breath, the intruder's deep breaths told where he was getting to and confirmed the furtive nature of his mission—if it had ever been in doubt. There was no way to know if Watson was awake and aware of the danger, but Holmes doubted it given the hour and the comfort a real bed would provide. In any event he would have to act as if Watson would take no part in the action for which they had prepared themselves. Had there been light, their visitor might have wondered at the absence of Avery Stockton's invalid chair. As it was, he nearly tripped over the room's rocking chair and the bundle of blankets that was on it.

Holmes was near equally at a loss as he peered from inside his self-made shroud, but as the intruder moved around Holmes he came between the detective and the curtainless window and his movements became a great deal easier to trace. The man—and Holmes could see it was a man—moved from out of the room's shadows to be silhouetted against the window. He was at the bed now and still there was no movement, no sound from where Watson lay. The intruder's one hand was raised high over Watson while he cast off his covers with the other hand. Holmes was out of his chair in an instant, sending the rocker rattling across the room, and shouting his colleague's name for all he was worth. The clatter and Holmes's voice broke the intruder's concentration for the moment. The moment was all it took for Holmes to throw himself onto the man's body sending him sprawling across the bottom of the bed and the object that was in his raised hand to go sliding along the floor.

Watson, now wide awake and surveying the scene at the foot of his bed, saw that Holmes had gained control over his would-be assailant and was tying his hands with a piece of rope he had brought in anticipation of just such a need. He spoke to his colleague in a deeply apologetic tone. "I'm sorry, Holmes. I am profoundly sorry. I must have fallen asleep for a while. You seem to have things well in hand regardless. Does this mean we've got our man?"

Before Holmes could respond, they were joined by Penelope Stockton and her three children whose looks of confusion were superimposed on the fatigue they all felt having been wakened from sound sleep. As Penelope lit the bedroom lamp, a chorus of voices sought clarification of the scene now suddenly illuminated.

"What is all this, Mr. Holmes? What's going on?" Joy alone asked the question that was essential to achieving that clarification. "What's Dr. Montgomery doing here?"

Holmes did not answer immediately, instead asking Watson to help Avery Stockton into his chair and have him join them. Watson did so after first picking up the object that was in Montgomery's hand with which he was about to assault him.

When all were assembled, and Dr. Montgomery had been placed in the rocking chair with Holmes at his front and Watson at his back, Holmes began to clarify for the Stocktons what they had witnessed.

"First, let me reintroduce Dr. Montgomery. You know him as the good-natured country doctor on whom you can rely for care. In his other life he is a murderer, although not the cold-blooded killer one reads of in the sensational fiction so widely available." Holmes looked to Watson, whose grimace told Holmes to get on with it.

"Dr. Montgomery does not murder for gain or out of rage or passion but to right the wrongs he sees as having been done by others, and perhaps to make up for his own contribution to those wrongs." Holmes looked to an audience as fully attentive to his words as he expected them to be. Penelope, seeing that Joy and Jonathan were part of his rapt audience, asked Olivia to remove them from the corner of the bed to which they appeared to have become attached, promising them biscuits when they left. It seemed a poor recompense for missing out on a story of murder by their family doctor, but they left peaceably regardless. Her children dismissed, Penelope again gave Holmes her full attention. Stockton listened warily as if he, like Montgomery, was hearing a story whose ending he already knew.

"I don't understand, Mr. Holmes. What 'wrongs' are you talking about?" Penelope asked.

Holmes turned to a sullen looking Montgomery. "Perhaps you would like to answer Mrs. Stockton's question, Doctor?" Holmes paused but no words broke the silence he'd created.

"I thought not. Then let me explain." Had the lamp Penelope had lit been a spotlight, it could not have been used to greater effect by Holmes. Moving artfully from light to shadows, he described the actions and motivation of the silent physician.

"You see, Dr. Montgomery was involved in an activity more than forty years ago that hasn't given him a moment's peace since. He was a young doctor just starting his practice and he was called upon to fulfill a request he knew to be wrong but believed he could not refuse. Mrs. Stockton, Mrs. Candace Stockton, was about to give birth. To twin boys as it turned out. Not identical twins, fraternal twins who wouldn't necessarily look alike as they got older. And that was important for what was to come.

"The first child required a forceps delivery. That can be tricky for any doctor, and maybe especially for a new doctor whose patient is the wife of a very important man, a man who made no secret of the pride he took in his family's farm or of his concern about the inheritance of that farm by his oldest son. But the first child born— the oldest son—was born with severe bruising around his head that the doctor knew would translate to later impairment, the extent of which could not be known at the time. The second child was perfect, and it appeared a simple matter to say the second child was, in fact, the first born. Indeed, within the small circle of the doctor and the people at the Stockton farm it was a simple matter to deny there was any other child. There was only one problem—other than the moral dilemma, of course. Avery Stockton could not deny his wife what was virtually her dying wish. She wanted to give her sons Biblical names, more than that, she wanted to follow the alphabet and give the boys Biblical names in accord with their birth order. And so, Aaron became a child of the forest while Balthasar became lord of the manor when he came of age. All of that became clear after a trip to the registry office and the discovery of Roger Stockton's true given name." Holmes managed a cold smile for Montgomery, "Have I left anything out, Doctor?"

Holmes's question was answered by a man suddenly freed to tell the story he had had to keep to himself for more than forty years.

"You seem to have captured the major points, Mr. Holmes. However, as I'm sure you know, I was not alone in falsifying records. I take responsibility for my actions, but the truth is I was directed to do so and threatened that if I didn't, my career 'would be over before it started.' I believe those were the words you used, Avery. Of course, I tried to convince myself that it was alright. In fact, Aaron was likely to be so compromised he wouldn't be able to assume responsibility for running a farm and I was promised he'd be well looked after. It was what I wanted to believe and is no justification for my conniving with others to do him out of his birthright—a decision that has haunted me through all these years.

"I could never take the satisfaction others did from their practice. If I saved a life—and I saved many—I was plagued by thoughts of the life I'd bartered away. I never married, I never had really close friends because of the terrible secret I would have to share with them if I allowed that level of intimacy."

"All of that was so terribly long ago," Penelope's contorted features reflected the bewilderment she felt. "Why now, why seek your revenge now and why Roger? The choice to inherit was made for him by others just as it was made for Aaron. And if you believed a great wrong was done, why a killing to right that wrong? Why not bring it to the attention of the authorities?"

"The choice was made for Roger and he reveled in it. He lived a life he knew he had no right to and never said a word. Neither he nor Avery ever met with Aaron or did anything more for him than to send money to strangers to keep him out of their lives." At the last, Stockton decided he had heard enough.

"You weren't dragged kicking and screaming into our ... arrangement. You jumped right in and became good old Doc Montgomery, always doing for everybody. Yes, and leading a comfortable life while you were doing for everybody." Avery Stockton's voice rose gradually as he spoke, and at the last threatened to wake the Fiddlemans in their rooms over the stables.

Montgomery's voice was softer and reflected the discussions he'd had with himself many times over the years. "I was weak, and I admit that. I wanted a career. Lord help me, I wanted time to minister to people's problems and I made a devil's bargain. But you, Stockton, you acted out of greed. You traded a man's life simply for the potential of maintaining a piece of property." At the last, Montgomery's voice became suddenly plaintive. "Aaron was your son. You were supposed to take care of him. Not farm him out to a convenient keeper."

Montgomery collected himself and with a shrug of dismissal for Stockton, he turned back to Penelope. "You ask why now, why so many years later, and why not go to the authorities. Those are fair questions. First, as to the authorities. I thought about it, of course, but I realized it would never work. It's not just that it would be my word against theirs. It was the records at the registry office, or rather the records that weren't at the registry office. There's nothing to indicate there is or ever was an Aaron Stockton. There's nothing to show there was a baby boy other than Balthasar. In short, Aaron doesn't exist. Still, I suppose I could have taken the case to the authorities, argued with them that in spite of my signature on the one birth record, in spite of Stockton's claim about one child being born and the Fiddlemans backing him up, that, in fact, another son existed and was being cheated out of his inheritance. Reality is we would be years in the courts and when it was done, we would most likely lose.

"But you should know that Roger Stockton wasn't my primary target. It was, of course, Avery Stockton as you came to figure out, Avery. That's why you had Penelope come upstairs with me whenever I came to see you, and that's why you keep a shotgun by your bed. You would never let me see you alone, much less unprotected. Not that I regret ridding the world of Roger. He was a bully and a wife beater. I saw the marks on your sister, Priscilla, and on you as well, Penelope, but neither of you was willing to report him lest you suffer more violence. And he was prepared to stand in the way of Olivia's happiness to satisfy his own selfish concerns. There was even his willingness to consider a scheme to get rid of

175

much of the woods for the money its lumber would bring, in spite of the fact that such action would likely destroy his brother's makeshift home. He happily joined in the denial of his own brother's existence and took full advantage of the opportunity that denial provided. In short, while no one else may choose to say it, I can tell you that Roger will not long be missed, and several people will be happier for his being gone.

"As to why I have acted now, I believe Dr. Watson can address that."

Watson minced no words. "Dr. Montgomery is a dying man. He has cancer and, if I'm not mistaken, is in the late stage of that disease. I must admit I was slow to the diagnosis, thinking his fatigue, lack of color and apparent loss of weight were the consequence of the frenetic pace of the country doctor, but learning of his correspondence with a leading cancer specialist gave all those symptoms a different and more tragic interpretation.

"But I fear you have not told the whole story," Watson raised the object that had been knocked from Montgomery's hand during his tussle with Holmes. "In the dark you mistook me for Stockton, whom you'd visited in this room many times, and you were about to inject him—in this case, me—with whatever is in this syringe that was knocked from your hands. I intend to have the contents of the syringe analyzed but feel quite certain it contains enough morphine to have its intended victim dead by morning. Stockton would be seen as having died of natural causes which is how the death certificate would read as filled out by the attending physician who is also the local coroner. Tell me, Doctor, were the Fiddlemans next on your list? Is that why they have been packing to leave?"

"I think I've already said enough, but I congratulate you, Doctor and you, Mr. Holmes, on your extraordinary deductive skills. But tell me, how did you first get on to me?"

"There were two things right at the start," Holmes replied. "There were first the tracks from your buggy. The tracks of different vehicles are really quite distinctive you know and the spacing of wheels and extent of indentation only fit a buggy, your buggy as opposed to Mrs. Stockton's which was also at the crime scene and could be seen, like yours, to have stopped and started again, but hers showed evidence of making a revolution—making a complete turn to go back to the farmhouse. Yours showed evidence of stopping and starting again—without turning. That was because you had come to the edge of the woods after a late-night visit to your scarlet fever patient and a nap at your patient's home until early morning as is the custom with such visits. You found Roger Stockton on his constitutional as you knew you would, and your two shots were lost in the noise of hunters in the woods. You took care of your business and continued on your way.

"The second thing that pointed to you was the state of the murder victim as reported by my colleague, Dr. Watson. To make certain of his death, he was turned over and shot through the very center of the heart as determined by the doctor. Assuming it was not a lucky guess, it would take someone schooled in anatomy to make such an exacting shot. Still, it was not a great deal to go on, and to make certain of our suspicions, we first had to eliminate from consideration each of Roger Stockton's more obvious enemies before setting our little trap for you.

"Which reminds me," Holmes looked to Penelope and Olivia, who had rejoined them, "I must congratulate you both on your playacting. I'm a man who enjoys a good performance and you both, and the two youngsters, performed marvelously. I will, of course, let the two of them know how well I think they did."

Tactfully, Holmes ignored the fact that Penelope had never been informed of the part Jonathan played in pretending to be sick, or that his supporting cast, having been informed, encouraged the call to Dr. Montgomery essential to solving Roger Stockton's murder. It had been Mrs. Hudson's firm belief that no mother could be convincing about a child's illness unless she believed that child to be truly ill.

"Now, I believe it is time for bed. This has been most interesting, but we will have a full day tomorrow. I believe everyone is due at eleven. Watson, I think we can free Dr. Montgomery's hands, but please take possession of the doctor's bag lest he have access to anything that would keep him from meeting with Inspector Lestrade. Also, Mrs. Stockton, I'll need a key to the room to lock Dr. Montgomery in for the night."

"I assure you, Mr. Holmes, I won't be going anywhere, and I do need my sleep."

"Regardless of what he says, I, for one, will sleep better knowing Montgomery is locked in," Avery Stockton announced.

The key was found, and Montgomery was locked in the room for reasons other than to ensure Avery Stockton's sleep.

As it turned out, everyone slept fitfully except Montgomery, whose sound sleep was only interrupted by the early morning arrival of Constable Chase. Chase informed a bewildered Mrs. Fiddleman that he had come to take the prisoner to the Bow Street Station. Holmes, being a light sleeper, was wakened by the commotion at the door, wrapped himself in his mauve dressing gown and joined the two of them where he did what he could to clarify the situation, and speed Montgomery on his way. Holmes directed Chase to leave word for Lestrade that he would be in contact with him later in the day to explain everything, but for the present to keep Montgomery under lock and key.

By eleven, Percy Dickson, his mother, Lady Dickson, Alfred Thompkins, Daniel Olyphant, and Penelope, Olivia, Joy and Jonathan Stockton were all gathered around the Stockton dinner table most with cups of tea provided by Mrs. Fiddleman. Holmes took a position at the head of the table with Watson seated close by, armed as always at such times, with his accounts book and Number 2 Eagle pencil. The group was joined finally by Avery Stockton complaining bitterly about his treatment at the hands of the several men who carefully, if not lovingly, carried him downstairs.

Stockton was settled at the foot of the table causing Lady Dickson and the other invitees to take seats as near as possible to the head of the table. Penelope and her three children took seats that set them as a buffer between Stockton and the guests while the Fiddlemans, after a futile search for seats remote from those they regarded as their betters, took chairs finally at the foot of the table at as much of a respectful distance as they could manage from Stockton and after bowing their heads apologetically in his direction.

Having made certain that everyone had been properly introduced, Holmes explained that because all of them, with the exception of Lady Dickson, had been questioned at length, and most had been seen as suspects in Roger Stockton's murder, he felt obliged to share with them the results of the investigation. In fact, all those

178

in attendance had by now learned of Holmes's late-night activity and the resulting arrest and detention of Montgomery. They, nonetheless, appeared to hang on every word of Holmes' retelling of first the discovery of Aaron's history and hereditary rights, and then the trap laid for Montgomery and the near demise of Watson in the process of capturing and detaining Montgomery. When he was done, he paused more to allow his audience to catch its breath than for any such need on his part.

"I believe," Holmes began after a suitable pause, "there are two people with us for whom much of what I've said comes as no surprise. Isn't that so, Mr. and Mrs. Fiddleman?"

Heads turned and all eyes came to focus on the Stockton's servants.

"I'm sure I don't know what it is you're thinking, Mr. Holmes," Fiddleman said, "but if you're suggesting me or Mrs. Fiddleman has got anything to do with the killing of Mr. Roger, you are one hundred percent wrong."

"That is true, Mr. Fiddleman, but it's not enough. You and Mrs. Fiddleman chose to collaborate with Mr. Stockton in keeping secret Aaron's existence for which you were no doubt handsomely paid. But with Roger Stockton's death, there was suddenly real danger associated with that collaboration. That's why you had your bags packed and were ready to leave even if it meant denying yourselves a bequest from Roger Stockton's will."

Once again silence descended on the group. All eyes turned back to Holmes, waiting his next revelation. Instead, there was a question raised in the high-pitched voice of a twelve-year-old.

"Will they hang Dr. Montgomery?"

The questioner's earnest expression caused Holmes to battle back a smile with only modest success.

"Dr. Montgomery is very sick and, according to our own excellent Dr. Watson, may not survive long enough to be tried in court. I dare say his punishment will come in his being reviled by all those who previously held him in high regard, and the realization that his place in the collective memory will be that of a murderer rather than the healer he sought to be."

"How about the others? How about the Fiddlemans or grandfather? They're not sick. Can any of them be hanged?" Jonathan was not to be denied the possibility of the ending he saw as appropriate to Holmes's narrative.

With Jonathan's second question, Holmes was unable to suppress an indulgent smile, while the subjects of Jonathan's call to justice cringed in their places at the end of the table.

"I'm afraid there will be no hangings, Jonathan. The punishment has to fit the crime and hanging might be seen as excessive. For now, we might explore what we can do to make up for at least some of the harm that's been done to Aaron."

"How would we do that? How can we possibly undo all the hurt that's been caused?" Percy Dickson asked.

"If I might speak as someone who is not part of the family, but who thinks a great deal of the family." Thompkins paused, then looked around the table to see if, indeed, anyone took exception to his speaking.

Stockton did. "We all know who in the family you think about but you're not a member of the family yet and you never will be if I have anything to say about it."

"Well, of course, you've nothing to say about it, you silly man." The new voice was forceful, angry, female, and wholly familiar to Holmes and Watson. "You and your son have done all you could to ruin the lives of my girls, but your interfering days are over. You committed a crime and directed others to … is the word 'abet', Mr. Holmes?" There followed a long and solemn nod in reply. "To abet your action. It's only my daughter's soft heart and a change in your behavior that will keep you out of prison. And it would be well for you to remember, I don't have one—a soft heart that is." Lady Dickson stared down her dumbfounded, if not contrite adversary, then continued after making a suitable change in the timbre of her voice, "Now, what is it you were about to say Mr. Thompkins?"

Thompkins looked to Lady Dickson every bit as awestruck as Stockton, if with far less cause for alarm. Thompkins's open-mouthed astonishment was, in fact, the familiar expression shown by those meeting Lady Dickson for the first time. He collected himself finally and taking note of her supportive smile, he nodded his appreciation and resumed the talk he had earlier begun.

"I just wanted to say that we can't make up for all the wrongs that have been done to Aaron—certainly, not all at once—but we can pick and choose things that can get us started. As some of you may know, I've been made interim head of the Wilberforce Bank and Trust, and I'm certain that, in my new position, I can work with the bank's lawyers to draw up guardianship papers for Mrs. Stockton or Mr. Dickson—or the bank if you prefer—to make certain someone who cares about his interests is available to Aaron."

"Thank you, Mr. Thompkins, that's a most constructive suggestion. Is there something you can do, Penelope?" Penelope had neither the will nor the capacity to refuse her mother.

"We can … we will move him from the woods to his own room in the house."

"Aaron can sleep in my room," Jonathan happily volunteered.

"Aaron will sleep in his own room." Penelope's statement led to a pained expression on the part of Jonathan and a small smile from Joy.

"That still leaves the farm to manage. You gonna give that to him as well." The challenge to the group came from its acknowledged outsider.

"Much as I hate to admit it, Stockton's got a point," Olyphant spoke to an issue about which he felt he knew a good deal. "Managing a farm is more than just milking cows and feeding chickens. I'd be happy to help out, neighbor to neighbor, just until you get the hang of it. And with my Benjamin getting back to home, I suspect he may want to spend some of his time at your farm— maybe more than 'some'." He stole a mischievous glance to Olivia, and she countered with a broad smile. "Benjamin's learned a lot about farming—having had an excellent teacher—and I've no question he can be a help."

"You watch him. What he wants is our farm," Stockton called to no one in particular. Nonetheless, he roused the concern of one person.

"Grandpa promised the farm to me. Do I still get the farm? Can I keep the horses?" Jonathan did not find the laughter that followed his questions reassuring. He was, however, comforted by Olyphant's words.

"There will be nothing and nobody to keep you from getting the farm, Jonathan. You're too good a neighbor for me to let anything come between us."

Having organized things at the Stockton farm to her satisfaction, Lady Dickson was prepared to move to a new field of battle. "Then, that's all settled, Mr. Holmes. I believe we should be off to see your housekeeper about a certain recipe I believe I'm owed."

Holmes was not prepared to cede control of the meeting to Lady Dickson. "Not quite all settled, Lady Dickson. May I assume, Mrs. Stockton, that your father will continue to be staying with you?"

"Continue to be staying with her! It's my bloody farm. I'll let her stay with me if there's any letting to be done."

Holmes ignored Stockton's outburst as did everyone else. "Are you of a mind to stay, Penelope? I dare say you and the children could be accommodated elsewhere."

"We've come to know each other, Mr. Holmes. I think it best we all stay together."

"And what of the Fiddlemans?" Watson turned to look to the couple. "Are you still planning to join your cousin in Yorkshire?"

"As soon as we can, Doctor, although we may just stay to hear Mr. Stockton's will—as long as we've been held up this long."

There was an audible groan from Watson, wordlessly expressing sentiments that were widely shared.

"And now, I think we're ready to leave for Baker Street, Lady Dickson."

"Fine, I'll just get my things."

As people prepared to leave, they were stopped for the moment by comments from the youngest people at the meeting. "We can't be done yet. It's not right." Joy and Jonathan had been conspiring together and they now posed a question to their mother. "Can we get Aaron and bring him home?"

For answer, Penelope hugged her children tight.

Chapter 10. Three for Sussex

Mrs. Hudson was well pleased with the progress Holmes was showing and was now convinced that he could, in fact, be given large responsibility for the conduct of investigations. There had, however, developed one serious impediment to her implementing that plan. Mr. Holmes had suddenly evidenced an inexplicable fascination with bees and had even mentioned to her the possibility of devoting his future life and energies to working with those insects. It would be a subject for later discussion, probably prolonged discussion. For now, Mrs. Hudson had business to conduct with Lady Dickson. In preparation for their encounter, the table was laid with the good china, her mother's silver, and with cloth napkins recently purchased at Debenhams.

When her colleagues arrived with her guest, Watson hung back far enough to give her a broad wink signaling the success of their mission, a conclusion she had already reached from observing Holmes's uncommonly cheery disposition. After exchanging greetings with Lady Dickson, she, nonetheless, asked the question expected of her, if only for the sake of appearances.

"Did things go well, Mr. 'Olmes?"

"I'd say better than well, Mrs. Hudson. I can confidently say that our murderer is safely locked up and that things, in general, are much improved in the Stockton world."

Mrs. Hudson gave a nod of satisfaction for the success of her plan which Holmes took as a congratulatory nod for himself, accepting her unspoken applause with a broad smile.

After a brief and uncomfortable silence, Watson spoke to what he knew to be Mrs. Hudson's wishes. "I believe you two have some things you want to discuss. Holmes and I have some things we need to get to as well." With that, he shepherded his bemused colleague to the stairs.

Holmes was not, however, to be denied some reward for his labors. "As soon as you can, Mrs. Hudson, tea and some of your delightful scones."

The look Holmes got from Mrs. Hudson suggested the wisdom of his employing a food taster before biting into one of her "delightful scones."

"Lady Dickson, might I invite you to join me for tea and scones. They're fresh baked and the raisin filled that I believe you're partial to."

Any misgivings Lady Dickson might have had about sitting at table with the woman she regarded as Holmes's housekeeper, melted away at the memory stirred of her baking and its ties to Lady Dickson's purpose in returning to Baker Street.

"That would be lovely, Mrs. Hudson."

After pouring tea for them both and placing the plate of scones strategically near to her guest, Mrs. Hudson reviewed issues of Lady Dickson's health, the health and well-being of her children and grandchildren, and her satisfaction with the events of the last couple of days. After receiving the expected positive responses to all her queries, Mrs. Hudson spoke to her objective in gaining Lady Dickson's return to Baker Street.

"I wonder, Lady Dickson, if it's still your plan to see your family in 'Alifax, Canada?"

"It is, and it will be more than just to see them. I hope to live there if I can arrange something for Evermore, my estate in Sussex."

"Well now, it's exactly that I'd like to talk about."

Lady Dickson was sufficiently nonplussed that she rattled the teacup she was about to put to her lips back down on its saucer. "Mrs. Hudson, don't tell me you are interested in acquiring an estate?"

Mrs. Hudson smiled at the prospect. "No, Lady Dickson, it's not for me. I 'ave in mind some young friends. You are per'aps familiar with the Buffalo Bill Wild West Show?" Lady Dickson answered the question with a cautious nod.

"There's two lovely young people from America who will be leavin' the show and will be wantin' a place in England where they can raise 'orses. The young man 'as been a trick rider with the show and the young woman trains 'orses. I was thinkin' they could lease the estate from you for their 'orse farm. I know them to be 'ard-workin' and I'm sure they'll take the best care of everythin'. I know Mr. 'Olmes and Dr. Watson will vouch for their character."

Lady Dickson did not commit herself but looked thoughtful which Mrs. Hudson took as a good sign. "Tell me, are they already married and why are they leaving the Wild West Show?"

"They're plannin' on gettin' married just as soon as they 'ave a place to live. I can tell you they're very anxious to get married." Lady Dickson gave a pensive nod.

"About why they're leavin' the Wild West Show it's not because of any bad feelin' between them and Colonel Cody. I can tell you they leave on the best of terms with Colonel Cody which I know 'e would say 'imself if 'e was 'ere with us. It's just as I say they're ready to settle down and to use their know 'ow about 'orses to raise some of the finest animals in England." Remembering Joy's correction, she added, "some of the finest 'orses in England." There was again the pensive nod.

Mrs. Hudson took a deep breath and continued. "There is somethin' more you should know. Like I say, they're from America and one of the reasons they want to live in England is to escape the bad feelin' and real danger they'd find if they got married in America. You see, the young man is an Indian and the young woman is not. They want to be together somewhere where people won't attack them for bein' what they are."

Lady Dickson did not meet Mrs. Hudson's revelation with another pensive nod. There was instead a look of grim determination. "Well, if they believe that England can do the right thing where America can't, we have a responsibility to prove them right." Lady Dickson straightened in her chair preparatory to making her declaration. "I'll do it. I'll sign a lease with your friends allowing them to live in the carriage house and take their meals in the manse on two conditions."

Lady Dickson paused for dramatic effect. "They are to marry before going to Evermore, and I must have the recipe for your scones."

Mrs. Hudson paused but it was not for dramatic effect. The request, that was not a request, demanded a respectful moment of consideration. The first part was easy. She was certain Sudden Thunder and Jane Morrison wanted to marry at the earliest opportunity and the availability of Lady Dickson's estate provided that opportunity. Making available her recipe for scones demanded a respectful moment of study. In the end, there was, of course, no real choice. She had long since committed herself to do everything she could to support the marriage of Sudden Thunder and Jane Morrison, although she had never anticipated her recipe would be part of that everything. And still she had the consolation that the woman was going to Canada, and while some portion of that country might have access to her baking secrets, the risk of her recipe achieving widespread circulation seemed remote.

For Lady Dickson, beyond access to the best scones she'd ever tasted, she would enjoy not only the income her tenants would generate, but also a rationale for keeping Betts and her housekeeper/ cook employed as well as the considerable satisfaction of startling her neighbors from a distance of more than three thousand miles.

The bargain struck, Lady Dickson assumed responsibility for scheduling the lease signing and Mrs. Hudson assumed responsibility for scheduling the wedding. At her request, Lady Dickson was given an address for Jane Morrison and was promised an invitation to the wedding.

In truth, there was little for Mrs. Hudson to do. She renewed contact with Mr. Carruthers, the superintendent registrar, whom she correctly assumed would not have forgotten her, and through him reserved a room for the day and time of the wedding that met the wishes of the affianced couple. She informed Penelope and Lady Dickson of the schedule, then of the plans for the wedding as requested by Sudden Thunder and Jane Morrison. Penelope was delighted with the parts her family was to play. Mrs. Hudson was pleasantly surprised to learn the part she was to play.

The day of the wedding was bright and clear with just enough of a nip in the air to make certain everyone was aware that fall had come. The Baker Street trio arrived well before the scheduled ceremony since one of them had a part to play in the wedding. When she joined the other participants and found them being put through their paces, Mrs. Hudson was only mildly surprised to find Lady Dickson the field marshal for the operation. She made certain each person in the wedding party was clear as to when to appear, how to walk, where to stand, and how to act. She spent by far the most time with Joy and Jonathan who did, in fact, make up nearly half the wedding party. When the call came for the ceremony to begin, she put on a brave smile, pronounced her students ready, then lined them up in the order of their scheduled appearance. In a room that might have held fifty people there were less than twenty well-wishers, all of them jockeying for positions along the aisles of the several rows. Nor was attention paid to the custom of the bride's friends on the left and the groom's friends on the right for the very good reason that the bride's friends were the groom's friends. The only exceptions were Holmes and Watson who, together with Percy Stockton, filling in for his sister who was once again in mourning, were the only ones among the assembled unknown to either the bride or the groom. While it was true that Sudden Thunder had allied himself with Holmes long enough to rescue Mrs. Hudson from a fiery end in the settlers cabin, their bonding at the time consisted of a nod of appreciation by Holmes and a grunt of acknowledgment by Sudden Thunder, neither action seen as heralding a lasting friendship.

Moreover, the Sudden Thunder Holmes now saw was a far cry from the Sudden Thunder who was a part of their shared heroics. The man who had entered from a side entrance stood alone on the left hand of Carruthers, having declared himself without need of a better man. He wore a top hat, frock coat and striped trousers, and had two long braids overlaying the front of his coat, while moccasins could be spied beneath the trousers. Mrs. Hudson reasoned that Sudden Thunder was still working out how English he intended to be. Carruthers, meanwhile, did his best to pretend an interest in the papers on the lectern before him but kept stealing glances at the groom, then at the audience, half of whom, he thought, should be chasing after the other half if the posters around town were to be believed. He felt certain of only one thing; this would be a wedding unlike any he had ever performed.

And then it was time for the matron of honor to walk down the aisle as Lady Dickson unnecessarily reminded her. She gathered up her bouquet of wildflowers, their bright colors accentuated by her high-necked pale blue dress reaching near enough the floor to all but obscure her black leather shoes. She gave a final defiant tilt to her broad brimmed hat with the single ostrich feather—the hat admired by Tobias if no one else—and proceeded in measured steps down the aisle to stand finally opposite the bridegroom.

187

Next came the flower girl carrying a bouquet of white roses, and the ring bearer holding a white cushion with a ring attached to it by a single thread. Joy's pale blue dress matched Mrs. Hudson's while Jonathan's ruffled shirt, dark jacket and trousers made him something of a match for Sudden Thunder. In accord with Lady Dickson's tutelage, they wore somber expressions equally appropriate for weddings and funerals. Mrs. Hudson was certain that their outfits came from the same source as their solemn looks. After everyone in the audience had had a chance to jab his or her neighbor to point out some aspect of the children's manner or dress, Joy came to stand on Mrs. Hudson's right, Jonathan on Sudden Thunder's left as all four waited the bride's arrival.

She came down the aisle on the arm of William Frederick Cody, dressed in the buckskin outfit of Buffalo Bill only absent his Stetson hat, removed in deference to the occasion. For once, however, he commanded less attention than the person beside him. For the audience of Wild West performers Colonel Cody's appearance was no novelty. Jane Morrison's appearance was.

A small lace cap was set atop auburn hair that suddenly seemed to take on a near golden hue, and a cashmere cape extending well below her waist made elegant someone they had previously seen as pedestrian, even dowdy. Beneath her cape showed a pale blue blouse matching the dress of her matron of honor and flower girl, and a fringed buckskin skirt matching the dress of her escort. She took the flowers from Joy while Sudden Thunder removed the ring from Jonathan's outstretched cushion. Then they each turned to face Mr. Carruthers. As they did, Mrs. Hudson looked to the back of the room where the bridal party had initially gathered. As she expected, the area was deserted. Lady Dickson, having done what she set out to do, was gone.

Carruthers spoke the words he had long since memorized. He stumbled briefly over the groom's name, and he hurried past the part of the service about anyone speaking up now or forever holding his peace, his feeling being there was no way of predicting what might happen at this wedding, and there was no point taking unnecessary risks. When, at last, it was over, he shared a relieved smile with the newlyweds before hurrying off for a cup of tea or maybe something stronger.

In short order, the hall was empty, ready, after a modest cleaning, for another ceremony. Mr. and Mrs. Sudden Thunder would go first to Evermore, their newly leased estate and horse farm in Sussex. Later they would make arrangements to transport Colonel Cody's wedding gift of the four ponies they had chosen from the Wild West Show stables. Percy Stockton gathered up his exuberant niece and nephew to take them home to the Stockton farm, stopping briefly for ice cream along the way. Colonel Cody, after first insisting Holmes accept a thick envelope and a vigorous handshake, bowed gracefully to Mrs. Hudson, nodded to Watson and gathered up the remainder of the wedding attendees, making use of several carriages to get his people back to the fairgrounds. The Baker Street trio used a single carriage to return to 221B. Their talk about the wedding soon ran down but their smiles lingered to the end of the ride.

Once home, the members of the trio gathered in Mrs. Hudson's kitchen for reflection and refreshments. Mrs. Hudson went to put the kettle on and to set a collection of plain and raisin-filled scones on a serving platter while Holmes and Watson took seats at her table.

"I had hoped we might see Mrs. Stockton and Miss Stockton at the ceremony," Watson commented, "although, of course, I do understand about the period of mourning."

"Utter nonsense if you ask me," Holmes responded, "why should a woman—or anyone for that matter—put their life on hold for a year to pine for someone no longer with us—especially when that someone was an utter rotter like Roger Stockton."

"You have a point, Holmes. I suppose it's simply tradition. What is your thought, Mrs. Hudson?"

She had come to join them at the table while the tea steeped and sat now in her accustomed place at the head of the table.

"I think the true period of mournin' will depend on the person who's been lost. I will mourn my Tobias until the day I die, and what Mr. 'Olmes has to say about such as Roger Stockton is, I think, true. There's those we never want to forget and those, and may the Lord forgive me, we may not want to remember."

"The Lord forgive you?" Holmes winked to Watson. "I don't believe I've ever heard you call on the Lord before, Mrs. Hudson."

"I suppose that's true, Mr. 'Olmes," she said as she left to get the kettle, "There's so many with real problems, I don't like botherin' 'Er with mine."

The men's laughter followed her to the stove and welcomed her back to the table.

When the laughter had subsided, Holmes shared the bombshell he'd been long holding back. "There's no good or easy way to say this, but I have to tell you that all the recent talk about Lady Dickson's estate in Sussex and the attractions of country life have put me in mind of retiring from crime detection, taking a cottage in Sussex and doing what I've long wanted to do, which is to say, keeping bees."

"You're not serious, Holmes," Watson looked at him wide-eyed, a partially eaten scone held briefly away from his mouth. "Where does this come from?"

"Watson, in another year I'll be fifty and shortly thereafter I'll be starting the decline that is inevitable in all our lives. If I am ever to pursue interests beyond criminal investigation, it must be now."

"I can understand that, Holmes, but why bees? What could you possibly find intriguing about a bunch of stinging insects?"

"Not necessarily stinging, Watson. If you are careful about invading their territory you can avoid being stung and still have the benefit of honey to sweeten your food. But that's not what intrigues me. It's their society of hard-working subjects with a queen in charge that fascinates me. For some reason, I feel I understand that organization and might even choose to write a book about it." He shared a second wink with Watson, fully aware that Mrs. Hudson couldn't miss this one anymore than she could have missed the first. "What do you think, Mrs. Hudson?"

"I'll say nothin' against the bees, Mr. 'Olmes. I will say your announcement surprises me. In truth, I was thinkin' of turnin' more of our business over to you. You've been makin' such a contribution of late—especially on the Stockton murder—I thought it was about time you 'ad greater independence in gettin' the job done. Besides which, I've been thinkin' that it's all gettin' to be more than I sometimes think I can 'andle and I'm ready to step back a little and give you and Dr. Watson more of a chance to step up."

Watson, having had time to collect himself from the initial shock of Holmes's revelation, now sought to forestall the change his words promised. "I dare say the esteem in which Holmes is held will drive the demand for his services—which is to say, our services—whether in Sussex or on Baker Street. As for there being a need for you to cut back on your activity, Mrs. Hudson, I can truthfully say as a physician and a friend, I see no evidence in you or Holmes of any diminution in spirit or ability. Truth be told, I was rather hoping to continue with my little stories of our group's accomplishments for many years to come. You must know the editors at *Strand Magazine* are depending on us. Can we at least agree to make no rash decisions now that we may come to regret, or find it necessary to undo later. Instead, let us pledge that by the end of this year, 1903, we will revisit all plans and ideas for our future, and make our final determinations then."

For the second time in recent memory Watson and Mrs. Hudson joined hands across a table, this time together with Holmes, each of them wondering how many more times they would be together to celebrate the triumph of justice over injustice, and whether, when the year was out, they would ever see each other again.